among

the sins

of my

father

BLACK SWAN

PART THREE

by Sabre Rose

For more information about the author visit:
www.sabreroseauthor.com

ISBN: 9798582605478

"Dance is the hidden language of the soul."

– Martha Graham

Black Swan Trilogy Reading Order

Daughter of a Monster

Searching for Hope

Among the Sins of my Father

SABRE ROSE

chapter one

Jericho holds Hope in his arms. I can see their reflection mirrored in the darkness of the car windows. His head is bent over her protectively as though shielding her from the world. She clutches him, her fingers and knuckles white, her head pressed to his chest. Naked.

Her body is frail, her hair is damp and sticks to the side of her face. She looks both filled with sadness and tremendous relief. They cling to each other, talking in low muted tones that fail to reach the front of the vehicle. There's desperation and need in their connection. And even though I've lived with the knowledge for a while now, it's the first time it truly hits me.

The man I love is loved by another.

He belongs to her.

She is his wife.

I am not.

My chest feels as though it's being ripped open inch by inch. Slow and torturous. And I feel guilt. Guilt because she has done nothing wrong. Guilt because she has suffered in ways I can't imagine. Guilt because most of that suffering was at the hand of my father. Guilt because she's now safe.

And I despise her for it.

I fold over on myself as a wave of anxiety hits. It's violent, this one. A small wail forces its way out of me as the flashes start.

A hand on the back of my head. Pushing. Shoving. Pressing me downward. Flesh—both soft and hard—forced into my mouth. I bite. The hand on my head fists into my air and yanks my head back. I'm greeted by dark eyes flashing in anger. A low and menacing growl sounds. And then a wound opens on his neck. Raw and gaping. Blood starts to trickle.

"Are you feeling sick?" Barrett asks, his eyes darting between me and the dark and winding road.

I want to say yes, but I don't. I can't tell him that the stress of the evening, of seeing Jericho and Hope together, is causing my brain to fire weirdly, spitting unwanted flashes of dark and depraved images into my mind. I can't tell him they excite me. I can't tell him I'm that sort of sick.

So instead I sit back up, giving him a hesitant smile. "It's the winding road." I nod out the window. "I guess it has just brought on a little nausea. I'm fine though."

Fine. It's such a non-descript word. Fine. Not good. Not bad. Fine. It's nothing but a lie.

"Sure," he replies, drawing the word out with a chuckle.

He doesn't believe me. No one would. He knows the sweat that dots my head, the raised hairs on my arms, the paleness of my skin and the swirling nausea in my stomach don't come from motion sickness. But he doesn't push it.

The car clings to the road as it slices through the darkness. Barrett keeps looking behind as though he's expecting flashing lights in the distance. Part of me expects them too. Even the whir of the engine reminds me of the sound of the gunshot.

Closing my eyes, I attempt to count to five and breathe deeply and slowly. I picture myself forming the first five positions in ballet, moving through the motions and trying to take my mind away from the events that brought us here, escaping through the darkness, eager to get back to the Sanctuary.

But it's pointless. That sound of gunshot has brought back memories I thought long banished.

Flames leap up a building. A sinister smile spreads across a face too handsome to be recognized as evil. Cold metal between trembling fingers.

"Keep the gun on him, Everly."

The voice is faded and distorted. The past collides with the present and Aaron Keating's face dances in the shadows of my mind. I'm holding the gun, fingers trembling. Keating laughs. Another wave of nausea twists violently in my gut.

"Stop," I plead quietly, not knowing whether I'm talking to Barrett or the mangled memories in my head. I open the door even though the car hasn't slowed.

"Fuck," Barrett mutters as he reaches across my body and yanks it shut again. "Okay, okay. I'm pulling over. Just wait, okay?"

"What's happening?" Jericho's deep voice sounds from the backseat.

No one answers him as the car slows and Barrett guides it into the gravel on the edge of the road. I open the door and basically fall out, using my hands to crawl, not caring when the small stones dig into my flesh. When I feel the damp grass, I press my head to the softness.

Ragged breaths wrack my body. It's as though I can't control them. They're brutal and harsh as I struggle for air.

Please stop, I beg myself internally. Not now. Not with them all watching. Not after everything that's happened.

7

Hope is the one just rescued from a life in captivity, but I'm the one broken and useless on the ground.

A car door opens. I hold my hand behind me, begging them not to come over. I don't want comfort. I don't deserve it.

Dragging myself to my feet, I don't look behind as I stumble further into the field. There's a copse of trees nearby, offering me a place to hide.

"I just need a minute." My voice comes out less desperate than I feel, something of a relief. Hopefully they can't see how messed up I am. Hopefully they truly believe it's just motion sickness.

"Berkley." His voice is low and deep as he says my name. Everything within me wants to turn around and throw myself into his arms. I want to find comfort and solace there. But I can't. Not now. Not after everything Hope has been through.

A pathetic laugh stutters from me. "I just need some fresh air. I'll be back soon." I still don't look at him as I say it. I know I will crumble if I do.

It only takes a few strides for him to catch up with me. He grabs my arm, whipping me around to face him. "Berkley," is all he says.

"Don't." I pull my arm away. I can't stand for him to touch me right now. It hurts too much. "I just need a minute, just a minute."

I half stumble, half run into the woods, falling to my knees only when there's no breath left inside me. My throat tightens as I try to suck in air. The edges of my vision begin to blacken and I squeeze my eyes shut.

"No, no," I silently plead with no one. "Please, not now."

Images burst like fireworks through my brain. The scar on my shoulder burns.

A ragged wound weeping as someone laughs. My knees sinking into blood-soaked carpet. Lifeless eyes. Nails digging into my hips. A bullet bursting from the barrel of a rifle. Keating's face melding into Dominic's.

Strong arms hook under mine and I'm pulled to my feet. I know it's Jericho even before he speaks.

"First," he chants. "Second." He moves my arms, pulling them out to the side. "Third. Fourth. Fifth."

A small amount of air reaches my lungs as I'm able to breathe. Jericho starts again, chanting softly in my ear, his chest pressed to my back as he leads me through the positions again.

"You can stop now." I pull away, leaving the comfort and security of his embrace. "I'm okay now. Go back to Hope."

Even as the words leave my mouth I know how pathetic and spiteful they sound.

"Berkley." The way he says my name brings a wave of emotion crashing over me and tears well in my eyes.

I cover my face but he peels back my hands and stares deeply into my eyes. So deeply it hurts. I lower my gaze.

"We should go. The police might be coming for us."

"There's no one coming for us, Berkley." He tips my chin up but I can't look at him. I'm too ashamed. All I have to deal with is these images in my head. Hope had to live them. And yet, I'm the one having a breakdown while she waits patiently in the car.

"I'm so sorry you had to see all that."

He's talking about Keating. About the way he gave the order for Barrett to kill him merely by the nod of his head.

He swallows and I focus on the bob of his throat, unable to bring myself to look him in the eyes. "I never wanted you to see that side of me, that side of humanity. I should have been the one to shield you from it, not expose you to it."

I jerk my chin up, pulling it away from his touch. "I don't need to be shielded."

"Berkley." And there he goes, saying my name again.

I push my tears away with the back of my hand. "I'm fine," I say. "It's over." I still don't look at him as I shove my way past and back to the car.

Jericho follows in silence.

Hope is wrapped in his jacket when we return. Without a word, Jericho slides into the backseat and I return to the front. Barrett lifts his brows and I give him a nod before he pulls back onto the road.

The car is filled with hushed tension. The whirr of the engine is loud. I stare at the trees as they pass, their gnarled and twisted branches, the slice of the moon, anything to keep my mind empty of violent thoughts. The gates to the Sanctuary groan as they open.

I press my head against the cold glass of the window, looking up high to catch a glimpse of the decorative framing. For the first time, I notice the iron curves and curls into the shape of swans. The whir of the engine slows as tires crunch over gravel. The Sanctuary looms above, gloriously moody in the dim light. My eyes are drawn to the ledge I jumped from. It seems like a lifetime ago that I tried to escape this place. Now, I'm coming willingly, with the full knowledge of who Jericho is, what he's capable of and who he belongs to.

A sharp pain twists in my gut and I take a deep breath, trying to quell the rising tide of apprehension. Motion from the back catches my eye, and Hope sits forward, tears running down her face as she stares out the window.

Mrs Bellamy waits on the front steps just as she did when I first arrived. It's not raining this time but it feels like it should be. There's a chilling quietness about the night which is unsettling. The wind teases my dress as I step out of the car. Jericho holds Hope's door open and she gets out cautiously, her eyes scanning over everything, darting here and there as though looking for danger.

"It's okay," Jericho says, offering her a somber smile. "You're home now. You're safe."

She takes his hand, holding the sides of Jericho's jacket together with the other. She looks so small against the majesty of the building. Her blonde hair stands out against the harsh gloom.

Mrs Bellamy stands with her hands held over her mouth, her eyes shining with tears.

"Is it really you, my dear?" Her voice is a whisper that almost gets carried away by the wind.

Hope merely nods as she embraces her and together they cry. Mrs Bellamy pulls away and holds Hope's face in her hands, her cheeks squished between her fingers.

"It's really you."

I think she's saying it more to herself than to Hope. It's like, even though Hope stands before her, she still needs confirmation.

"It's me," Hope says. Her voice is deeper than I expected. Tougher. Harsher. Almost defiant.

"Let's get you inside and cleaned up before you see Ette," Jericho says, threading his fingers through hers. There's such familiarity in the action. As though they've done it a million times before.

The smile Hope offers him is brief but pure.

Barrett opens the oversized door and Jericho and Hope are swallowed by the Sanctuary. Their home. It used to feel like mine too.

Now I'm not so sure.

chapter two

BERKLEY

I stand on the stairs, the sound of Jericho's, Mrs Bellamy's and Hope's voices floating down from above. Mrs Bellamy is telling Hope about the room they have prepared. The room they've had prepared for years. It's beside Ette's. Part of the family wing.

I know I suck for having these feelings of resentment. I know I should be happy. Relieved. Excited even. But the violence of her rescue has tainted it for me. And the fact that something changed between Jericho and I the moment he laid eyes on her. It's unfair of me to think it but I know it's true.

Mrs Bellamy is offering to run Hope a bath. Hope cries as she tells her she hasn't soaked in a bath for years. They decide to leave Ette asleep, planning for a reunion tomorrow once everyone has had a good night's sleep. That doesn't stop Hope from seeing her though. I creep up the stairs, cautious of the creaks and groans, and watch hidden among the shadows as Hope peers into Ette's room.

I can't imagine what it would be like to lose someone and then find them again. Jericho holds Hope close as she weeps. It's tender and sweet and I slip back down the stairs annoyed at myself for my reaction to their reunion. I'm walking to my bedroom as I hear him say he should leave, let her get some rest. She begs him to stay.

She's scared.

She needs him.

Of course he stays.

My room is directly under hers. I open the door, ready to climb into my bed and fall asleep, but I know I won't find any peace there. My mind is too filled with images I want to forget and questions I don't want to answer. So instead, I creep slowly back down the stairs, slip through the dining room and head towards the basement. I need to remind myself of what was at stake here. Of the whole reason for my existence in this place.

My father is lying on a stretcher. It wasn't here last time I came to visit, but clearly someone felt sorry enough for him to provide him a place to rest. I rest my forehead against the one-way glass, watching as his chest rises and falls.

What will Jericho do with him now that he's no longer needed?

Will he nod at Barrett, silently signing his death warrant?

There is nothing special about my father in this moment. He doesn't look like a monster. He looks like a mere man. An old and fragile man. A man who should be bouncing grandchildren on his knee. Instead he is rotting in a cell paying for the crimes he committed.

But evil doesn't have a face.

It's an action. A choice. A decision.

Part of me wants to barge inside and tell him of our success. Explain how I fooled them all. How I got Gorman to reveal Hope's whereabouts all because he thought he was doing it for him. My father. The monster.

But I don't. I put my back to the door and slide down until I reach the ground. And it is there I fall asleep, the nightmares kept at bay by the monster at my back.

I'm sore when I wake. My joints are stiff, my bones cold. The house breathes and sighs as I make my way back to the stairs. The moon is lower in the sky now, almost dipping out of sight behind the trees which sway in the breeze. I can just make out the black shapes of the swans floating on the surface of the water out of the window. They have no idea of the turmoil inside the Sanctuary, of the lost woman now found.

My bed beckons but instead of answering its call, I change into my swimsuit and head down to the pool. I watch the sky turn from dark to light as I float, imagining myself as unaffected as the swans.

It feels as though I could walk around the Sanctuary and not see another soul, such is the extent of the empty and lonely feeling inside me. I feel as though a part of me is missing. No, not missing. A part of me has been torn away, despite my efforts to keep it. It's like it's been wrenched from my hands, pried from my fingers, ripped from my chest.

And that's how I spend the rest of the day. Alone. Isolated. Trapped by the morbidity of my own thoughts.

Because although I'm not crippled by flashes, I still can't get the memory of what I witnessed out of my head. I can't stop thinking about Mary. I can't stop wondering where Dominic is. I can't stop seeing Keating's blood on the carpet.

My ears strain for the sound of sirens.

My heart beats in fearful anticipation of the truth coming out.

A woman begged me to save her. And I did nothing.

I don't bother drying myself when I emerge from the water. I walk through the hallways, leaving wet footprints in my wake. At dinner time, I drag myself downstairs, preparing to face them. Him. Her.

I'm the first one there, so I pull out a chair and sink into it, grateful for the extra moments of time to prepare myself. I haven't seen Jericho since the night before. He's been busy caring for Hope. As he should. But only seconds later, the door opens and they both walk in.

Jericho's gaze zeros in on mine so I drop my eyes, and stare at a glass of water. I don't look up even as Hope settles herself opposite me and Jericho takes his usual seat at the head of the table. There's a nervous energy about Hope. Her hand floats about her face, touching her cheeks, her chin, pushing stray strands of hair behind her ear. Her eyes keep darting to the kitchen door. I don't know what to say to her. I don't know what to say to either of them. How do you greet someone who spent years in captivity at the hands of your father?

"Mrs Bellamy will bring her in soon." Jericho reaches over and covers Hope's hand with his own. My eyes get stuck on their connection, only lifting when Jericho clears his throat.

"Hope, this is Berkley."

I offer her a wobbly smile and she offers me one back. There's a question in her eyes. She wants to know who I am, why I'm here, but Jericho doesn't offer any more information. When the kitchen door swings open and Ette walks in, hyperactively chatting away to Mrs Bellamy, Hope stands abruptly, knocking her chair to the ground.

Her eyes well with tears as they scan over her daughter hungrily, drinking in the sight of her. Ette stops walking and stares openly at Hope.

"Who are you?" she asks, a frown pressing between her brows.

"Ette," Jericho walks over, crouching in front of her. "You know how I told you I'd find your mother and bring her home?"

Ette nods solemnly, looking skeptically between Jericho and Hope. "She's my mother?" she asks matter-of-factly.

Hope holds out one hand, stretching it toward her daughter. "Odette," she says, her voice breaking.

"No one calls me that," Ette replies sharply.

Hope swallows. Mrs Bellamy nods to Jericho and disappears through the kitchen door. I want to follow her. I don't belong here.

"Ette," Jericho's tone is a warning, but Hope steps in front of him and crouches down.

"You don't remember me?"

Ette shakes her head.

"That's okay, we can get to know each other again. There's plenty of time for that now."

"Are you staying with us?"

Hope nods. A smile stretches over her face. "If that's okay with you."

Ette shrugs. "Well, we do have lots of rooms."

Hope laughs. It's a carefree laugh but the end of it is cut off by a choked sob. Ette strides past her, heading toward the table.

"Do you want to sit with me?" Hope asks.

Again, Ette shakes her head. "I want to sit with Berkley. She's my best friend."

Hope swallows back the hurt as Ette waltzes over and plops herself beside me, blinking innocently at her mother without an ounce of guilt. She doesn't understand. All she knows is that her mother was missing and now she's found. She can't comprehend the nightmare Hope went through before she got here.

The door barges open and a whirlwind of motion flies through the door and throws itself at Hope. There's a wail and a gush of air as Hope scrambles away, dropping to the ground and crawling under the table.

"I'm so sorry," Gideon says as he realizes his mistake. "I was just so happy..." His voice fades as he takes in the cowering Hope under the table. She's breathing deeply, rocking back and forth as she hugs her knees to her chest.

"For fuck's sake, Gideon! What were you thinking?" Jericho hisses, his head ducking beneath the table to check on Hope.

Gideon runs his hands through his hair, desperation making his eyes wide. "I didn't think. I wasn't thinking. I was just—" He crouches down. "I'm so sorry, Hope."

Hope takes in deep breaths, trying to calm herself before crawling out from under the table. "Don't be sorry." She opens her arms, allowing Gideon to walk into them. "I'm just a little messed up," she whispers in his ear. "My god, it's good to see you."

Gideon squeezes her tight, then loosens his grip, concern wrinkling his angelic face.

Hope laughs. "It's okay. I'm not going to break or anything. I just got a fright before. It's going to take a while for me to adjust."

The staff come and take their seats at the table, each carrying a dish which we help ourselves from, instead of being served by Mrs Bellamy. Hope asks Ette about her schooling but in her typical child-like way, she doesn't want to talk about it, instead regaling her mother with recounting the various dance steps she's learned over the past few months.

Hope's gaze flicks to me curiously. You can tell it's hard for her to hear Ette talk about another person with such affection when she's been denied the chance of knowing her for years.

Each mouthful of dinner tastes like dirt. I keep chewing and chewing but no matter how hard I try, I can't seem to swallow. My mouth is dry so I take sips of water but nothing seems to help. Everyone talks around me but their voices are muted and I can't focus on any of them.

I push my chair away from the table. No one looks my way. I clear my throat. "I'm so sorry, but I'm going to have to excuse myself." I offer a pathetic smile. "I didn't get much sleep last night."

I keep my eyes down as I leave the room. It's not until I reach the door that I hear Jericho call after me. "Berkley, wait," he says.

I pretend I don't hear and let the door swing shut. He catches me just as I'm at the base of the staircase.

"Berkley," he says, his voice sharper than it was before. He knows I ignored him.

I stop and wait, but every part of me wants to race up the stairs and lock myself in my bedroom. For some reason, facing him hurts. It reminds me of all I'm about to lose.

He reaches for my hand, but I take a step upward, putting more distance between us. His eyes narrow, but he chooses to ignore it.

"We did it," he says, not being able to help the broad smile that stretches over his face.

"We did," I repeat, attempting to mimic his enthusiasm, but I can't. I chide myself for my inability to let him enjoy the moment. It's selfish. He's so happy about Hope's return. As am I. But something feels different now. I feel out of place. I don't belong here anymore and Hope's return has made that clear.

Jericho moves up to the first step, our heights aligning. "Ette has her mother back and it's all because of you." Grabbing my shoulders he crushes me against his chest. I hesitate, but only for a moment. Being here, secure against him, every sense drowning in him reminds me of every reason I want him. And it hurts. But sometimes I like to feel pain so I wrap my arms around him, clinging to him tightly as though it's the last time. Because that's how I feel.

Like this is it. This is the end.

I can't help the tears that well. I dig my fingers into his shirt, bunching the material. I don't want to let him go but he doesn't feel like mine anymore.

He's hers.

Then the door swings open and Jericho drops his arms, stepping back and putting distance between us as Hope looks on with an accusation in her eyes.

"Hope," Jericho says, his voice breaking a little as though he's ashamed.

A small frown presses between Hope's brows. "Are you—"

"Hope!" Ette calls, running over to her mother. "You need to come watch me dance." Ette looks up at me. "Can we show her our dance, Berkley? Can we?"

"You're the dance tutor?" There's a coldness to Hope's voice. Or maybe it's relief. Whatever it is, it's clear she feels as uncertain about me as I do her.

I nod. "I'm sure you can show your mother without me, Ette."

"But it's a duet!" she protests, her bottom lip wobbling.

"Berkley is very tired—"

"It's fine," I say cutting Jericho off and pushing past him. "Ette wants to show her mother her dance so that's what we'll do."

Ette reaches for my hand and threads her fingers through mine squeezing tightly. Then she stretches out her other hand to her mother. Hope moves her gaze to meet mine over the top of Ette's head. We lock eyes for a fraction of a second before she drops her gaze to her daughter, smiles and takes her hand.

chapter three

It's a simple dance. We begin kneeling on the floor. We're supposed to extend our right arm, use it to frame our face then push to the other side, but Ette, in her excitement, starts the wrong way. Instead of moving in unison, we're mirror images, reflecting each other. It's okay, we can work with that. Once we're on our feet, Ette's three-step turn somehow turns into four, but at least she does it in the same direction as me so we don't bump into each other. She does the press down dramatically though, her body slumping as though defeated before rising to a lock. Ette has never been one to tamper down the theatrics of dance. She does the motion of 'wiping the sweat off her brow' as I explained it to her in practice with determined melodrama. Our routine is unfinished so we end while the music still plays, having just completed our pas de bourrée in perfect unison.

Hope breaks into applause with tears streaming down her face. She stands close to Jericho, her body tilted toward his. Gideon smirks at them from where he's leaning against the wall. He wiggles his brows at me and a small knot twists in my stomach.

Doing my best to ignore it, I offer Ette a high five, commending her on the way she pointed her toes at all the right moments, something she struggled with while she was learning the routine.

"Did you like it, Hope?" Ette says, eyes shining brightly.

"I sure did," Hope says exaggeratedly. "I had no idea what a wonderful dancer you are!" She crouches down so she's eye height with Ette. "You know you can call me Mother, right?"

Ette rolls her eyes. "It's a little too soon, Hope. I'll get there one day." The way she says it makes her sound years older than she is. There's almost a sadness to her tone, or mistrust, but she's still allowing the possibility of the term coming to her naturally. One day.

Before I realize what I'm doing, I walk over and scuff the top of her hair.

Hope's head whips up. "You're awfully familiar with her for a dance teacher."

"She's not just my dance teacher," Ette replies, lifting her chin a little. "She's also my best friend and Mr Priest's best friend." Her blue eyes twinkle with mischief.

"Hey," Mrs Bellamy bustles over, feeling the tension from the other side of the room, "I thought I was your best friend?"

Ette rolls her eyes. "You're also the person who tells me to go to bed every night and brush my teeth and wash my face and eat all my vegetables."

"You mean all the things which keep you happy and healthy?" Mrs Bellamy wraps her hand around Ette's. "How about we see if your mother is as good as doing voices as Mr Priest while telling stories?"

Ette turns to Hope and loudly whispers with a laugh, "It won't be hard."

Once they leave, I feel the weight of Gideon's and Jericho's stares on me. Neither of them says anything so after turning off the music, I head towards the door, citing my earlier excuse of tiredness as a way of escape.

"Berkley, wait," Jericho says as I pass him.

"I'm tired." I throw the words over my shoulder, not wanting to look at him. Because I know if I do, I will crumble. I will relent and find myself in his arms again when I know that's no longer my place.

27

"Miss Berkley!" he says sharply and grabs my arm. "Please wait." His demeanor is both threatening and pleading, the two sides of him fighting for dominance just like the dueling swans etched into his skin.

His eyes are so dark it's hard to see any hint of blue. They're like the night sky during a storm. You know the blue is there but it's hidden behind the layer of turbulent clouds and blanketed in darkness.

He stares at me, chest rising and falling with each breath. His fingers tighten as I test his aggression, pulling away ever so slightly.

"You can leave now, Gideon," Jericho commands, his eyes still locked on mine. The line of his jaw bulges as Gideon chuckles.

"I'm good where I am."

"Leave. Now," Jericho orders.

The thunder to his voice rumbles through me and I shudder under a wave of delicious arousal. Neither of us look at Gideon as he pulls himself off the wall and wanders nonchalantly away. It's not until the door slams shut behind him that Jericho speaks.

"I know what you're doing."

I pull my arm from his grasp. "I'm not doing anything."

"Yes," he tips up my chin, demanding I look at him, "you are."

"Then what? What am I doing?"

"You're pulling away from me."

"I'm not the one who's—"

"We both knew this day would come, Berkley. We knew that things would be different when she returned. Difficult even."

"Difficult?" I repeat, my voice rising. "She's your wife, Jericho. Your wife. She needs you."

"And I need you."

"It's not the same."

"No, it's not. But it still doesn't change anything. You're mine, Berkley. I choose you. I want you. I need you." The way he says 'you' gets more desperate with each repetition.

"Have you told her that?"

"Do you think now is the time? I will if that's what you want. I will go and talk to her right this very moment."

I drop my head, staring at my bare feet pressed against the wooden floor. "No."

I sigh, frustrated at the mixed feelings twisting about inside. Already I can feel tears welling. Again. I grit my teeth together, begging them not to fall.

"How have you been sleeping?" Jericho's voice is gentler this time.

I merely shrug as a response. I don't know how to act. There's a side of me that wants to cry and scream. I want to say how unfair it was that he made me love him when this was a possibility. This feeling of loss. This feeling of being cast aside. This feeling of betrayal. And what's even worse is I don't have any claim to feeling this way. He's not my husband. I wasn't the one who suffered years of abuse at the hands of my father. I wasn't the one who lost my child. Lost everything.

I risk a look up at him, knowing what it could do to me. "Does she know who I am?"

He's staring at me intently, the thunder clouds still evident in his eyes. "Who are you?" he asks.

"The daughter of the monster who kept her."

He shakes his head. "Nor does she know that we're keeping the monster in the basement." He takes a deep breath and runs his hands through his hair. "There's so much to tell her, but to throw everything at her all at once would be cruel. She needs time. She needs space to breathe, to feel free. I don't think I should tell her anything until she's stronger."

A snort of air escapes. "After everything she's been through, I think the last thing you can call her is weak."

"And your flashes? How have they been?"

"You don't need to worry about me."

"That's where you're wrong, Berkley. I do need to worry about you because I can feel you pulling away from me with every second. I feel it each time you drop your gaze, each time you deny my touch."

I want to protest. What about him? What about him dropping his embrace as soon as Hope saw us? But I already know the answer to that. I know why he did it. To protect her. As he should. As we all should.

He wipes a tear away from under my eye with the pad of his thumb. The tenderness of the motion causes a sob to escape.

"Don't," I say, as though his touch caused me pain. And it did. It reminded me of everything I can't have. The tightness in my chest increases. It's been there constantly since the night we rescued Hope. Since I saw Barrett slit the throat of the man who, as far as I can tell, was guilty of nothing but an affair with a young Hope. Since a woman looked into my eyes and begged me to save her life.

A familiar knot twists in my stomach

"Don't." It's his voice that says it, not mine. My hand is swatted away from where it lays on his chest. He grips my wrist tightly, twisting it until my entire body crumples with the pain and I fall to my knees. "Stay," is his next command.

Jericho's stance straightens. It's like he grows inches as he takes in a breath and lifts his shoulders, towering over me. "I'm not going to let you do this to us, Berkley."

He moves past me to the door and twists the lock shut. It makes a loud sound in the barrenness of the room.

"Get undressed," he growls.

"I'm not going to—"

He takes my fingers, just my fingers, toying with them before looking into my eyes and repeating the words. "Get undressed." He leans close as he says it, his breath washing over my ear. "Then kneel and wait."

The commands alone bring a sense of relief. The twisting in my gut stops. Obey or rebel. The choice is easy. He's recognized the mangled indecision within me.

He's taking control.

chapter four

My fingers tremble as I take the hem of my sweater and lift it over my head. He nods once, moving past me and flicking off the lights, leaving only the light of the moon filtering in through the windows. Then he leans against the mirrored wall, crossing his arms and narrowing his eyes. He stays like that as I undress, my heartbeat rising with each movement.

My leggings come off next. I peel them from my skin slowly, aware of his eyes watching my every move. I'm left in nothing but my underwear. In the mirror my skin glows in the light of the moon. One side of me is illuminated while the other is hidden in shadows.

"Keep going," Jericho instructs. His voice is thick and deep, almost another growl. The desire to press my legs together, to drown in the sensations he's causing to run through my body is strong, but instead, I do as he says, reaching behind me to undo the clasps of my bra and then slide my underwear over my hips, stepping out of them and tossing them away.

He just stares at me for a while, his eyes running over my body and igniting my skin, licking it with fire. There's a low vibration trembling deep inside. I don't know whether it's anticipation or foreboding. All I know is I like it. I like that he's taken control. That I'm under his command. My mind quiets. My stomach stops twisting. But my heartbeat keeps beating rapidly.

"Kneel." His voice is deeper this time. Almost broken.

I lower myself slowly until the cold wood kisses my knees. I sit back, pressing my butt to my heels. My hair flows loose and long, tickling my shoulder blades. I feel every cell of my being as Jericho pulls himself from the wall and slowly stalks toward me.

My hands are resting on my lap, but they are not still. I am not still. I'm quivering, trembling in anticipation of him. I push my hair behind my ear and place my hand back on my lap. Jericho is behind me now. He walks slowly and with purpose, inspecting me as I kneel in silence. I squirm, moving the placement of myself over my heels. I'm certain he must be able to hear the rapid beat of my heart. It's a rhythm track to my need. Pulsing. Electrifying. Rousing.

"Be still," he commands.

I school my body into obedience. Because I want him. I want him badly. All other thought has fled my mind. All I see is him.

I want his touch. I want it strong and firm and rough. I want his growl as well as his bite. I've always tried to suppress my darker side, the side that craves to control and be controlled, but Jericho has only made those feelings stronger. And this time, I'm willing to submit.

He comes and stands before me. I raise my gaze slowly, starting at his shoes and letting it trail over him until I meet his eye. Reaching out, he lifts my chin with a single finger, not allowing me to look away.

I swallow and the movement feels strange, forced.

"Still," Jericho repeats.

I nod as he removes his finger. He keeps his eyes locked on mine as he starts to undo the buttons of his shirt. He moves leisurely. Slowly. Painfully slowly as though he wants to torment me.

His buttons fall open one by one until there's a strip of his flesh visible between the lines of material. Then he shrugs his shirt over his shoulders, catching it with his fingers before it falls to the floor. He doesn't let it fall;

instead, he walks over to the side of the room, folding it over the chair. His movements are languid and exaggerated, as though he knows the torture going on inside me. As if he knows exactly how the sight of seeing him shirtless and bare makes me feel. As if he too can feel the warmth that floods between my legs. As if he knows how strong the desire is to squirm against myself, to give myself some freedom from the desire that tugs deep inside.

After removing his shoes, he pops the buttons of his jeans one by one. He doesn't look at me as he does it, but he knows how intently I'm watching him. I couldn't tear my eyes away even if I wanted to. I'm drawn to him. Pulled by some magnetic thread that won't let go.

The swans on his back continue their fight as he twists and turns, tugging his jeans off and placing them over the back of the chair.

The darkness of his eyes has deepened when he walks back to me. No longer are they filled with threatening thunder clouds. They're ink. Cataclysmic and ruinous.

He comes to stand behind me. My skin prickles and I shiver, though I'm not sure if it's from the coldness of the air or the anticipation of his touch. I watch him in the reflection of the mirror. His body is bathed in the same moonlight as mine, cut into light and shadows, half-hidden, half-exposed. His fingers brush over my shoulders as he adjusts my hair, moving it to fall down my back like a veil. My head is perfectly placed to disguise his hardness in the mirror, but the rest of him is fully exposed.

The cut of his shoulders. The swells of his chest. The ridges of his stomach and the way the deep lines of his muscles dive to his groin. Feathers from the fight of the swans dance over his arms, taking flight in the moonlight.

He's so exquisite he takes my breath away.

In the reflection of the mirror, his gaze scorches mine. Bending down, he pulls me to my feet, wrapping my arms around the back of his neck, arching my body and exposing it fully. His hand floats down my side, leaving behind a trail of fire. His fingers brush so softly against me, it's hard not to writhe with the agony of it.

I want to meld into him. I want to collapse against him, allowing him all control, all power. I want to surrender my body to him. Do with me as he wills.

Without warning, he cups my breasts aggressively, eliciting a sharp gasp as he twists my nipples. The connection of my hands behind his back breaks. I fold over myself, grabbing my breasts and shielding them from his assault.

His head cocks to the side. Black fire lights his eyes. His lips brush over the curve of my neck. "I told you to be still." His eyes drop to where I'm covering myself. "Remove your hands."

I shake my head. Not because I don't want to remove them. Not because I don't want his touch. But because I want his anger. His wrath. I take a step away and Jericho's left eye twitches, the vein beneath it pulsing.

He strides toward me. "Remove your hands."

I'm clutching my breasts, the flesh oozing between my fingers as I stare at him defiantly. I don't move. I don't take a step backward. I lift my chin, my tongue darting out to moisten my bottom lip as he takes another step, his body so close to mine I can feel the heat of him warming the air between us.

With one fluid motion, Jericho rips my hands away, twisting me around and holding both my hand securely behind my back with one of his. The position makes it hard for me to resist. He presses himself against me, his hardness pushing against my hands. I grab for him eagerly, but he moves, jerking his hips away and denying me the pleasure.

He tuts in my ear, scolding me. "Now, now, Miss Berkley. You know better than that." The darkness of his voice sends delicious waves of arousal through me. "I'm the one in control here. Not you."

Even though he says the words, I know I could stop him with one single command. I know if I wanted to, I could order him to the floor and walk all over him, push my heels into his chest and he wouldn't complain. In fact, he would welcome it.

Tugging downward on my hands, he forces my shoulders back, my chest out. He walks me toward the mirror, watching me in the reflection as his free hand moves to encase my breast. He massages roughly and I press into it instead of shying away, biting my bottom lip and crying out when he twists my nipple.

"There she is," he says before running his tongue up the side of my neck. His hand moves to my other breast and I gulp back a gasp as he repeats the same motion. When his hand trails over my stomach and dips between my legs, I let my head flop back against his shoulder. He pushes two fingers inside.

"Open your legs."

I don't hesitate to do as he says, eager to feel him deeper inside me. He teases and taunts, pushing in and out a few times before shoving them into my mouth.

"Suck," he commands.

I obediently lick the taste of myself away. His eyes close as I run my teeth over the pads of his fingers and his hips thrust against me. My hands search for him, the feel of his hardness desperately but he always moves just out of my reach, pushing me forward so my hands move further up my back. His cock pushes against my ass and I writhe against him, wanting—no—needing to have him inside me. It's an exquisite need that manifests as pain. A pain so visceral and deep I would do anything to sate it.

Dragging me over to a chair, he sits down and pulls me over his lap, letting go of my hands long enough to direct them down the legs of the chair.

"Hold," he says.

The coldness of the metal is soothing. I wrap my fingers around it, grateful for something to cling to as he begins to caress the cheeks of my ass. He rubs, his fingers sliding over me before he slaps me gently. If I lift my head and twist it to the side, I can see the reflection of us in the mirror.

His legs are spread wide and I'm splayed over them. His eyes dart over my body stretched beneath him as though he can't choose which part of me to focus on. His hand is repetitive as it rubs over my ass, back and forth, slipping occasionally between my legs to tease me before a sharp slap resounds.

I gasp.

He slaps again. Harder.

I gasp and grip the legs of the chair tighter.

I can't tear my eyes away from the reflection of us. The light of the moon shines from behind, spilling over his shoulder and illuminating only parts of me. One slice of my ass is exposed by the light and it's a shade of pink, reddened by his hand. My breasts are crushed against his thigh. My toes are spread over the floor, gripping into it to stop myself from sliding and to provide me some resistance against him.

He increases his pace, his cock bouncing against my stomach in the same rhythm as his slaps. The repetitiveness of it, the sharpness of it intensifies. A groan of pain escapes me.

"Tell me to stop," Jericho growls.

But I don't want to. The pain is mixed with pleasure I never thought possible, so I writhe on his lap, pushing my ass higher, closer to his hand. This causes him to moan deeply and I feel the reverberations of it. His slaps start again. A stinging, cleansing punishment. One hand presses between my thighs and I open myself further, craving his touch. He inserts a finger, groaning at my wetness as I push my ass into the air, welcoming his discipline. He adjusts me over his lap, tilting my head closer to the ground. I hold onto the metal bars of the chair as he slips another digit inside, finger fucking me with aggression.

He slaps me again. Harder than he ever has before and tears spring to my eyes. But still I don't pull away and I make no motion to escape because I don't want to. My ass is both on fire and numb. I want the rest of my body to feel the same.

My tears turn to sobs.

"Tell me to stop," Jericho begs.

But I don't. To cry like this without the overwhelming flashes running through my mind, without the twisting knife in my gut, feels like freedom. It feels as though someone has lifted a weight from my chest and let my heart soar.

"Goddammit, Berkley." Jericho leans down and peels my fingers from the legs of the chair. He pulls me up and to his chest, letting me sob against him.

Desperation floats through my veins. I want to crawl under his skin. I want to drown in him. I want every inch of my body singed by his touch. Peppering kisses over his chest, I claw my way up his torso, digging my fingers into his shoulders before I sink onto him.

He moans low and slow as he fills me. And then I just cling to him, grinding my hips in a slow circle, breathing in his scent, tasting his sweat, stabbing my nails into his flesh.

"Don't ever doubt me," he says, as I ride him. "Don't ever doubt how I feel about you. Don't ever pull away from me." He runs his mouth over me, his lips dragging against my skin. "Do you hear me, Berkley?"

I nod, barely able to muster the strength to concentrate on anything but the feel of him.

"I need to hear you say it. I need to hear you say that you know I'm yours."

"You're mine," I breathe as ecstasy tingles deep inside.

"No one else's," he says.

"No one else's," I repeat.

He holds me tight as he rises from the chair, keeping himself firmly planted within me as he lowers us to the ground. And then he holds me, my back propped up by his embrace as he drives inside deeply. My body shakes with each thrust until I erupt and convulse, my flesh turning to jelly as he continues his punishment until he too comes undone.

Once our breathing returns to normal, he presses soft kisses to my skin, over my forehead, my cheeks, my lips and my neck. "You're mine, Miss Berkley. You'd do well not to forget it."

chapter five

BERKLEY

Jericho rolls onto his back and pulls me with him, sprawling us both over the dance studio floor. I snuggle against his chest, contentment washing over me at the stillness of my mind. His naked flesh is warm beneath mine, still flushed by the heat of our encounter.

I could fall asleep like this. The steady thud of his heart echoes in my ear. The pressure of his hand holds me in place. And he smells like home. Propping my chin on his chest, I grin, dizzy with delirium.

"What?" he asks, noting the way I'm looking at him.

I laugh. "My ass is rather warm."

Jericho chuckles and moves his hand down my back, rubbing across the tender flesh. "You should have told me to stop."

"I didn't want to." I move, placing my cheek back on his chest and start tracing lines on his skin, connecting the floating feathers. "For some reason, I like the way it feels. But I don't at the same time. I mean, it hurts, but I like that it hurts. I like that I cry. Afterward, I feel like I'm clean again."

Jericho doesn't say anything. He pulls me closer and presses a kiss against the top of my head. I don't want this moment to end. I just want to stay here with him forever, lying on the floor, wrapped in his arms. It's safe here. I'm happy here. Even if I don't fully understand why.

Jericho clears his throat and the sound rumbles in my ear. "So, are we good now?"

I nod, my cheek rubbing against the hairs of his chest. Right now, it's hard to remember a moment when we weren't good.

"I promise I will tell Hope about us."

"There's no hurry," I say. "I was just feeling a little fragile, I guess. But we need to give her time. She's been through things most people couldn't even imagine."

"But she needs to know. Otherwise, it's just delaying the inevitable."

"She does," I agree. "But not right now."

Then Jericho curses. "Fuck, I wasn't wearing any protection."

"Don't worry," I mumble against his skin. "I'm on birth control."

"Good, because fuck that felt amazing." Letting out a sigh, Jericho moves, encouraging me to move too.

"You're not going to tell her now, are you?" I ask as my ass hits the cold floor. I wince a little but it doesn't really hurt. It's more of a gentle burn. A reminder.

"There's no point in delaying it. I need to be honest with her. There are a few things I've been putting off talking to her about." Jericho walks over to where his clothing is draped over the chair and pulls on his jeans. Getting to my feet, I stroll over and wrap my arms around him from behind, stopping him from being able to put on his shirt. My head presses against his tattoo. There is so much of him and this house that is about her. About Hope. She's etched on his skin, stained in the windows, wrought into the iron.

Jericho covers my hand with his, pulling my fingers to his lips and brushing kisses over my knuckles. "Are we good now?" he asks again, as though he needs reassurance. I nod. "Good," he says. "I just want to be able to rest in the knowledge that I'm not going to lose you. After everything I've been through over the past few years, I reckon that would be the thing that would break me."

I squeeze tight. "I'm not going anywhere. I'm yours."

He pulls me around him so he can look me in the eye. "And I'm yours. So no more doubt, okay? No more pulling away from me. No more worrying about how I feel about Hope. It's you I want, okay? It's you I love."

He says the words so easily it would be effortless to believe them. And I do. Now. Here. Wrapped in his arms. But out there is a different story. Out there with flashes running through my mind, memories of slit throats and echoes of gunshots, it's harder to cling to the feelings I have when it's just him and me.

He grabs my cheeks. "Okay?"

I smile. "Okay."

He slings his shirt over his shoulders as I reluctantly pull my own clothing on. I don't bother with my underwear and hold them in my hands as he finishes doing up his buttons. It's just about bedtime anyway, and tonight, after this, I might actually be able to sleep. A small smile dances across my lips at the way my body feels.

Used. Pleasured. Satisfied. Tender. Sore. Loved.

Unlocking the door, Jericho pulls it open slightly before turning back to me. "So you'll remember all this tomorrow? I won't wake to find you pulling away from me again?"

I stretch onto my tiptoes and press my lips to his. "Promise."

"Good. The back and forth was getting a little exhausting." He chuckles.

"Hey! There were extenuating circumstances. You tricked me into coming here, remember? And then you locked me up. Like literally."

Jericho cocks a brow playfully. "What about the fact that I'm fucking the daughter of the man who stole my wife, circumstances like that?" He laughs as he pulls the door open fully. Then he says, "Oh, shit."

I peer around Jericho to see Hope standing on the other side of the door. She blinks, then her gaze moves from Jericho to me and back again. Tears well as she turns on her heels and starts to walk the other way.

"Hope!" Jericho reaches for her, grabbing her arm.

She jerks away as though his touch burns and hisses, "Don't touch me!"

Jericho holds his hands up. "Hope, let me explain."

"Explain?" Her eyes flash with moistened anger as they dart between Jericho and me. "How—Is she—I knew there was something familiar about you." She advances on me. "There's something in your eyes, something evil and dark just like his." She spits on the floor then turns her anger toward Jericho. "How could you do this to me? How could you—" She doesn't finish her sentence and instead, storms away.

"Hope!" Jericho calls, but then he turns back to me, hesitant.

"Go," I say. "Go after her."

Further down the hall, Gideon leans against the wall, a smirk covering his face. "Sorry, were you two busy in there?"

"I'll deal with you later," Jericho growls as he passes him.

"How could you do that?" I say to Gideon.

"What?" he claims innocence even though the gleeful look on his face contradicts it. "How was I to know what she'd overhear?"

"Why do you hate me so much?"

He laughs. "I don't hate you." His eyes scan up and down my body in dismissal. "It's my brother I hate and you know why."

I shove my face in his. "There's a lot you don't know about your brother, Gideon Priest."

"That's rich coming from the girl he fucked without telling her he was already married."

I groan in frustration. "You're so bloody-minded."

"And you're too naïve to see what's in front of your fucking face." His eyes lower to where my fists clench at my sides, my discarded underwear bunching between my fingers.

I want to blurt out the truth to Gideon. I want to tell him his brother isn't the kind of monster he thinks he is. But it isn't my secret to tell. "He gives you everything, Gideon, and asks for nothing in return."

"I earn my way."

"How?"

Gideon's eyes narrow. "You're awfully feisty today, aren't you? Did he not perform properly? Is there an undercurrent of frustration I'm sensing here?" He steps closer, leaning to whisper in my ear, "I could help you with that, you know."

"You're unbelievable, you know that?"

He laughs, throwing his head back, curls bouncing. "And you're too easy to rile up."

I glare at him for a few moments before turning away and storming off. I can't deal with him right now. But Gideon doesn't want our conversation to be over. He follows, chasing me down the hallway.

"I earn my way by gambling."

I snort.

"What? It's the same way Jericho earned his start."

"And how's it working out for you, huh? Managed to buy your own home yet? Run your own business? In fact, have you managed to do anything but lounge around drinking?"

Gideon sucks in an exaggerated breath. "Someone's found her claws."

Frustration slices through me and I turn around and shove him, both hands planted into his chest. He stumbles back but manages to regain his footing. I start to run up the stairs, needing to be away from him but again, he follows.

"Look, I'm sorry. I didn't mean it. Well, not all of it anyway. It's just you're so cute when you're angry."

I let out a second frustrated wail, earning another laugh from Gideon. He holds up his hands and stops following me. "Okay, okay. I'm being an asshole. I'll stop now. I just want to talk for a bit. Sometimes I feel left out of my own life. I don't know whether it's because Jericho thinks he's protecting me, or he doesn't trust me, but it's hard. It's lonely."

His words stop me from walking any further. There's real hurt in his voice. He doesn't know the truth. He still thinks Jericho killed their father. I sink down to sit on one of the steps and Gideon comes to join me. His fingers wrap around the railing of the banister. The muffled but heated voices of Hope and Jericho float down from above.

"Did you know they'd found Hope?"

"I was there."

A flash of pain cuts across Gideon's face.

"It all happened rather suddenly."

Gideon nods, his fingers tightening around the intricate railing. "Too suddenly to even let me know it was happening?"

"Believe me, it wasn't anything you wanted to see. Hope was—" I pause, thinking of the best way to word it. "Hope was scared. She was handcuffed when we arrived."

"Fucking Keating," Gideon mutters. "I always thought it was him but Jericho would never listen to me. He listens to Barrett but never me."

"It wasn't Keating. It was his son."

A frown pressed between Gideon's brow. "His son? I didn't even know he had a son. Why?"

I sigh, leaning back as I think of Dominic. He has such an easy smile and easy manner; it's still hard to think of him capable of such a thing. It was like two different people were residing in the same body. Makes me wonder how many others are like that.

"He said he did it to make his father proud but I thought he'd always hated his father."

Gideon tilts his head, leaning it against the banister. "I suppose I can understand that, hating someone but still wanting to make them proud." He smiles sadly. "Kind of like me and Jericho. I hate him, I honestly do, but sometimes there's nothing I want more than for him to actually notice me."

I don't know how to answer that. Jericho stays away because he knows his younger brother despises him for what he thinks he did, but he still refuses to tell him the truth.

"But they—" He clears his throat. "They got rid of Keating, didn't they? Did they get rid of Dominic too?"

I swallow, the image of Aaron Keating falling to the floor blinding me for a moment. In the end, all I can do is nod. "But not Dominic. In the middle of it all, he took off."

"So he's still out there?"

I nod again. "Somewhere."

"And who did it? Who was the one to—" he runs a finger across his throat "—do the deed?"

"It was Barrett," I say quickly. I don't add that Jericho gave the order. Nor do I add that Jericho and I sat in the car while Barrett dealt with Mary. The thought of it makes me feel nauseated and my stomach twists. I take a deep breath, willing away the flashes as Gideon watches me curiously.

"You still don't see it, do you?"

"What?" I ask, letting my breath out in a gush. Overhead the voices grow louder but they're still too muffled to hear any words clearly.

"What he's really like. Who Jericho really is."

"And I suppose you're going to tell me."

"He's a cold-hearted killer. There's something wrong with him," Gideon taps his head, "up here. He can't see that what he does—"

"Just stop," I say, getting to my feet. "I know you hate him and I know why. But maybe you don't know everything, Gideon. Maybe there are things he's protecting you from."

Gideon doesn't respond. He sits with his head hung low. But then he swings it up and peers at me. "How's your father doing? What do you think Jericho will do now that he has no use for him?"

"He can do whatever he likes. I don't care."

Gideon smirks. "Yes you do. You haven't suffered enough to truly understand the desire of wanting someone dead. Deep down, it's not something you'd ever have the courage to do."

"And I suppose you would?"

Gideon pulls himself up. "Nope. But that's the difference between my brother and me. He thinks he has the right to take someone's life." He shrugs as though we're talking about something insignificant. "I don't."

chapter six

I follow Hope into her room. She sits on the floor, back to the wall, knees drawn to her chest. She scowls when I lower myself to sit beside her. I don't say anything, just sit in silence, waiting for her to talk.

"I thought I'd be happy once I was free." She speaks so quietly I have to lean in closer just to hear her. "I thought I'd walk around, grateful for every breath of air, just pleased to be alive."

"And you're not?"

She shakes her head slowly. The years have been both gentle and harsh with her. Her hair is long, trailing far past her shoulder blades. It's thinner than I remember. She used to keep it cropped in a tight bob, always perfectly framing her face. Now it hangs in unkempt strands shouting of her time spent in captivity. Her clothing hangs loosely from her frame, covering her arms, but I've already seen the scars. The state of her broke my heart when I saw her naked and scared, handcuffed to the bath. It was a moment of pure joy and sheer terror. Relief and sadness. But she's just as beautiful as she's always been. Her smile is the same, and her laughter, both things I've only witnessed when she's been around Ette.

"I'm angry, so, so angry. It's like there's this rage inside me and I can't get it out. I want revenge."

"On Dominic?"

"On everyone," she says. "On every man who thought he had the right to control me, to own me, including the father of your little fuck-bunny." She glances at me. "She even looks like him."

I snort, choosing to ignore the first comment about Berkley, only focusing on the second. "She does not."

"You wouldn't know. You haven't looked into his eyes."

She has no idea I've had him locked away for months. She doesn't know how many times my fists have flown into his flesh. She doesn't know I've looked into his eyes and seen the evil reflected in there. They are nothing like Berkley's.

"The set of them is the same, not the color, but the shape." I don't correct her. There's no point. But she adds,

"I can't believe you're fucking her," and I flinch at her words.

She moves, sitting on her knees and yanks up one sleeve of her sweater. "Look." She holds her bare arm out. "This was the only control I had over my own body, the only option I had to exert a little power."

I stare at her arms and the thin pale lines that run down them. It's as though someone has forced their nails deeply into her skin and dragged them down her arm.

She tugs her sleeves back down. "He hated it. He told me that my body was his to scar, not mine." She slinks down as she talks, growing smaller with each word. "He put a collar around my neck and chained me to his desk after I did it. He kept me there for days. Like a dog. He'd click his fingers and I'd have to crawl to him. And I'm finally set free to find you're fucking his daughter."

"It's not her fault. She didn't know who he was."

"It's not what she did or didn't know that's upsetting. It's what you knew. I never expected you to wait for me. I mean, our marriage was hardly normal, but I never considered that..." She lets out a big sigh. "Did you know who she was when you. . . when you..."

She looks up at me. There's an expectation in her eyes. An expectation to deny I knew who she was. To claim my innocence. But I can't.

"Yes. I knew exactly who she was. That was the whole reason I hired her. I had a plan. I was going to use her to make him talk."

"So why didn't you?"

"He was in jail." I know I'm lying to her but I'm not sure she's ready to know the truth. She seems strong. She seems ready to tackle life, but I know what trauma can do and I don't want to overwhelm her.

"They caught him?"

I'm surprised. "You didn't know?"

She laughs but it's cold. "Strangely, my subscription to the Captive Daily didn't always make it."

"His place was raided the day after the auction." I don't look at her as I say it. I know how devastating it was for me discovering she was missing. Again. I can't imagine what it must be like for her, hearing how close she was to safety.

She just sits for a while, staring at a blank space on the wall. Even though the familiarity is there in her features, she's a stranger to me now. She's hard where she used to be soft. Tough where she used to be weak. Scarred where she used to be flawless. And I can't help feeling like it's all my fault. Like she blames me.

I need her to understand the things I did. The decisions I made, so I plunge into the story, giving her only the details she needs.

"When you were taken, the first person I thought of was Keating. I thought he'd organized some way to simply get rid of you in order to get custody of Ette. So I lied. I told the police she was taken too."

Her eyes widen. "You did what?"

"According to the official police record, Odette is missing, just like you. I did it to protect her. I did it so I could keep her here, away from him, and no one would question it. I kept Mrs Bellamy on and she's been with me ever since. She's been like a mother to the girl. I hired tutors and swore them to secrecy. I've done everything I can to give her a life you would have wanted for her."

I can't read the expression on Hope's face so I blindly keep pressing forward, spilling all the secrets I've kept for years.

"I've dedicated my entire life to you and her, Hope. I spent all my time, all my money just trying to find you. I hired Barrett to watch Keating but he found nothing. He was convinced that Keating had nothing to do with your disappearance so we moved onto other theories. We chased the idea of you all over the world. I went on wild goose chases that resulted in nothing." I move closer to her, hoping she can hear the sincerity in my voice. "After years and years of chasing ghosts, I finally got confirmation that you were with him, with the monster before he was jailed. I became obsessed. I sought information on his wife, his children, the women he'd held captive, the people who'd worked for him, anything and everything I could. And then finally, I came up with a plan."

"And Berkley was part of it," she says, as though she's resigning herself to hear the part of the story she doesn't want to.

"I made up a position for a dance tutor and hired her. I tricked her into coming here, living here with us and it was during that time she got under my skin."

"Under your skin or under your clothes?"

Her crudeness annoys me and I lash out without thinking. "Well, it's not as though you didn't fuck others." Pain flicks across her face. What a callous thing to say. I reach out to her but she jerks away. "That was stupid. I didn't mean it, Hope. I'm sorry. I just lashed out without thinking."

"People have said worse." She shrugs as though unaffected but I know how cruel my comment was.

"She's the one who got the information about where you were. It was her contacts, her charm that enabled me to find you. If it weren't for Berkley, you wouldn't have been found. You owe her some thanks for that."

Hope jumps up, her hands fisted at her sides. "I don't owe anyone anything! You included!"

"I didn't mean—"

"Look around you, Jericho. You talk as though your life has been difficult. Oh poor me, searching for my stolen wife. You got to spend your life surrounded by people who respect and admire you." She twirls on her heels, arms wide, head lifted to the ceiling. "I mean look at this place. You live in a fucking castle!"

I stand, trying to resist the temptation to yell back at her. "Everything in this place is for you! Every day I've been filled with the guilt of what happened to you. Guilt that I got to live my life, I got to spend it with Ette while you were fuck knows where, getting exposed to fuck knows what."

I rip my shirt open, tossing it to the floor and turn to expose my back to her. "I've been haunted by you, Hope. Reminders of you are fucking tattooed on my skin. You're the reason I bought this place. There was a part of me, a fucked-up part that always imagined you here. Imagined you staring out the stained-glass window in my room, watching the swans just like you used to. I was just focused on finding you. Nothing more. Just finding you. I expected nothing more. I never counted on…" I let out a deep breath. She doesn't need to know the details of how I fell for Berkley. "Anything you want, I'll give it to you. This house, my business, the clubs, money, anything. But no matter what you ask for, nothing can ever make up for what you've been through."

She's calmed down. She looks so small in her baggy clothing, as though the outfit is attempting to swallow her whole. She clutches at one arm with the other, sort of holding onto herself.

"And what about you, Jericho. What is it you want?"

I answer without hesitation. "Berkley."

Again, pain flicks across her expression. She takes a step back but then schools her face into something cold and void of emotion.

"Well, I want the head of her father on a fucking platter."

It's then that I realize hiding the monster's presence isn't protecting her. It's giving her the only thing she's asking for. Vengeance.

I hold out my hand. "Come with me."

She looks at my outstretched offering and narrows her eyes.

"Trust me," I assure her.

She follows me to my office, not saying a word the entire time. The person she used to be filled silence with words. The person she is now is comfortable with it.

I flick on the switches to the monitor and wait for the picture to load. Hope peers at the screen and then recoils when she sees the image.

"You have cameras in prison?"

I push a seat over and she climbs into it. "Not exactly," I say, leaning over her to switch on the other screens. The rooms of the Sanctuary come to life. "I have cameras here."

Hope watches the man who once owned her, laying on his stretcher, staring mindlessly at the ceiling. She reaches out to touch the screen as though it will somehow prove the reality of it.

"He's here?" Her voice shakes.

"He was getting a retrial and his lawyer was able to get him released on bail. I took the opportunity to relocate him."

"Here?" she says again, eyes glued to the screen as though if she looked away he might escape.

"In the basement."

Her fingers clutch at the table. Her face has paled, her eyes wide.

"He's yours. You get to decide what gets done with him. It's the least I can offer you. If you want his head on a platter, I'll give it to you."

"Does she know?" She flicks a glance my way, but it's brief.

"She does. She isn't like him, Hope. She's one of us."

Hope doesn't say anything. She tucks her legs up, resting her chin on her knees and simply watches the screen.

"Is it really him?" she says after a few minutes. Then she shakes her head. "Is it okay if I just stay here and watch for a bit?"

I glance at the clock. It's late. "Stay as long as you want. Would you like me to stay with you?"

Again she shakes her head. "I'll be fine."

"Okay," I start walking towards the door. She's fixated on the screen, a small line pressed between her brows. "Goodnight then."

She doesn't even hear me. I close the door just as Barrett approaches.

"Everything okay?" he asks.

"I just showed Hope the camera."

Barrett's gaze ducks past me as though he can see her through the door. "How'd she take it?"

"Not sure yet."

"Would you mind if I hung around, just to make sure she's okay? I'll stay out of her way. I won't go in. I just want her to know someone's here if she needs it."

I clap Barrett on the shoulder. He's a good man.

"Oh, and sir?"

"What did we agree on using that word?"

"We didn't agree on anything. But you asked me not to call you that." Barrett grins, then straightens his stance, his usually serious demeanor taking over once again. "I just wanted to let you know we've found him."

"The kid?"

"Yeah. Dominic. You want me to collect him?"

I nod, not wanting to voice it out loud. I feel like somehow Berkley could hear me and I know she's fond of him, despite everything she now knows. "I'll come too. We'll leave the day after tomorrow."

My eyes skip back to the closed office doors. I don't want to leave Hope alone. I don't want to crowd her. Truth is, I feel like I'm constantly on edge around her. I'm unsure what to do.

Barrett clears his throat. "I've got this, sir. Go do what you need to."

Without me having to say a word, he understands. I nod in recognition and head off in search of Berkley. I find her in the bathroom. She's soaking in the bath, headphones on, legs crossed and draped over the edge, her body submerged in milky liquid. Her hair floats in the water, swaying as she moves in time to whatever music she's listening to. The swells of her breasts break the surface of the water, two perfect circles, nipples peaked and pink.

I lean in the doorway, arms and ankles crossed and watch her. A smile teases the corners of her mouth. Her eyes are closed and the movements of her body create ripples in the water. She's so innocent and pure yet she slides between submission and aggression. Between sinner and savior. Damnation and deliverance. She's a riddle I'm desperate to solve.

She doesn't notice me until I step fully into the room and then she pulls the headphones out, looking up at me with apprehension.

"How'd it go?"

I shrug as I start undoing the buttons of my shirt and pushing off my shoes. "About as well as can be expected, I guess."

"She hates me, doesn't she?"

I push my jeans over my hips and let them fall to the ground. "She doesn't. Make room."

Berkley sits up and I lower myself into the water. The scent of jasmine floats up. As soon as I'm sitting in the water, Berkley lowers herself between my legs, her head resting on my chest. The curve of her lower back brushes over my already hard cock.

"I told her about your father."

"She knows he's here?"

I nod, resting my chin on the top of her head so she can feel the movement.

"What are you going to do with him?" Her voice is quiet.

I bring my hands to rest on her thighs. Her skin is smooth and soft. Right now I don't want to talk about her father or Hope. I want to get lost in her. She's my only respite. But I know that would be unfair to ask of her. She's owed the truth as much as anyone.

"What do you want me to do with him?"

"I don't care." The tone of her voice belies her words.

"I told Hope she could make the decision. Considering."

She turns in the water, her breasts pressed to my stomach, her arms on my chest and her eyes peering into mine intently. "What about Dominic?"

"What about him?"

"Don't pretend you don't know what I'm asking, Jericho. I know you'll be looking for him. I know what you did to his parents."

"I didn't—"

She places her finger on my lips and shakes her head. "Don't lie to me. You may not have done it, but you still gave the order."

It's strange for me, viewing my decisions through someone else's moral compass. "We're still looking." It's almost the truth. "I don't know where he is."

She bites her bottom lip. Her stomach presses into my groin, making it almost impossible for me to concentrate on the topic at hand. "Promise me you won't hurt him."

"He was the one who held Hope captive."

"But he didn't harm her. I can't believe he did. He's peaceful. He's a dancer. Maybe there's more to the story than we know. Maybe someone was holding something over him, forcing him to keep her."

I chuckle at her naivety. "You don't think that keeping someone against their will is harming them?"

Her body stiffens. "I don't know. Maybe you should be the one to answer that."

"Berkley," I say her name as a sigh. "What happened in that head of yours while I was talking to Hope?"

"I remembered who you were and what you've done."

"Everything I've done was for a good cause. Finding Hope."

"Do you truly believe that?" She looks up at me with those eyes. Those eyes that make me want to agree with everything she says just so they will look upon me with affection and desire.

"I believe that things can't always be separated into good and bad, right and wrong. Sometimes it's more than that. Sometimes it's less. All I know is that people have hurt Hope and turned her into someone I barely recognize anymore. And I want to make them pay for it."

chapter seven

I wake curled on the chair of Jericho's office. My body is cramped and sore. I stretch slowly. The screen still shows him, my old master, lying on his stretcher in his cell. He's sleeping.

It's strange being able to watch him the same way he used to watch me. Nothing is appealing about it other than having the security of the knowledge that he's trapped, unable to hurt anyone else. I watch him with detachment, as though he's merely a villain on a television show. The man I see now is nothing like the man who I called Master. That man was evil and wicked and cruel. That man took pleasure in my pain. There were times he was gentle, even kind. But I was never fooled by those times. I know them for what they were. His. Everything was his. His choice. His time.

But it was my life.

Now, here, surrounded by stone and metal, he looks old and weak. He doesn't look capable of cruelty. He does not look like a man I should fear, and yet as I sat here last night, my body shook. Every part of me trembled until exhaustion set in.

It must be the wee hours of the morning as the world beyond the window is gray and dim. Cloud blocks the rising sun and mist filters its way through the trees. The swans on the pond sleep with their heads tucked under their wings, content and safe. It's a feeling I'm still not used to. I know I'm safe, I know I'm free. But I don't feel it.

As soon as Jericho left last night, I pushed the door to his office back open. I don't like being trapped behind a barrier, even if I know it's unlocked. It's irrational and illogical but I can't help it. My heart started to race and I kept looking at the door, getting up and testing to see if it was unlocked. So it was easier to just leave it open. That way, one glance was all it took to reassure myself.

With one last look at the monitor, I leave the office, almost tripping over Jericho's head of security as I walk out the door.

"What are you doing there?" I gasp, my hand held over my chest as my heart pounds.

He wakes, pulling his legs away from where they were stretched over the floor. "I must have fallen asleep." He looks at me sheepishly as he gets to his feet. "I thought you might feel safer if someone was at the door."

"That was very kind of you, but it probably would have been best if you'd let me know you were there in the first place."

He smiles and bows his head. "I didn't mean to startle you."

"Barrett, isn't it?"

He nods and holds out his hand. "It's a pleasure to finally meet you, Hope. It's nice to put a face to the name after spending years searching for you. Not that I didn't know what you looked like. It would have been a little hard searching for you if I had no idea what you looked like." He laughs uncomfortably as I shake his hand. He squeezes gently as though he's afraid of breaking me.

"Well, thank you for searching for me. Although it would have been nicer if I didn't have to wait years to be found." His face reddens and I feel a little mean for my sharp retort. "But I do appreciate what you've done."

"Are you heading back to your room? Would you like me to walk you there?"

I shake my head. "I'm fine, but thank you for the offer. It was nice officially meeting you, Barrett."

He salutes as I walk away. Strange man.

My room has been decorated in the colors I used to like. Blues and golds and grays. I don't know what colors I like now. It seems unimportant. Clothes are stuffed into my drawers, presumably placed there by Mrs Bellamy, but again, I don't know whether I like them or not. I'm not used to having a choice. For now, I'm dressed in oversized sweatpants and a long-sleeved top. It seems safest.

Breakfast will be served shortly, but I don't go down, even to see Ette. I don't know what's worse. Worrying your daughter might forget you, or knowing she has.

Nothing is the same as I left it.

Ette has grown into a young girl, a graceful, smart and beautiful young girl, all of which has nothing to do with me. She tolerates my presence, putting up with it like one might an elderly great-grandparent that your parents insist you visit. Her smile is hesitant and the term 'mother' is nothing more than a word. Seeing her interact with the people who have brought her up causes me more pain than I'd ever had while imagining her life without me. Inside my head, it was only a fear, nothing certain, but out here I can see the way she clutches Mrs Bellamy's hand, the way she rolls her eyes in annoyance at her governess and how she smiles and runs to Berkley every time she sees her.

The feeling that washed over me when I first saw Jericho stride through the bathroom door is nothing like I've experienced before. I can't even describe it. He held me close, whispered reassurances in my ear, wrapped me in his jacket, and kept me safe. The last time we'd been together, his legs had been twisted in mine. His body had been less developed then. Lithe and lean. But now, having witnessed the change when he showed me the tattoo, time has made him hard and defined. His face was dusted in hair that never used to grow. And his eyes have a rigidness that never used to be there.

I barely registered the girl who was with him at the time. She was nothing more than a background player, someone clearly disturbed and needing help, going by her reaction in the car. I never considered her to be of consequence until Ette ran to her. I never suspected her of holding Jericho's heart until I saw the way he watched her as she danced. And I didn't have an inkling she was the daughter of the man who kept me captive for years, until I looked deep into her eyes and saw him reflected there.

How Jericho could do this was beyond me. He's fallen for the daughter of a monster. And children of monsters usually turn out to be one themselves. I should know.

There's a knock at my door, even though it's open. I glance up and see Ette peering at me, so I force a smile and tell her to come in. She takes a step closer but doesn't move past the door.

"Mr Priest said I should check on you since you didn't come down for breakfast."

"I'm fine," I quickly assure her, patting the bed, hoping she'll come in and sit beside me for a few moments. "I just slept a little too late."

She notes my hand patting the bed but she doesn't move. "Mrs Bellamy never lets me sleep in even though I try to every single morning. She says it's the trait of lazy people to lie in bed all day if they're not sick."

"Well, she's probably right. I will get up. I was wondering if you'd be able to show me the library, actually. I'd love to find a book to read."

A small frown presses between her brows and her bottom lip pushes out as she thinks. It's a look so like when she was a toddler, I can't help the tears that gather.

She takes a few cautious steps toward me and holds out her hand. "It's okay, I'll show you the way. You don't need to cry."

My words are choked. "Thank you."

She's silent as she weaves downstairs, through rooms and along hallways. The building is magnificent but confusing. It's taking me a while to figure out where to go and how to get there.

"Here." She stops abruptly at the doorway to the library.

"You're not coming in?"

She shakes her head. "Miss Jones doesn't like it when I'm late for my lessons. She's not fun like Berkley."

"You like Berkley, don't you?" I ask, ignoring the way my chest constricts as I say the words.

"She's one of my favorite people in the world," Ette says proudly. Then her face falls a little and she starts toying with the hem of her dress. "Can I ask you something?"

"You can ask me anything."

"Where were you?"

My throat thickens to the point I feel like I can barely breathe. How do I answer her? How do I tell my own daughter of the atrocities that were committed? Do I lie? Do I tell the truth?

"Away," is all I say in the end.

"But where?" she presses. "And why didn't you come back?"

I smile through tears. "I did come back." I hold my hands to the side and attempt to laugh. "See? I'm here."

She nods, considering the information and then turns on her little heels and leaves.

I don't hold back my tears once she's gone. I allow myself to collapse to the ground and let them fall freely. I sob. Giant, gut-wrenching sobs that I try to stifle, but it's pointless.

"Are you okay?"

The voice startles me. I lift my eyes to find Berkley peering at me, concern framing her eyes.

"It's you," I say coldly, pulling myself up off the floor and wiping my tears away. Somehow it seems worse that she is the one to witness my breakdown.

She points behind her. "I was over there. I didn't mean to interfere."

She's too doe-eyed and young, nothing like I thought Jericho would go for. Her hair is thick and long and lush. Her body is that of a dancer, elongated, graceful, defined. She's wearing one of his shirts. It's over-sized and hangs down to the middle of her thighs. Her legs are bare. Her feet are covered in small white socks.

An undeniable surge of hatred swells within my chest. I don't hate her because he loves her. I hate her because of who she is. Whose daughter she is. I hate that she was free when I was not. That she got to dance with my daughter and hold her hand when I couldn't.

My eyes drop to the rolled-up newspaper she's clutching in her hands. I can only read part of the headline. Murder-Suicide.

"I stole it before it got to Jericho." She sort of waves the paper and gives an uneasy chuckle. "He likes to read his news pressed in ink."

She talks as though I don't know him. And I suppose I don't anymore, not like she does, but I still can't help the annoyance that creeps inside me just at the sight of her. Jericho and I never loved each other. Not like that. But he's still part of my family. A part I want to protect.

She's uncomfortable with the silence between us. She moves closer, coming to sit on the overstuffed chair in front of me. She tucks her knees to her chest and hugs them.

"It's strange to think we lived in the same house and never met."

I close my eyes and try to think of her there. I wonder what sort of a man she knew my master to be. Was he the same with his family as he was with us? Was he arrogant and conceited? Did he consider himself a god? Did he ever show his violent side?

I can tell how much the silence is getting to her, so I merely shuffle across the floor until my back is pressed to one of the chairs. I keep looking at her expectantly without saying a word. It unnerves her. I enjoy it.

"Did you know my mother?" she asks finally. When I still don't reply, she adds more as if to prompt me. "Lily. She often talked about Iris. That was you, wasn't it?"

I haven't heard that name in a long time and it brings back waves of emotion. I steel myself against them, focusing on the part of information I didn't know. "Lily is your mother?"

She nods eagerly, pleased to have found one subject we can bond over. "She was rescued during the police raid. I never knew who he really was until that day. I didn't know he was my father and I didn't know he was a monster."

I swallow the knot of pain in my throat. Lily is free. The news both fills me with joy but also with self-pity.

Berkley adjusts herself on her seat. "She told me that in some sort of fucked-up way, she thought he loved her." She picks at her socks. "Do you think he loved you too?"

"He isn't capable of love."

"I'm sorry," she's quick to say, noting the vehemence in my tone. "I didn't mean to imply…" she lets her voice fall away.

"I've fantasized about his death." I watch her intently as I say it, waiting for her affection for the man to shine through, but she remains impassive. "I've imagined wrapping my fingers around his throat and just squeezing and squeezing until his face turns purple and he finally just stops breathing." She still doesn't react, so I push some more. "I've imagined running a knife up his veins." I demonstrate with my fingers against my skin, following the lines of scars that are already there. She flinches and a small flicker of satisfaction burns within me. "I'd just sit back and watch him bleed to death. I'd stand over him as the blood drained from his body and spilled into the dirt where it belongs."

Her skin pales. It's as though I've triggered some sort of memory. Her gaze falls to the newspaper still clutched in her hand. Part of the photo beneath the headline is visible now. It's the face of Aaron Keating. She closes her eyes and counts to five under her breath.

"What are they saying?"

Her eyes spring open. They take a few moments to focus on me, as though she was far away and attempting to pull herself back. She holds out the paper.

"Attempted murder-suicide."

"Attempted?" I question, scanning the small text beneath the photo.

"Mary was shot, but she didn't die."

The article says if the bullet wound had been a little more to the left she would have died instantly, but as it was, she lay there bleeding slowly until she was found. The son, Dominic, has not been seen since and is wanted by the police for questioning. When I finish reading, I glance up to find Berkley studying me. She opens her mouth as though to say something and then thinks better of it. Shuffling to the edge of the seat, she props her head on her hand.

"Did he hurt you? Dominic, I mean?" Her face flushes. "I mean I know he hurt you, he kept you captive. But the person I know could never do that, so I was just wondering how he treated you because it just doesn't sit right in my head."

"You knew him?"

"I thought I did. He was so gentle. I just can't imagine him…" She doesn't finish her sentence and lets the words hang between us.

"And you've been known as such a great judge of character in the past."

She smiles sadly. "Yeah, I know. It seems I'm an easy target for lies. He was just always so kind to me. It's hard to imagine him as anything else."

"There were times he was kind. I could tell his heart wasn't in it, you know? That the person he was trying to be wasn't really him. Sometimes it was like a friend popping by for a visit. We watched a movie, played a game." I laugh coldly. "If you ignored the fact that I couldn't leave." Berkley's looking at me intently, drinking in the information regarding her friend. "But then there were other times he'd come in and it was almost as though he carried this dark cloud with him. He was moody and sullen. He was repulsed by me. It's almost as though there were different versions of him."

"Did he ever talk about his father?"

I shake my head. "He never mentioned his family at all."

Berkley rises from the chair, her movements fluid and graceful. Jericho's shirt is too big, floating around her body as though she's an angel drifting on a cloud.

"It's strange to think he's Ette's half-brother," she says quietly.

"Family are the people you choose, not the ones dictated by blood."

Her gaze burns my soul. "I wish everyone felt the same as you."

I realize what I've said. I've let her off the hook for the sins of her father. I curse myself inwardly as she goes to leave. When she reaches the door, she turns around, leaning her forehead to the frame.

"I didn't know he was married." Her eyes plead with me to understand, to offer her some semblance of forgiveness or acceptance.

I don't.

She drops her gaze to the floor. "But even when I did find out, I didn't leave." She bites her lower lip before looking back up at me and I almost curse Jericho then and there for falling for her charm so easily. "I loved him. I love him still. He's the family I choose."

I don't say a word. I let the discomfort of my silence grow until she gives up and slips away.

chapter eight

It's commonplace for the staff to join in at the dinner table now. Our meals are provided on platters in the center and everyone helps themselves. The result is a more laid-back feel. Less stuffy. But tonight, the tension is palpable in the air.

To everyone except Ette.

She sits, stuffing her face and chatting easily. No one tells her off for talking with her mouth full. Not Jericho. Not even her governess Miss Jones. No one corrects her when she prattles on, mispronouncing words and telling nonsense stories. We all smile and nod while trying to avoid looking at each other.

Gideon sits opposite me, grinning the whole time. It's almost as though he enjoys this strange dynamic. He chews with his mouth open, flicking his gaze between Jericho, Hope and me, and wiggling his eyebrows every time I happen to look up.

Hope watches and interacts with Ette. No one else. It's like she's got blinders on and she's determined not to remove them. Jericho just eats, seemingly oblivious to it all.

But then he does something unexpected. After finishing his meal and laying down his cutlery, he reaches across the table and lays his hand over mine. It's a quiet movement with no announcement but it's as though the entire table collectively gasps. It's innocent in relation to the affection he's shown me in private, but my heart still starts racing and my cheeks flush. Gideon's brows almost pop off the top of his head, and Hope's eyes slide over and fix on our connection.

"You're holding Miss Berkley's hand!" Ette crows, announcing to the table which had already, quite literally, stopped and taken notice.

"I am," Jericho says, offering her a smile.

"Are you two boyfriend and girlfriend now?"

"We are." Jericho squeezes my fingers a little.

She screws up her nose. "Do you kiss her?"

Jericho laughs. "I do."

Ette shrugs. "I'm going to kiss my boyfriend one day." She shoves another forkful into her mouth, mumbling through the mess. "When I get one."

And that's it. That's the announcement to the household, the confirmation of our relationship.

Jericho clears his throat and all eyes turn to him. "Barrett and I will be leaving for the night. I've made sure there are extra guards to allay any concerns. We'll be returning tomorrow."

I look at him questioningly, but he doesn't return my look. He pushes back his chair and proceeds to leave. I rush after him.

"Where are you going?"

He places a kiss on the tip of my nose. "Just into the city for the night. There's some business I need to attend to."

I frown, fearing what he's going to do. "What sort of business?"

He lowers his voice to a growl. "My business."

Why do I always get so hot and bothered when he uses that tone? It makes me want to just melt at his feet.

"It's not about Dominic, is it?"

"I told you I don't know where he is. Keep an eye on things here for me, would you? Make sure Hope feels safe."

"Maybe you should assign someone else that job. I don't think she likes me."

"You'll be fine. She'll be fine." He pulls me close and I grumpily wrap my arms around his waist and press my cheek to his chest. I breathe in deeply, drowning in the scent of him. I don't want him to leave. I want us to spend the evening together, and the night, and all the next day. I want to lay in his arms. I want to climb on top and sink onto him. I want, just for a few days, for everything to be normal, without drama. Ignore the monster in the basement. Ignore the outside world and just live in our own bubble.

"Are you going to be gone all night?" I sound like a sullen child.

His chuckle is loud and deep, rumbling about his chest. "I've set most things up so I can operate from home, managers I trust in the clubs, staff to boss around and do all the work I don't want to, but occasionally my presence is required. Like tonight. I need to show my face, play a couple of hands, attend to a couple of issues."

"Can't I come with you?" I say, my voice muffled by the material of his shirt. I need to stop. Just stop. But for some reason, I can't. There's this panic inside at the thought of him leaving. I tell myself it isn't because I'm worried what he'll do, what revenge he might exact, but I know I'm lying.

"Not this time." Jericho pulls himself away. "I've got to go."

And he leaves me in the hallway, watching his retreating back. I don't return to the dining room. I pull myself up the stairs and flop onto my bed. A while later, through the rain-streaked window, Barrett pulls the car toward the front of the Sanctuary and Jericho climbs in. He's wearing a dark navy suit and a white shirt. As usual, his shirt is without a tie, and the top button has been left open. His hair is slicked up and back into groomed perfection. His chin is dusted in dark stubble.

Just looking at him makes my heart ache.

I feel foolish pining after him like some love-sick schoolgirl. But it's how I feel. And it seems the weather is mimicking my mood as the rain isn't thunderous or powerful. It just trails down the windows pitifully, almost as though they're crying.

My sleep is fitful. It's filled with dreams of smiling mouths that twist into evil smirks. Fragments of memories mixed with fears of the unknown. Dominic laying in a pool of blood instead of his father. Mary pleading with me to save her life while clutching at a gunshot wound in her stomach. The blood seeping through the material of her dress and staining her fingers. And Jericho in the background, leaning against an invisible wall, just watching.

I wake with dread lodged in my chest. Something is wrong. I know it. My heart pounds so hard it feels as though someone has taken a hammer to my chest. I sit up, pulling my knees to my chest and hugging them as I watch the rain pelting against the window. It's far more tempestuous out there now. The gentle tear-like rain of yesterday is gone and now it is as though the outside world is screaming in rage. The swans on the pond are all huddled under the branches of the willow trees which droop over the water, creating some sort of shelter.

My room is deathly cold. There's condensation on the inside of the windows and they're foggy at the edges, giving the world a melancholy feel. I breathe into the room and it billows white before dissipating.

I don't go down to the pool. I don't go down for breakfast either. I don't want to run the risk of seeing people. Not Hope with her accusing eyes and cold glare, and certainly not Gideon with his smirks and mocking laughter. Instead, I spend the day in the dance studio, running through old routines interspersed with periods of just staring out the window and trying to shake the coldness that's settled in my bones.

By the time Ette arrives for her lesson, I've managed to work some warmth back into my limbs. I decide not to focus on any set moves or routines and instead we have some fun. At first, Ette rolls her eyes when I suggest we move to the music as though we're mimicking animals, but after she sees my impression of an elephant dancing, she laughs and joins in. So, when I suggest doing classic dance moves like the twist or simply spinning but as slow as we possibly can, she agrees without hesitation. We play freeze dance and I finish off the lesson by teaching her the start of the 'Thriller' dance, much to Miss Jones's disapproval. She stands with her arms folded and a scowl on her face in the doorway.

"I would have brought her up," I say, attempting to catch my breath. "You know, like I usually do," I add with a tight smile.

"Her mother asked me to come and collect her."

"Oh."

Miss Jones looks at me as though I've done something other than my job as a dance tutor. "Master Gideon was looking for you earlier. It seems as though having one man in this household twisted around your finger isn't enough." My mouth drops open as Miss Jones strides past me and grabs Ette's hand, pulling her from the room. "Perhaps it's time you consider moving on. You've done quite enough here, don't you think?"

I'm still a little shocked as the door slams shut. After a few beats to recover myself, I jerk the door open, determined to give Miss Jones a piece of my mind, but instead I find Gideon striding down the passageway.

"There you are," he exclaims. "I've been looking for you."

"So I've been told," I mutter, peering behind Gideon so I can at least level a laser-eyed glare at Miss Jones's retreating back.

Gideon saunters past me and into the studio. He looks around, leveling his gaze at the ceilings and walls as though inspecting the place. He gives himself a wink when he catches his reflection in the mirror.

"Look, now's not a great time for me."

Gideon raises his brows. "Are you expecting another student?" He grins and runs his tongue over his teeth. "What about me?" He performs some sort of wobbly pirouette and then bows deeply.

"What do you want, Gideon?"

"You really are in quite the mood today, aren't you?"

I just cross my arms, jut my hip to the side and look at him expectantly.

"Fine." He lowers himself to the ground, flopping down to lie on his side, his head propped up on his hand. "I was just wondering what sort of secret mission Jericho was on, since you seem to be in the know these days."

"Well, I'm not."

"You're not what?"

I roll my eyes. "I'm not in the know."

"So, you don't know about this little mission he and Barrett are on?'"

"No, I don't. All he said was something about playing a few hands so I'm guessing it has to do with the club in the city. Maybe a poker game or something he has to attend."

"But you're not sure?"

"I've already told you that."

Gideon picks up a stray piece of fluff from the wooden floor. "So you don't think it has anything to do with your friend? The one who had Hope?"

I level my gaze at him.

He shrugs. "It's just interesting is all."

I take the bait. "What's interesting?"

"You're the daughter of the man who kept Hope for years. He sells her and guess who she turns up with? Someone you're rather close with from all accounts."

"Perhaps that has more to do with the fact that his father is also Ette's father. Something I had nothing to do with, just like I had nothing to do with her involvement with my father."

Gideon jumps to his feet and wipes his hands together. "Interesting way of wording it. Involvement with your father." He snorts. "Like it was a choice."

"What are you trying to get at, Gideon?" Frustration leaks into my tone.

"I'm not trying to get at anything. I was merely asking questions. Let me know if you hear from your friend again, like ever." He strolls past me with a smirk. "Have a good day."

My stomach is growling by the time dinner comes around but instead of joining the others, I head outside, not caring when the rain drenches my clothing. I run through the garden and make my way to the gazebo on the edge of the pond. It's peaceful here. The rain pelts down like a blanket, cutting off the gazebo from the rest of the world. Occasionally lightning strikes, flooding everything in light and then the thunder starts to rumble. It's so loud it reverberates through me.

I can't stop thinking about Dominic. What he did and the person I know simply don't match up in my head. Dominic was kind; sarcastic, but kind. He would never want to harm Hope, I just know it. I wish I could talk to him, find out exactly what he did to her while she was locked away in the bunker on their property.

Surely, that fact alone should chill me to my bones. He kept her trapped against her will. There is no coming back from that. But does it warrant death, or does it warrant being locked away, just like my father is?

The world is turning black by the time I see headlights cut through the trees as a vehicle makes its way along the winding road. I watch as Barrett pulls the car to the front of the Sanctuary and Jericho disappears inside. He moves with purpose, as though he's on a mission and it only takes a few minutes for him to come striding through the rain, his mouth in a tight line, brows pushed together. The dread that has sat in the pit of my stomach all day rises and gets caught in my throat. I lift my hand, as though begging it to stay there and not rise to the surface and confirm the nightmares that have been swirling about my head.

"What are you doing out here?" he asks, ducking to step under the shelter.

"Did you find him?"

Jericho's gaze drops. And that's when the dread in my throat escapes and I let out a little gasp of anguish.

He opens his mouth, but I don't want to hear the words that I know are coming. So I talk before he does. "He's a good person. He's a kind person. Someone must have forced him to do what he did to Hope. There's no way he could have done it on his own. No way he'd want to. He isn't that sort of person. Ryker, my brother, he had to—"

"We were too late," he says, cutting me off and reaching for me.

I move out of his grasp. I can't help it. I can see the truth in his eyes, but I don't want to acknowledge it. I don't want to believe it. I don't want him to touch me with the same hands that…

"Berkley," he growls. "You don't know the full story."

"Then tell me."

I lower myself to the seating that runs around the closed-in section of the gazebo. It's as though the world has gone silent around us. The rain no longer sounds when it hits the gazebo roof; the wind doesn't howl. Thunder doesn't rumble. Lightning doesn't crash. My heart doesn't beat.

"Barrett found out where he was hiding. By the time we got there he'd already taken his own life."

I stand again, needing distance between us. I cross my arms over my chest as though they will somehow protect my heart from breaking. "I don't believe you."

His gaze is unflinching. "He hung himself, Berkley. There was nothing I could do."

A sob is wrenched from me. I fight the tears, fight the images of Jericho hoisting Dominic's limp body into the air. My fists ball at my sides. I take another step back and then another until I'm exposed to the rain.

"Berkley," Jericho steps toward me, but I turn and run, wanting to be anywhere but where he is.

chapter nine

Dominic's easy laughter and rolling eyes flash through my mind as I push myself harder and harder through the rain. I enter the Sanctuary through the kitchen and sprint down the hallway toward the dance studio, not caring about the wet footprints I leave in my wake. The doors slam when I shove my way through them, the sound echoing around the empty room. I push the buttons on the stereo frantically, bringing up the song to which Dominic and I danced a duet long before any of this mess happened. Back when I was just a girl who wanted to dance, and he was just a boy who shared the same dream.

And then I lay in the middle of the floor with the lights off, my body soaked and cold, and just listen. I let the music carry me away to a world unperverted by the desires of the men around me.

When we performed for the company, Dominic danced alone at the start of the song. He would start by leaning over me, my head turned to the side while he shadowed my movements without touching. Then I stayed on the floor, just as I am now, as he powerfully twisted and turned his body, having trained it to perfection.

It's as though something or someone controls me when the music gets to the part where I joined in. My body rises from the floor and I imagine Dominic beside me. Our movements are schooled by violent and savage choreography. We kick high into the air. We fight and we fall. Wild tears run down my face as the music fades, knowing that our routine was left with Dominic reaching for me, lying alone on the floor.

But when the next song plays, I keep dancing. It's messy and angry and sad. I dance until I'm exhausted. I dance until the image of Dominic fades. I dance until I can barely breathe. And when I'm finally done, feeling ragged and torn, I look up to find Jericho leaning against the wall, arms crossed, watching me.

I'm on the ground on all fours, chest heaving, wet clothes clinging to my body. Jericho just stands there with this look on his face. It's part arrogance, part lust, part indifference.

Music fills the air once again and I crawl across the floor, drawing out my movements, keeping my eyes fixed on him. He pulls himself away from the wall, uncrossing his arms to let them fall at his sides as he watches. There's desperation and pleading in my movements but, as the music swells, so does the feeling inside and I pull myself to my feet, standing in front of him, almost pressed to his chest.

We're face to face. Eye to eye. I don't know whether he's going to grab me and crush me against him or toss me aside. His breath washes over my face as his nostrils flare. It's as though we're battling in an invisible war. He takes a step closer. So close his chest pushes against mine.

Then his hand wraps around the back of my neck and forces my mouth onto his. I fight with my impulse to grab onto him, let him devour me, and my impulse to push him away.

The latter wins. I shove him, pushing him against the wall and he stays there, a wicked grin on his face, eyes flashing with provocation. He runs his hand through his hair as he straightens himself and advances on me again.

"What is it you want from me, Berkley?"

I take a few hurried steps backward. "Did you kill him?"

He keeps striding forward, his face twisted into beastly glee.

"Did you kill him?" I yell.

My heart thuds so hard it hurts. My skin prickles with fear or anticipation or excitement. But he just keeps stalking forward, hunting me like prey.

"Why won't you answer me?" My voice breaks this time. I walk so far across the room, I back into the piano.

"Because you don't really want to know the answer. You don't want to know the truth of who I am."

"Yes, yes, I do." I lift my chin even though it trembles.

He leans forward, brushing my hair behind my ear before growling quietly. "What do you want me to say?" He bites my earlobe gently, sending a shot of lust into my core. "Do you want me to say no? Do you want me to say I never hurt a hair on that boy's head, that he was so miserable, so filled with regret that he took his own life? Do you want me to say all that so you can fuck me without guilt? Or do you want me to say yes, so you have an excuse to fuck me like you hate me?"

I shudder as waves of lurid desire crash over me, drowning out my senses, my mind. Everything but him.

I hate that he does this. I hate that he challenges me, pushes me, insults me, and yet all I do is come back for more.

"Tell me to leave and I will." His voice is a growl.

But I don't. Because I don't want him to. I want him to claim me, dominate me. I want him to make me forget everything.

I love that he does this. I love that he challenges me, pushes me, insults me, and leaves me yearning for more.

I close my eyes as he hisses in my ear. "It's your turn to tell the truth now, Berkley. So what will it be?"

He turns dark eyes filled with euphoric ferocity on me. He towers over me, hands pressed to the piano at my back, caging me in. With a surge of aggression, I lift my leg and knee him in the groin. He winces, but then his eyes narrow and a true tremor of terror ripples through me.

"As you wish," he says, grabbing me by the back of the neck again and crushing his mouth against mine.

Our movements become a tug of war. Back and forth. Attacking and retreating. Each time I try to run away, he drags me back, and I melt against his mouth once again. We battle, tearing at each other's clothes, scraping our nails over each other's flesh. His hand fists in my hair, holding me in place as his tongue runs over my neck and jaw. I flail wildly until the buttons of his shirt spill onto the floor.

Jericho lets me go long enough to tear his shirt off. I don't go anywhere. I wait with heaving breath until he comes at me again, confused by the range of emotions colliding within. He lifts me, taking me away from the piano and pins me against the wall. Our mouths fight for dominance. I wind my fingers into his hair and tug hard. He moans and presses against me harder, so hard I find it difficult to breathe.

"My god, Berkley. You drive me insane," he growls, nipping at my bottom lip, biting down until I feel the metallic taste of blood seep into my mouth.

But I can't pull away.

I can't escape him.

I don't want to.

He claws at my breasts, his mouth falling to follow suit when his hands tear at my leggings. He rips them from me, the pressure cutting into my flesh before tossing them aside, leaving nothing between us. He fumbles desperately with his pants, dropping them to the floor before plunging inside me.

The air leaves my lungs.

He's vicious and feral and savage. There's nothing I can do but cling to him as he drives inside, thrusting with all the frustration and anger that ripples through his body. I press my hands to his chest, trying to push him away even though I only want him closer. He just holds me firmer as grunts of aggression spill from his lips.

Tears gather, but they're not tears of sadness or pain. They're tears of relief, tears of anguish, and tears of need. It's like Jericho looks into the darkest recesses of my soul and knows what I want, what I need, even before I do.

All the fight leaves me, and I become nothing more than a ragdoll, tossed by Jericho's demented thrusts. The friction of my damp skin against the wall brings knife blades of pain that only make me wetter. Lifting limp hands, I wrap them around his neck, holding on as though my life depends on it.

He does nothing but use my body for his own pleasure, but it's what I need. I want my body sore and my mind empty.

"What is it you want from me, Berkley?" he growls, his words accented by grunts as he continues to thrust into me.

"You," I sob. "Just you."

He slows, grinding his hips in a circle rather than driving into me. Tilting my chin up, he forces me to look into his dark eyes.

"You have me. You'll always have me."

It's as though a coil unwinds at his words and I gasp as the suddenness of a climax shudders through my body. Jericho thrusts one last time, then holds himself still as he pulses inside. His head drops to my shoulder. I let my legs fall from his hips and we stand, forehead pressed to forehead as the world and the room and the music materializes back into focus.

When he lets me go, I slide to the floor, curling into the fetal position and letting cathartic tears fall freely.

"He wouldn't have felt any pain." Jericho stands over me, his naked body on full display. "It was quick."

A sob is wrenched from me as he walks away. Because it's in that moment I realize I've fallen in love with my own monster.

I lie alone on the floor, memories ripping through my mind, jumbled and confused. Jericho, my father, my brothers, all dance around me, their movements distinctly different, until the image blurs; their bodies start to meld together until they merge into one monster with two heads. Each side of the monster mimics the other. They're the same but one side is bathed in light and the other in darkness.

I close my eyes tight, willing the image away. It's not a flash, it's not a dream, it's a curse. A spell that's washed over me.

I don't know how much time has passed when Jericho creeps back into the studio. I feel his steps reverberating through the floorboards rather than see him. I'm where he left me, curled into a ball, naked on the floor. He lowers himself behind me, dragging a blanket to cover us both and wraps his arm around my middle, pulling me close.

He doesn't say anything as we fall asleep. He doesn't need to. Everything he could say, everything I could say, is trapped in my head. But none of it matters.

I am his.

I will always be his.

Nothing will change that.

chapter ten

It hasn't stopped raining for three days. The world outside Jericho's bedroom window is dark and dreary. The moon is hidden behind clouds. The branches of the trees sway in the wind. But the rain is so gentle it doesn't make a sound as it falls against the glass.

Beside me, Jericho sleeps. He's lying on his stomach, stretched over the mattress, and almost hugging the pillow. He hasn't shaved in a few days, so his jaw is covered in dark stubble. He's naked and the sheets are tugged low, so his tattoo is on full display. Even in sleep his brows are pulled into a frown.

I want to reach out and touch him, trace the lines of the swans in battle that grace his back, but I don't want to wake him. He hasn't had a lot of sleep lately, going to bed well after midnight and waking in the early hours of the morning. Then he locks himself away in his office, his raised and tense voice often slipping through the cracks of the door. So it's good to see him resting. He almost looks peaceful. Almost.

Moving slowly, so as not to wake him, I creep out of bed and walk over to the window, grabbing my cardigan to wrap around my shoulders. Even though it's not cold inside the room, it feels like it should be. I press my forehead to the glass and stare out one of the segments of stained glass. It turns everything blue.

I've kept myself locked away of late. I don't want to see the hate reflected in Hope's eyes. I don't want to see the distrust in Gideon's. Once again I've become the thing I fear the most. Nothing more than the daughter of a monster. All I want to do is hide. Or run away. Again.

There's a part of me that tells me to creep silently out the door, leaving everyone and everything behind. I could start again. Just like I've done before. I could escape to a small town where no one knows my name. Or I could hide in a big city and blend in with the throng.

But when I think about leaving Jericho my heart twists violently. He is the only reason I haven't gone. He's the one thing I crave too much to abandon. He is my reward and my punishment.

I imagine him chasing after me, pursuing me to the corners of the Earth just to bring me back to him. Like he did for Hope. But that would be cruel to ask of him. I cannot ask him to abandon his life here, the life he's built. Even if he built it for another woman.

My feelings for him are a double-edged sword. He's everything I want. He's everything I need. But he's also everything I want to avoid. The threads of his life are too wrapped up in the parts of me I want to forget.

"What are you thinking about?" Jericho's voice is low, scratched by the lingering need for sleep.

"I didn't mean to wake you."

He's rolled over now, resting on his back with his hands propped behind his head. There's a smattering of dark hair on his chest that fades, leaving the ribbed muscles of his stomach smooth. He's undeniably gorgeous. Instantly a wave of need and longing crashes over me.

"Come back to bed."

He pats the space beside him and I pad my way back, letting my cardigan fall and climb under the sheets. He lifts his arm over my shoulder allowing me to snuggle into his side and rest my head on his chest. His heart beats steadily as he pulls me close. I wish mine had the same rhythm. Instead, it rapidly rises and falls, leaving me exhausted by its unpredictability.

"What were you thinking about?" His lips are pressed to the top of my head as he speaks.

I give a small laugh as my hand travels across his chest, once again tracing the connection of the tattooed feathers. "Just my life. Being here. Everything."

"This is your home now, Berkley. You belong with me."

"But there are so many reminders of who I am here."

"You are more than his daughter."

"Sometimes it doesn't feel that way. Sometimes I feel like I'm never going to escape him. There's always going to be someone who looks at me in a certain way, who doesn't trust me merely because of the blood that runs through my veins."

"Are you talking about Hope?"

"Not just her. Anyone who knows the truth."

"Do you want me to talk to her?"

I shake my head, rubbing my cheek against his chest. "It just makes me seem pathetic. I am pathetic. Look at what she's gone through, what's been done to her, and here I am complaining because she doesn't like me." I sigh. "I thought this was all behind me, that coming here was a sort of escape, but now I'm trapped here, in a place where everyone knows the truth of who I am."

He adjusts himself and tilts my chin so I'm looking up at him. "You feel trapped here?"

"Trapped by my own doing, of my own accord. I'm trapped by my feelings for you, Jericho. I don't want a life without you, yet I can't see myself ever escaping who I am with you by my side."

"Fuck, Berkley." He sits up, leaning against the headboard and pulling me between his legs. My thighs wrap around his hips, my arms around his neck. "I don't ever want you to feel trapped by me. I want you to want me, to need me, but I don't want you to be unhappy. It kills me to think that I'm putting you through some sort of—"

I finish his sentence. "Torture."

"Is that how it feels?" His brows are pulled together dramatically, and his mouth is a thin line of concern. Those dark eyes of his skip between mine as though they are searching for a truth he wants to see behind my words. One where I'm not tortured by my affection for him, where I'm not in a constant state of tug-of-war. "What can I do?" His voice breaks on the words. "Anything, Berkley. Anything you want of me and I'll do it. I just want your happiness." He sighs deeply. "I thought I was giving it to you."

"You are," I say, hugging him tight. But honesty pulses with each beat of my heart. "But you're also the source of my pain. I want you. I want you so badly that it causes me pain because to be with you is to be her. The daughter of a monster. The monster who hurt your family. It's who I will always be when I'm with you."

"You don't mean that." He presses a tender kiss to the curve of my neck, transforming the waves of confusion to waves of lust. "That is not who you are." His mouth moves up the side of my neck, leaving warm, wet trails in his wake. "To me, you are a pool of cool water on a hot day, or a warm bath on a cold day. You frustrate me and inspire me. You are graceful and beautiful and fierce and bold. I'm in awe with the way you stand up to me, defy me, fight me and I'm in awe with the way you submit to me and crave me."

He cups my face. His fingers dig into my jaw and cheeks as though he's desperate for me to hear the truth in his words. "You give me hope, Berkley. You make me believe there's more to this world than greed and power and control. When I felt as though everything good had been taken from me, you came into my life and reminded me that I could have a future. A future of happiness and love."

Pulling me close, his mouth crashes against mine in a delicious collision of need and longing. His hands cupped around my face keep me in place as he tries to relay the feeling in his words into the action of his mouth. My nails dig into his shoulders, needing a release for the pent-up passion building inside.

"Remember this, Berkley. Remember my words. And promise me if you ever want to leave, you'll talk to me, you'll tell me. I don't think I could stand it if you left. I can't even imagine how empty my life would feel without you."

I nod as his gripped fingers hold me in place, the desperation of his plea translating into the physical as his hands move to my shoulders, digging into my flesh and reminding me that it's only his touch that melts me like this.

"Promise me, Berkley. Promise me you'll talk to me before doing something rash, that you'll let me know what's going on inside your head."

"I promise." My words come out breathless and desperate because the way he's touching me is making me forget everything I said, everything I felt. In Jericho's arms there is no outside world, no monsters. No monsters other than him.

His hands slide down my back and he jerks me closer, opening my hips wider and allowing his hardness to press against my warmth. "I know a part of you wants to go, but let me remind you of one reason to stay."

He tilts forward, lowering me onto my back and crawling over me. His eyes burn darkly as he reaches up and runs a single finger down the side of my face. It's such an innocent gesture but it feeds the fire burning within. He lifts my hands above my head, trapping my wrists in his fingers and stretching my body out beneath his. Then he kisses his way down my arms. When he reaches the soft flesh of my upper arm, he bites gently, and I squirm as it sends sharp stabs of yearning into my core.

He runs his tongue down my right arm, darting sideways when he gets lower so he can torment my breast with pleasure. Even though my arms are no longer trapped by his, I keep them stretched above my head, offering my body to him. He sucks my nipple into his mouth, teasing it between his teeth and biting down with enough pressure for me to writhe in demented rapture.

He leaves no part of me untouched by his lips. His tongue runs over my breasts and along the dip between the swells. He latches onto the flesh of my stomach and hips, kissing and licking, sucking and biting. He nips as though tasting, sending sharp pangs that prickle my skin. He sinks his teeth into my hip bone, and I let out a low moan of pleasure.

My body is imprisoned by his touch.

Continuing his trail of kisses, his mouth drags over my skin and buries into the soft flesh of my thigh. My legs open willingly, of their own volition, begging him closer. But he ignores my blatant supplication and runs his tongue down my leg and over my ankle until he sucks my toe into his mouth, scraping his teeth across the flesh.

I gasp, my chest convulsing off the mattress, surprised by the intensity the action elicits. Jericho lets out a low growl and wraps his hands around my ankles, jerking me along the bed, tugging me closer to him. He lifts my legs, placing my knees over his shoulders, my feet dangling over his back. And then his mouth attacks my inner thighs again, dancing between them, biting and tormenting.

I'm a wound-up bundle of exquisite sensations. I want to run away and pull him closer. I want him to stop and never cease. I'm torn between needing release and drowning in pleasure.

I need his tongue between my thighs so I buck my hips, urging him to taste me, give me some release from this excruciating torture.

A wicked grin covers his face as he shakes his head. "So impatient," he tuts.

Grabbing my ankles, he flips me over, and begins the agony all over again, his mouth colliding with every inch of me, sending me to a place where I no longer know what I want. I'm consumed by him. Every part of me has been licked by burning desire.

I pant and I moan. I twist and I writhe. But Jericho doesn't stop. He's determined to undo me by the stroke of his tongue while never giving me what I need.

He bites into the flesh of my ass cheeks and runs his tongue along the backs of my thighs. My ass rises, desperate for him to reach between my thighs and sate my need. But instead of giving me what I wish, he sits back and clears his throat.

"Get on all fours."

I scramble to obey. He could ask anything of me in this state and I'd willingly heed his command. I'm desperate in my want for him. It's an ache. Something I can't ignore. It's controlling my movements, my thoughts. I cannot stop.

Twisting my head, I look behind. His back is pressed to the headboard of the bed. His cock is hard and thick and his fingers are wrapped around it as he strokes up and down. His eyes are fixed on where I'm open and exposed, ready for him. Heat flushes my cheeks when I think of how obvious my need for him will be.

"Touch yourself." His voice is almost a groan.

Embarrassment washes over me. "Jericho, I can't—"

"Touch yourself," he commands and my hand flies between my legs, my shoulders pressing into the mattress as my ass sits high in the air. I'm so wet it's mortifying.

"Berkley," he breathes as I run my fingers over myself. The sensation causes a small moan to escape. "It feels good, doesn't it?"

I nod and bite my lip in shame.

"Don't hide yourself. Don't hide the way you feel. There's no bigger turn-on than seeing you enjoy the way I make you feel, Berkley. I want to see your wetness. I want to see the way you're swollen and ready, desperate for me."

"Then don't make me wait any longer." My words come out as a choked plea as I twist around to look at him again.

He shakes his head. "I love seeing you desperate and begging. I love seeing how badly you want me."

I pull my hand away and turn around to face him. His eyes fall to my breasts, flushed and red from his touch. He reaches out to flick a nipple as he strokes himself, his head falling back against the headboard as a long and low moan escapes.

Leaning forward, I lower my mouth, eager to taste him, to feel his hardness push in and out of my mouth. Jericho's hand winds into my hair, taking control of my actions. He pushes me onto him, his hand gripping my hair as his cock hits the back of my mouth.

I gasp for breath and plant my hands on his thighs, reeling back, fighting the force of his hand wound into my hair. His eyes fill with illicit darkness when he jerks my head upwards. I fight against his grip, wanting to lower myself onto him again. He lets me lower my head, only to jerk me upwards again and crash his mouth against mine. We kiss,

114

our tongues tangling in a battle of passion before he separates us and pushes my head down again.

He holds me lightly this time, allowing me to take pleasure in the taste and form of him. I run my tongue from base to tip before taking him in my mouth and sucking hard.

He hisses and I revel in my dominance over him. His hips jerk when I try to take more of him into my mouth, forcing his cock to hit the back of my throat once more. My entire body convulses, and I reel back again, sucking in air.

Jericho slides down the bed, lifting my hips into the air so he can position himself under me. Then he guides me onto his cock, his eyes locking with mine as he fills me. I plant my hands on his chest and begin to rock back and forth, relishing the feeling of fullness.

I ride him with wild abandon, letting my lust control my movements, ignoring his pleasure and only seeking my own. He watches with the devil reflected in his eyes. His hand wraps around my throat, his thumb playing with the line of my jaw. He squeezes ever so slightly, and I push into his grip, wanting the desperation of the need for air to set my body on fire. Jericho's fingers crawl up over my chin and push into my mouth. He shoves them down my throat until I gag and convulse. His eyes roll back as I constrict around his cock.

He does it again and the sensation causes me to explode. I arch my back as the ripples of ecstasy rip through my body and then I collapse, my head falling to his chest, all strength leaving my limbs.

Jericho holds me tightly as his hips piston, driving himself into me until his own release gushes and we lie tangled in each other's arms, spent and content.

chapter eleven

HOPE

Ette is the only thing that brings me any fraction of joy. But even my time with her is bittersweet.

When she smiles, I think of all the happiness I've missed.

When she laughs, I think of all the fun we never got to share.

And when I watch her dance, I think of all the time that's been wasted.

I hate that part of my life was stolen. And I hate that I can't seem to put it behind me. Every day I'm wracked with anger at the memories that live inside my head. They twist and turn like a poison, stopping me from being able to truly enjoy the freedom I now have. Every action is tainted by my life before. Every thought of the future is ruined by my past.

"You're here again?" Jericho's voice startles me.

I'm in his office, staring at the screen that shows the man I called Master, lost in the bramble of my own thoughts.

Jericho walks over and sits on the edge of the desk. He threads his fingers together and places them in his lap. For some reason, the action makes me feel like a child about to get scolded by the teacher.

"I'm worried about you."

I keep my eyes fixed on the screen.

"This isn't healthy, all this time you're spending watching him."

I snort. "I think I'm allowed a little leeway considering the situation."

"True." Jericho nods. "But maybe you should talk to someone."

That makes me turn my gaze to him. "Like who? You? Berkley?"

"A professional."

"And you are going to let me go into the city to see one?"

Jericho frowns. "We've already talked about this. It's too soon. We haven't decided how we're going to handle your return in regards—"

I push back from the desk and get to my feet. I'm not having this discussion with him again. He insists he's protecting me, but his protection feels more like control.

"Hope." He sighs when he says my name. Like I'm a frustration. A hindrance. "Hope," he calls out when I ignore him and clump my way down the stairs. "You've got to—"

"Stop telling me what I have to do, Jericho." I whirl around to face him. "Don't you understand? That's all I've dealt with for years. I've lived by someone else's rules, been told what I can and can't do. I don't need you doing the same."

He's slightly taken back by my outburst. He blinks a couple of times and then descends the few steps to stand just above me. "I care about you, that's all. I want what's best."

"Well, maybe you should let me be the one to decide that."

He nods, accepting the rebuke.

I take a deep breath. "I want to see him."

"A therapist?"

"The monster," I clarify.

He sighs again. The sound does nothing but annoy me, so I turn and start walking down the stairs, ignoring the words coming from his mouth.

"I don't think you're ready, Hope. We don't need to rush anything. There's plenty of time for revenge."

But revenge isn't what I'm after. Not yet anyway. That time will come. For now, I want to look into his eyes and know he doesn't have power over me anymore. And I want him to know it too.

I want to confront my demon.

Maybe then he'll stop haunting me.

"Hope," Jericho calls out. "Where are you going?" He keeps following me as I stride across the dining room. "You know I'm not going to let you in there."

I walk through the kitchen and down the passageway. The dance studio is just ahead. Faints strains of music can be heard wafting along the hall to greet us. She must be in there. I push the doors open and Berkley freezes, mid-pose, arms held in an arc above her head, one leg extended behind her, the other tight and taut, balancing only on her toes. She wears a pale pink leotard and a short skirt. Her feet are covered by ballet shoes, the ribbons winding up her calves. Her hair has been twisted into a messy bun on the top of her head.

She looks nothing like the daughter of a monster.

Planting her foot on the ground, she brings her arms and legs down, looking at us curiously. Her eyes dart between Jericho and me, and each time she looks at him, there's a softening of her stance.

"Take me to your father," I demand.

She looks at Jericho instead of me, searching his expression for an explanation of my demand.

"Berkley," he says, striding over to her. His hand hovers protectively. I know he wants to reach out and touch her but for whatever reason, he's hesitant around me. He should know better. "Don't listen to her, she's—"

"You know the code, don't you?" I demand, talking over Jericho.

She nods dumbly.

"Then take me to see him."

"Why can't Jericho?"

"He refused. He doesn't think it's a good idea."

"You don't?" She turns to him with those stupidly innocent eyes of hers. The ones that remind me of her father even though his don't hold an ounce of innocence. The ones that are gray and blue and green all at the same time.

"She hasn't been back long. She doesn't need—"

"Stop telling me what I do and do not need!" My hands clench into fists at my side. I turn to Berkley, trying to control the rage that shudders through me. "You owe me this."

"She doesn't owe you anything," Jericho snaps back.

But I know I've won by the way Berkley's head drops. She feels the weight of her father's sins. I can exploit that.

"She's right, Jericho," Berkley says. "I don't think it's your decision to make."

She walks toward the door and I shoot Jericho a triumphant smile.

He scowls before striding after her and grabbing her hand. "Berkley," he warns in a low growl.

An almost visible tremor ripples over her. She looks up at him and for a moment I think she's going to be swayed, but then she lifts her chin a little and jerks her hand out of his.

"Fuck," Jericho curses.

I can't help but aggressively brush by him but when he reaches out to grab my hand, I reel away and hiss, "Don't touch me."

It's an automatic response now that I have a choice. Fear of people touching me without permission. Panic at being trapped behind closed doors. Jumping in fright if I'm startled. They are the new normal of my life.

Berkley strides down to the basement confidently, as though she's done it a thousand times before. Perhaps she has. Perhaps she's visited her father hundreds of times. Perhaps she's already told him I'm here.

She looks at me before keying in the code. I nod, giving both her and me the reassurance that this is what I want, but then, as she goes to pull the door open, I slam my hand against it, stopping her.

Suddenly my heart is pounding in my chest. Cold sweat dots my brow and my throat constricts, making it hard to breathe.

"Are you okay?" Berkley asks.

I'm not. But I don't tell her that. I just stand with my hand planted against the door as though I'm afraid if I let it go it will swing open and unleash the monster within.

"Deep breaths." Berkley demonstrates by breathing in deeply, her chest rising, her back straightening as though I don't fucking know how to do it myself.

Even though I'm pissed at her, I copy her breathing in the hope it will calm my own. But I can't suck in enough air. I'm hot. Too hot. Sweat drips off me and I start to shake.

"You're having a panic attack," she says, taking both my hands in hers and holding them tightly.

I shoot a glance toward the door, scared it will open but it remains secure and shut.

"Look at me," Berkley orders. When I don't, she shakes my hands. "Look at me."

I do. The sound of my heart beating thuds loudly in my head. It's almost deafening.

"I want you to count with me, okay?"

I want to slap her for how calm she's being. But instead, I merely nod as I try to suck in another breath of strangled air.

She begins to count, drawing in deep breaths between each number. It's pathetic. And stupid. But it also works. I mimic her, keeping my breaths in time with hers. She's staring at me with those wide eyes and for a moment, it's as though I see the blue sky reflected in them. She stays with me, holding onto my hands and counting and breathing until my heart rate slows and the air flows freely into my lungs.

"You don't have to do this. Not yet."

I pull my hands out of hers. "I thought I'd be fine."

"You don't have to be fine, either. It's okay not to be okay." She lets out a little snort of air. "I should know. I haven't been fine in a while."

I don't know what she could possibly know about not being fine. As far as I'm aware, the monster raised her as his own. She lived a life of privilege. She can't possibly know anything about what it feels to have control and choice taken away from you.

She sees the doubt in my eyes. Pushing her sweater over her shoulder, she exposes a scar. It's somewhat faded now, but you can still see the rounded hole and the spidery lines that jut from the radius.

"The day after you were sold, I was shot by my half-brother." She nods toward the door. "His son."

"Sebastian?"

She smiles faintly and pulls her sweater back into place. "I forget you know them."

"I still get panic attacks. And I haven't been through anything like you have. You're brave, Hope. You're one of the toughest people I've ever met. You've gone through all this, all this shit, and yet you're still here. You've still got love to offer Ette. You've still got a life to live."

Her words get to me, forcing a lump to grow in my throat. I blink away tears.

"You don't need to do this now, but that doesn't mean you won't ever confront him. You've got time. There's no hurry. He's trapped here. He's not getting out. You can make him pay if that's what you want to do. No one is going to take that choice from you. Not Jericho. Not me. No one."

A sob rips from my chest. It hurts. It tears. I stumble backward and fall against the wall, allowing myself to sink to the ground as the sobs keep coming. Berkley sits beside me. She doesn't say anything. She doesn't touch me or try to make things better. She just stays by my side as the tears fall. And it's enough.

When my tears finally dry, she gets to her feet and holds out her hands, waiting for me to accept her offer of help. I place my hands in hers and she pulls me to my feet. She just looks at me for a while, not saying a word. But it's all there in her eyes.

The worry.

The guilt.

The apology.

Even though we don't exchange words, something changes between us in that moment. An understanding. We walk in silence back to my room. Before she leaves, she turns to me and simply says, "I'm here if you need me." And then she slips away.

I know I'm not ready to face the monster yet. But I will be soon. And I need to be prepared. I need the skills to exact revenge.

I catch a glimpse of Barrett disappearing around a corner and chase after him. He looks startled when I call his name.

"Is there something I can help you with?" he asks.

My eyes drift over him. As usual, he's dressed all in black. There's a firearm slung from his belt and a knife strapped to his side.

"Would you teach me?" I ask, nodding to his belt.

"Teach you to what?"

"To use a knife."

chapter twelve

I'm plastered to Jericho's chest when there's a knock at the door.

"Not now," Jericho calls out, his voice pulling on the growling and commanding tone that makes me tremble.

"Ah, sir? I mean, Jericho, this is a matter of importance," Barrett's voice doesn't hold any of the commanding tone of Jericho's. It's unsure yet persistent.

Jericho lets out a huff of annoyance as I roll off him and he gets to his feet, pulling on a pair of sweatpants as he walks. The door creaks as he swings it open.

"What?" he snaps.

"Sorry, but there's been some new developments."

I'm hiding in the bed, sheets drawn to my chin. Barrett can't see me from the doorway, but I'm still not risking it.

"What is it?" Jericho's tone is a little gentler this time, but there's still an element of terseness.

"I believe there's been some retaliation."

That pricks my interest and I poke my head over the headboard. "Retaliation?" I question.

Barrett's eyes slide over to me and a little heat creeps up his cheeks.

"It's your mother," Barrett says, focusing back on Jericho. "She's gone missing."

"Fuck," Jericho curses. "You sure?"

Barrett just nods.

"Retaliation from who?" I ask. "You said Dominic was dead." Just saying the words out loud cause my throat to tighten and my chest to constrict.

Jericho glances my way. "We don't think he was working alone." Then he turns back to Barrett. "I'll be down soon. Get the car ready."

Barrett nods and Jericho closes the door, walking over to the rack that holds his clothing and sorting through the options until he tugs a shirt over his head.

Slipping from the bed, I wrap my cardigan around my shoulders and walk over to sit on the sofa as he does up the buttons of his shirt.

"Who do you think he was working with?"

Jericho doesn't look at me as he sits to pull on his shoes. "It's nothing for you to worry about."

"You can't just push me aside now that you've got want you want," I snap.

Jericho looks up, confused. "What are you talking about?"

"You used to tell me things, you used to listen to me but now that Hope is back, you're cutting me out of everything again. I'm not some little girl you need to shield from the truth. Tell me things straight. Don't sugar-coat it or make up some more palatable truth. There's always something you're not telling me, something you're holding back. You won't even tell me the truth about Dominic. Do you think I won't be able to handle it?"

Jericho sits back on the sofa, now fully dressed. He chews on his bottom lip, eyes narrowing. "I don't want you to know all the things I've done. I don't want to be the monster for you. I'd rather you look at me in suspicion than in disgust."

"It's a little too late for that."

His head cocks to the side as though he's deliberating just how much to tell me, then he sighs deeply before talking.

"We're not sure who, but we're pretty certain Dominic had help in acquiring Hope. It seems odd that he was simply able to purchase her with no ties to that world. That's why we've increased the number of guards around here. We also assigned one to my mother, without her knowing. He's been keeping Barrett informed on her movements. He must have reported something that's made Barrett suspicious. We're going to check it out but I'm sure it will be nothing. She's gone missing before, but she always turns up once she's sobered up a little."

"Let me come with you."

He shakes his head. "Please Berkley, just let me worry about one thing at a time. Having you there would be…" He pauses. The vein beneath his left eye twitches. "Just please stay behind, here, where you're safe. There are extra guards, cameras in action, and no one can enter the gates unless they work here. It's the safest place for you to be right now." He leans over and kisses the tip of my nose. "And it means I won't need to worry about you."

I pout. I know it will look childish but I don't care. "So you just want me to stay here and sit around for you to return like some sort of princess locked in a castle?"

He chuckles. "We'll only be gone a day or two and it's just for now. When I get back, let's plan an escape, just for the two of us. Away from all this."

"Promise?" I know I sound like the little girl who stopped crying when offered an ice-cream, but the thought of just Jericho and I together is an offer too tempting to resist. So I sink back into the sofa, determined to be content with my place in the current situation.

"Promise." He winks before he walks out the door.

I hate this person I've become. This whining, pleading, pathetic person but I don't know how to escape it without losing him. I'm trapped by my own desire.

I sneak down and steal some breakfast long after everyone else has eaten theirs. I skip lunch and instead, wander around the gardens, not caring about the gentle rain which settles on my hair and my clothing without ever sinking in. I feed the swans, taking with me leftover vegetables from the kitchen. They squawk and honk, one of them daring to come close enough to take some food right out of my hand.

"Jericho said we're not supposed to feed the swans," Ette says, and I turn to find her hand in hand with Hope, strolling along the edge of the pond. Hope holds a basket, resting it on her hip.

"We're going to have a picnic inside the gazebo. Do you want to join us?" Ette asks.

There's a smile on Hope's face but it falters when she looks at me, so I shake my head. "I better go get ready for our lesson later. You two have fun though, okay?" I gather the last of the swan food in my hand. "Here, you take this." I place it on top of the basket. "Just don't tell Jericho, okay?"

Ette laughs. I wonder if she noticed that Hope and I haven't said a word to each other. If she feels the tension that ripples between us. I don't know how to fix it. I don't know how to be someone I'm not.

I offer Hope a small smile as I turn away, but she doesn't look at me. She keeps her gaze fixed on Ette. I thought things might have become a little easier between us since she broke down outside my father's cell, but it's as though it never happened.

My afternoon drags by as though someone has put the world in slow motion. I keep to myself during dinner, only talking when someone asks me a question, and then I rush up to my room, eager not to feel the heat of Hope's glare. It's gotten to the point that I don't know if I'm reading into things, or if she really does despise me. I try to imagine what it would be like for her, to finally be set free and return to a home that has been built for her, only to find another woman in her place. But I'm not willing to let go of what I've got. Not yet at least. For now, I'll bide my time and wait for Jericho to return so he can remind me that I belong to him and he belongs to me.

Sleeping alone brings back nightmares and I wake, covered in a cold sweat and shivering. Only this time, I don't remember my dream. It's just the dread of it that lingers. I wish I could creep upstairs and crawl into Jericho's bed. The scent of him alone would bring me comfort. Instead, I bury myself further under the covers as the house creaks and groans, trying to ignore the thudding of my heart.

But the thudding of my heart is joined by other noises, footsteps and voices muffled through the walls. Despite the fear that settles in my chest, I get out of bed, careful to step quietly and open the door. The hallway is clear. I tread lightly on the stairs, avoiding the steps I know that complain under pressure and open the door to Ette's room. She's sleeping soundly, not disturbed by any of the noises. Further down from her room is Hope's. The door is open. There's a light on but as I approach, I hear the heavy breaths of her sleeping. Maybe the guards were simply talking to each other. Maybe it's early enough that Alma has got up to prepare the food for the day.

My bed is cold when I slip back under the covers. My door is shut, and the covers are pulled tight to my chin, but I keep my ears above them, straining to hear any more noises. Maybe I imagined them. Maybe I am still dreaming.

I lie awake until exhaustion overtakes. I dream of Michael. Well, not actually of him, but his presence is a major part of the reason I'm on my knees begging for Jericho's forgiveness. Because, in my dream, I did something to make him stop loving me and it involved Michael. Whether it was a kiss, or something more intimate, I'm not sure. All I know is the feeling of desperation as I plead, looking up at Jericho as he scowls. His face is blurred by my tears. And the feeling of having done something I can't take back is unbearable, even if it is just a dream.

I don't know whether it is that feeling which wakes me, or subconsciously I hear something, but suddenly I find myself awake, heart pounding and eyes wide.

The house is silent. Oddly silent. Instead of the usual sighs and moans of the building settling at the night, there is nothing. My heartbeat is loud in my head, as though it's beating on the outside. There's no splatter of rain. No howling of the wind.

Then a hand clamps over my mouth and I'm dragged from the bed. I don't have time to react before a gag is shoved in my mouth, and strips of material are tied around both my eyes and my mouth. Then my hands are twisted behind my back and secured by a zip tie. By the time I try to fight back, it's too late. I'm bound.

The sound of my heart is now deafening.

I'm grabbed by the crook of my arms and dragged across the floor. I try to cry out, make some sort of noise but with the gag in my mouth and completely blind, I don't manage anything more than a scuffle of my feet on the floor.

Panic hits as they pull me down the stairs, at times lifting me off the ground to keep me from falling. I try to lash out and kick against something, but my flailing proves pointless. Whoever has me moves with military precision through the Sanctuary. They don't talk. They don't hesitate. They drag me while ignoring my failed attempts to alert someone.

It's hard to breathe with the material they've shoved into my mouth. It scrapes against the back of my throat and I start to gag. I twist and turn, trying to free myself from their grip, but they just hold on tighter, to the point of pain. I'm not sure where in the Sanctuary we are when I'm shoved against a wall and the blindfold is ripped from my eyes.

Someone has their arm pressed across my collarbone. A face, covered by a balaclava, is only inches from mine.

"I'm going to free your hands. Do not fight back. Do not resist. If you do there will be consequences. Do you understand?"

I nod, knowing there's little else I can do. I'm turned around and my cheek is shoved against the cold wall as someone presses against my back and runs a knife through the plastic of the zip tie, freeing my hands. My immediate gesture is to rub my wrists. They hurt from where the plastic cut into me.

I'm in the hallway of the basement. The door to my father's cell is just in front of me. My heart drops. I know why they're here and what they want.

"Enter the code," comes the command.

135

I don't hesitate. What would be the point? Three men surround me, all dressed in black, all with their faces covered, all armed.

My hands shake as I key in the code. I see the look of relief on my father's face as one of the men enter his cell, and then the blindfold is shoved back on and my hands are twisted and tied behind my back again.

"About time you came," my father says. But he's the only one of them that talks.

I'm taken by the arms again as I'm dragged back through the Sanctuary. There's barely a scuffle of sound. These men know what they're doing. I know we're outside when the cold air whips around my t-shirt, the only thing I'm wearing. The stones of the gravel dig into my bare feet. A car door opens and I'm pushed inside, falling across what I assume is the back seat of a vehicle. I'm jerked back into a sitting position and then the door is shut again.

There's a moment of silence, more doors opening and shutting from other vehicles and then the seat bounces as someone else is shoved in the other side.

There's a muffled whimpering sound as the engine starts. As the tires crunch over the gravel, the whimpering gets louder and more desperate. Breaths are desperately sucked in through nostrils as someone hyperventilates beside me.

It sounds like Ette.

I struggle against my restraints, but they only dig in deeper, cutting into my skin. I try to scream but the sound gets muffled by the material shoved in my mouth. I breathe deeply through my nose, trying to keep myself calm as Ette continues to cry. I try to shuffle across the seat, but a forceful arm shoves me back.

"For god's sake take the gag out of the kid's mouth."

There's movement and a scuffle and then Ette starts to scream in earnest.

"Shut her up, would you?"

I jump and twist on the seat, trying to place myself between the men in the front and Ette. She's screaming and crying. No coherent sounds are coming from her, only terror. Then the material is yanked down from my mouth and I'm able to spit out the gag.

"Ette, Ette, it's me. Berkley. It's okay, I'm here," I say into the darkness.

"Berkley?" she cries.

"Yes, it's me. It's okay. You're okay. We're okay." I don't know if any of this is true, but my only thought is to comfort her before she works herself into an uncontrollable state of panic.

She keeps crying but there's less desperation to the sound now. "What's happening?" she says. "I can't see anything."

"We're in a car," I state the obvious because nothing else is obvious.

"Where are we going?"

"I'm not sure." I clear my throat, attempting to sound as calm and in control as possible. "Could you tell us where we're going? Who has taken us?"

"Now would be a good time to stop talking," comes the gruff reply.

Ette sucks in a labored breath. "Berkley, I'm scared. I don't like this. I want to go home."

"It's okay. We're together. I'll—" A sharp slap knocks my head back. Pain radiates over one side of my face.

"Berkley!" Ette screams.

I shake my head as though it will dislodge the ringing in my ears. Ette's sobbing. She can barely draw in breath.

"It's okay. I'm okay, Ette. I'm right here."

"Quiet!"

I shuffle across the seat again until I feel the heat of her body pressed next to mine. "Shh," I say quietly. "We'll stop talking for now, okay, but I'm here. I'm right beside you."

She resorts to quiet hitches of breath. I wish I could hold her hand or look into her eyes to reassure her. But closeness is the only comfort I can offer.

I'm not sure how long we drive for, but eventually, we slow to a stop and coldness floods the car as the doors are yanked open. Ette lets out a pitiful scream as she's pulled from the car and I'm yanked in the opposite direction. I'm pulled over grass, the dampness coating the soles of my feet. And then I'm inside, on cold and hard floors. Our footsteps echo loudly.

"Ette?" I call out.

But the only response I get is another slap to the face and a command to keep quiet. A door opens, someone slices the plastic from my hands and then I'm shoved, sending me sprawling.

chapter thirteen

JERICHO

"She's probably holed up somewhere, tripping on whatever high she's addicted to at the moment."

Barrett doesn't say anything, merely stares at me briefly before returning his eyes to the road. He doesn't need to say anything. I already know. Retaliation was to be expected. We're just unsure by whom.

"Drop me at the club," I order.

Again he looks over at me but doesn't say anything. He flicks the blinker on and takes the next turn.

"I need to make an appearance," I answer his unasked question. "Things need to seem normal." Barrett nods. "You keep looking and keep me informed."

He pulls to the side of the road outside the club. Already there's a line, waiting to be let in. They cry out in protest when I stride to the front. I guess they don't know who I am.

The club is packed. It's good for business, I guess, but I hate it when it's crowded like this. Too many bodies writhing. Too many voices rising and falling. But I plaster on my smile and adjust the sunglasses slung over my pocket. They are my grounding, my reminder to be the man I portray to the world.

Barrett and I spent most of the day scouring the city for any signs of my mother. We asked in all the usual places, visited all her frequent haunts, but as yet, nothing. I expect her to be passed out somewhere, but there's also that niggle in the back of my head. Maybe it is retaliation. Maybe Barrett's not stupid for assuming the worst.

Pushing my way through the throng, I wave and smile to the people that call out and make my way to the back room. I must keep up the appearance I've always portrayed. Rich, arrogant, playboy. Too interested in gambling and partying to be of any consequence to anyone. I've neglected it of late, choosing instead to spend my time chasing the daughter of a monster. But I need to keep up the appearance, especially now that people may be watching more intently than they used to.

"Ah, Mr Priest," the dealer calls out. "We're just about to start, care to join?"

I nod as I pull out a chair and take my place at the rounded table. Familiar faces grin back at me. A national rugby player, a news anchor, a few nobodies with enough money to splurge, but there's one new face. One I wouldn't normally allow. The dealer sees my look of concern.

"Patrick Conway." He nods at the man who stands and stretches his hand toward me. I don't take it.

"Anderson vouched for him," the dealer offers.

"How come I didn't know about this?"

Color creeps up the dealer's face. "Darla said she'd informed you."

I grunt, remembering the pile of emails I'd ignored from the club's manager the day before.

Conway sits back down. "We've met before, actually."

"We have?" I keep my eyes on him as the cards are dealt. I know we've met, I recognized him the moment I laid eyes on him, but he doesn't need to know that. I want him to think his presence means little to me.

"I was one of the officers who came to question you after Sebastian Atterton went missing."

Some of the others around the table look at me suspiciously.

"Ah, yes," I reply. "Did you ever manage to find out what happened to him?"

Conway meets my gaze unflinchingly. "It's like he vanished into thin air."

"Well, I'm sure if anyone were to find him, it would be you and your esteemed colleagues." The comment earns a few chuckles. I lift the glass of whiskey that's appeared before me. "The more the merrier. Welcome to the Black Swan." I throw the contents of the glass down my throat and thump it back on the table. The waitress approaches to fill it again but I shake my head. I only like to give the appearance of drinking in situations like this. I don't like to be drunk.

I throw most of my hands, letting money bleed. It keeps the others around the table happy while giving me an excuse to leave if I need to.

There's something dubious about Conway's presence, but throwing him out of the club, or even just the game would arouse more suspicion than I want to attract at the moment. He keeps smirking at me each time he swipes the pot from the centre of the table. It's as though he thinks he has something over me, as though he's winning more than just money.

"Speaking of things vanishing into thin air, has anyone been keeping up with the Keating case?"

There are a few murmurs from the group, but Conway keeps his gaze locked on me, waiting for my reaction. He likes to sit with his tongue pressed between his teeth, as though there's laughter he's trying to stifle. It annoys the fuck out of me, but I'm careful not to react.

"Murder-suicide, wasn't it?" I throw some chips onto the table. "That's what I read in the papers anyway."

"Attempted," Conway corrects.

Someone clucks in disapproval. "Sad story all around that one. The wife was in a car accident a few years back. Her face is all messed up from the scarring." He winces as though picturing it. "I don't think things have been good for them ever since. The case went to court and all. She got done for drunk driving. The other driver died and all she got was a fine." He shakes his head.

"There were signs they were holding someone in a bunker in the backyard," Conway adds. The bet he places is a large one. I match it, earning a raised brow from him as I slide the chips into the middle of the table. "We haven't found the son yet, but we have our suspicions." Conway mimics a motion of someone hanging. "It's almost as though someone wanted to wipe out the entire family."

"You don't think it was the father that did it?" The news anchor asks.

Conway laughs. "Now don't you go reporting on any of this. As far as you're concerned all this is just hearsay. I don't think drunken conversations around a poker table can count as a credible source."

My phone vibrates and I slide it out of my pocket just enough to read the message. It's Barrett. He's found her. An immense wave of relief rushes through me. It wasn't retaliation. She really was just holed up somewhere drugged out of her mind.

My chair slides noisily across the floor as I get to my feet. Folding my hand, I throw it on the table. "Sorry lads, but duty calls." I lift my phone as though its presence alone provides proof of my need to leave. "It's been a pleasure." I doff an imaginary hat.

Conway grins, knowing I've just left a sizeable amount on the table. He thinks he has one over me. I nod in his direction.

"All the best for your investigation."

"Which one?" His brow hitches at the same time his smirk does. I swallow back the urge to whack it from his face.

"All of them."

Barrett is waiting in the car by the time I make my way through the crowd and outside the club. He merely nods in acknowledgment when I climb into the passenger's seat and pulls back onto the road.

"Where is she?"

"The warehouse on the corner of—"

"I thought we checked that place out earlier," I say, cutting him off.

"We did."

I adjust myself on the seat. I cannot get Conway's smirk out of my mind. It's clear he knows more about me than I thought. Or at least he suspects things of me. It's like there's a piece of the puzzle I'm not aware of. Mary hasn't spoken to the police, of that I'm sure. It's reported that she's gone to stay with her brother who has been keeping the police far from her while allowing her to recover. Barrett was clumsy for the first time ever. We haven't spoken about it. There's no point. It is what it is. Mary survived. It's a complication. Nothing more.

We use our phones as torches when we enter the building. Barrett takes me straight to where Alice is lying on a discarded mattress. She's warm, she's breathing, but there's little else to indicate her consciousness. The strip of material around her arm has been loosened. There's a needle on the ground. It's a state I've found her in many times before.

I crouch down, placing my hand on her forehead. I don't know why I do it. I think it's some sort of throwback to the times I felt like I had a mother. The times I was sick, lying in bed and she would come and press her hand to my brow and shake her head, declaring I still had a temperature. It didn't happen often, but those times still replay in my head. I think my memories confused the times of sickness with affection.

She's small and frail in my arms as I lift her. It's almost unfathomable to think that this creature was the one to give me life. It's always felt the other way around to me.

"Hospital?" Barrett pulls the door open so I can place her in the back seat of the car.

"Call the doctor and get him to meet us back at the Sanctuary. She's coming home."

"What about the lad?"

"It's time Gideon knows the truth."

"That's a change of tune for you."

I shrug as I shut the door on the limp body of my mother in the back seat and climb into the front passenger's seat.

There have been a lot of changes in me recently. And it's all because of her. Berkley. For the first time in my life, I've got someone I want to make happy. I want to see her smile and know that I was the one who put it there. I've never felt that way before. I've always been driven by my need to find Hope, my desire for revenge. It was my sole focus. It's only now, because of her, that I've begun to see things differently.

For the first time ever, when I think about the future, about what I want in life, there is an image in my mind. And it's of Berkley.

Berkley laughing.

Berkley crying.

Berkley dancing.

Berkley sleeping.

But there's still this fear that's settled in my chest. Berkley thinks we share the same darkness, but I've hidden the depths of my deeds. I've restrained myself around her. She hasn't been witness to the things I've done. She's innocent.

And I'm afraid if she comes to know the truth of who I am, she'll turn her back on me and never look back. Part of me knows that's what's best for her. But the other part of me, the selfish part, the part that craves her, can't imagine the darkness of my life without her in it. I don't want to return to the man I was before. The one who presents a lie to the world and then hides his true self in the darkness of his castle.

Berkley has shown me I can have more than that. I can have someone to love who will love me back. Someone who doesn't shy away from me. Who wants to know me. Even if I'm scared of showing her my darkest parts.

Barrett and I don't talk during the drive home. His mistake weighs on him heavily. I don't talk about it though, as I know it won't help. Barrett is a man who likes to stay trapped inside his own head. It's a trait I appreciate.

It's the wee hours of the morning by the time we pull up outside the Sanctuary. There's a full moon tonight, and the light gives the Sanctuary an eerie glow. The door creaks loudly when Barrett pulls it open and I carry my mother inside. She's in desperate need of a bath or a shower, but in her current state, all we can do is lie her down on a bed and wait for the doctor to arrive.

Barrett stays with her as I make my way to Berkley's room. There's almost a desperation to see her, as though the time apart has placed an invisible wound inside me that only she can repair.

The only light in her room comes from the moonlight seeping through the edges of her curtains. I creep over to her bed. I just want to slide under the covers and wrap my body around hers. I want the comfort of her. The pleasure of her. She reminds me that there's good in the world if we look for it.

But she's not there.

I storm from her room and into my office, flicking on the screens that show the security cameras. It seems to take an eternity for them to finally show the images. My eyes scan over them hungrily as the dread in my chest grows tighter. Room after room shows as empty. Even the cell which holds the monster. I slam my fist on the desk as my fear grows.

"Barrett!" His name echoes through the house. "Barrett! Gideon! Hope! Berkley!" I expect them all to come running out of their rooms in panic even though I know Berkley wasn't in hers. There's a part of me still clinging to some sort of hope of an explanation other than the obvious.

"Everything okay?" Barrett comes jogging toward me.

"He's gone," I snap.

"Who's gone?"

"Atterton." I start to stride down to the basement, panic pumping through my veins.

"What's happening?" Gideon appears, hair tousled, eyes blurry. "What's going on?" He starts jogging after us. "Where are we going?"

The pace of my steps increases as I rip open the doors and storm through them until I find myself standing outside the monster's door.

I take a deep breath before I key in the code and send up a prayer that it's a glitch with the cameras. Nothing more. But even as I hold out hope, my heart beats erratically because I know. Deep down, I already know.

I swing open the door to an empty cell. "Fuck."

Gideon pokes his head around the corner. "Where did he go?"

Ignoring his confused expression, I turn and bark orders.

"Barrett, go to Hope and check she's okay. Gideon, check on the staff and make sure everyone is accounted for. I'll go check on Ette."

I sound calmer than I feel. I'm not one to jump to conclusions. I need to check on everyone first, but deep down I know it's pointless. My mother was a distraction. This is the retaliation.

I don't bother to be quiet when I barge into Ette's room. I call out her name as soon as I enter, but only silence replies. Turning on my heel, I run back into my office and access the storage for the camera feeds.

I see men silently stalking through the house dressed all in black. The additional guards I'd hired were taken out before they even realized someone was there. The men in black split into two groups. They drag Berkley from her bed and drag her down to the basement. They carry Ette from the house. They leave everyone else alone.

I sink to my chair. For a moment, I feel nothing. No rage. No terror. Nothing. It's a strange feeling, this nothingness. My skin feels as though it lifts from my body, as though it's held in suspension, and then after hovering for a few moments, it crashes back against me, wrapping my bones in reality.

The monster is gone.

Berkley is gone.

Ette is gone.

They've been stolen.

The rage drives me back to my feet and I let out an anguished cry as I swipe my desk, sending the contents clattering to the floor.

Hope appears, rushing over to me. But instead of her presence being calming, it infuriates me more.

"Why didn't you stop them!" I yell.

She's confused. Of course she's confused. She doesn't know what's happened.

"Who? Stop who?" She places a hand on my arm, and I reel away from her, much like she's done to everyone else. She crosses her arms. "What's going on, Jericho?"

I drag my hand through my hair, tugging on the roots. The pain feels good. "They've taken them." I fall to a squat. Breathing has become difficult.

"Who's taken them?" She crouches in front of me. "Jericho, you're not making sense."

My eyes flick to the screens, but of course they're scattered over the floor now. "Ette." Her name comes out as an anguished breath. "They've taken Ette. And Berkley. And Atterton."

The color drains from Hope's face. She sort of falls backward, landing on her backside. "No." She shakes her head. "What are you talking about, Jericho?

She scrambles over and shakes me, but I can't talk. I can't offer her any comfort. Vomit rises and for a moment I think

I'm about to be sick, but I push it back down and get to my feet.

"What are you talking about, Jericho?" Hope clutches at me hysterically. "Where's Ette? Who has Ette?" Her voice breaks. Her eyes are wide with panic.

I stand and push past her. I can't go through this again. I can't have another person I love, people I love, ripped from me.

"Where are you going?" Barrett asks as I shove past him.

My mind is addled. My thoughts muddled. I can't make sense of any of it. The precision of the hit shows they knew what they were doing, where they were going, who they were taking.

"Jericho!" Barrett yells. "Stop!"

He grabs me from behind and spins me around. I greet him with my fist. He stumbles backward, the surprise of the punch knocking him from his feet.

"Jericho don't," he warns. "We've got to keep your head in a—"

"She's gone!" I yell in his face. "They've taken her!"

"We need to stay calm," he urges as he gets back to his feet.

"Calm?" I repeat. "When I find out who took them, I'm going to tear each fucking limb from their bodies."

chapter fourteen

BERKLEY

"Ette!" I yell into the emptiness beyond the bars. "Ette!"

My hands grip the bar and I push and pull with all my might. I don't know why I bother. They're metal, encased in concrete. There's no way they'll budge. But I still rally against them as though they are to blame. As though they are the only thing between me and freedom. Me and Ette.

I've lost count of the number of times I've screamed her name, but she never answers. I know it's pointless but it's the only thing I can do. The only thing I can cling to.

The cell I'm in is exactly as it sounds. A cell. Concrete walls, floor and ceiling. No windows. A toilet and hand basin in one corner. A bed with a single blanket and a pillow along one wall. Metal bars form the wall and door which faces out against a concrete corridor. In the hours I've been here, no one has walked past. No one has replied to my screaming.

I've never felt so alone.

And cold.

I'm still dressed in the over-sized t-shirt I wear as a nightgown. There's no underwear under the flimsy material. My feet are bare. The strip of material that blindfolded me lies discarded. There's a slight breeze that whistles down the corridor and slips into my cell, making me shiver. I glance over at the blanket neatly tucked around the mattress of the bed in the corner, but somehow it feels like defeat if I take it.

"Ette!" I yell again. My voice breaks on her name. My throat is sore and raw from all the yelling.

My knuckles are white as I hang on tightly to the bars and press my face against the cold metal. But no matter where I stand, or how hard I try to press my face to the bars, I cannot see more than a couple of meters beyond my cell.

Sinking to my knees, I knock my head against the bars in desperation. As though it will accomplish something. Anything. It's only after I've been quiet a long time that a voice speaks. My head whips up as I audibly scan for the direction of the sound.

"There's no point in all the yelling." The voice is quiet.

"Who are you?"

"It doesn't matter."

"Do you know where we are?"

"It doesn't matter."

"It matters to me."

"It won't soon," is the only reply I get.

"I came here with a young girl. Did you see her?"

The voice must be coming from the next cell. I wonder why it's taken so long for her to talk to me. Maybe she was waiting for me to scream myself hoarse first.

"They don't have kids here." She lets out a derisive snort. "Apparently they're not that sort of evil."

For some reason her reply makes me laugh. Not a chuckle or a snort, but a loud and raucous laugh. The kind that surprises you with its volume and ferocity.

"I don't know why I just laughed," I say to my mystery friend.

"It's because there's nothing else you can do."

We fall back into silence. I shuffle across the floor until my back is pressed to the cold concrete. There's no warmth offered in the room apart from the blanket on the bed. A single tear rolls down my cheek and I pull my knees closer to my chest. I almost fall asleep like that, but my fear keeps me awake. Every time my eyelids droop my entire body jerks, fighting the need for sleep.

Then I hear footsteps. They echo off the concrete walls as though their creator is in my cell. Shadows appear. Multiple people are walking down the corridor.

"Just do as they say," the voice in the next cell whispers. "Don't fight them. Save your strength."

But if I don't fight, if I just do as I'm told, what am I saving my strength for? I start to tremble as they get closer. But all I can focus on is Ette. Where they've taken her. What they're doing to her. If she's okay.

The steps get louder. The shadows meld into one menacing figure that stretches across the ground. One monster. My heart beats loudly. Then, without warning, nausea swells and I'm overtaken by a flash. I thought my concern for Ette had drowned out my anxiety.

I was wrong.

I'm on all fours. There's a chain around my neck and someone, or something, is jerking on it, propelling me forward. Gravel digs into my palms and knees. I beg for whoever is on the other end of the chain to stop but all they do is laugh and yank harder. I fall, my face grazing against the gravel.

I clutch my cheek as though the pain is real. I can feel the stones digging into my skin even though I can't feel them with my fingers.

The shadows loom closer.

The footsteps grow louder.

I examine my fingers for blood. Because that's how real it feels. Even though everything physical tells me I'm pressed against the wall of a cell, knees pulled to my chest, everything in my head has me pressed against the gravel, sharp stones digging into my cheek.

The chain is jerked up violently. Someone shoves their face in mine as my hands fly to my throat, trying to relieve some of the strain of the chain around my neck. "How do you like it? Do you like being treated like a dog?" the voice hisses, but I'm too desperate for air to respond. The chain jerks upward again and I scramble to find my footing before the air is cut off completely.

I'm stretched, rising to my tiptoes as the chain keeps lifting. My toes scrape over the ground, searching for firm footing.

A deep voice laughs.

"Everly?" I'm jerked out of my flash by the sound of my name on someone else's lips. It takes a while for me to focus on the three figures peering into my cell. The lights above them appear harsher than they were before. The buzzing is loud. Almost loud enough to drown out the clanking of metal as the gate is pulled open.

"Michael?" I say cautiously as he approaches. I'm not sure if I'm still caught in my flash or not. It's like reality and my visions are mixing to such an extent that I don't want to trust my own eyes.

"Everly!" Michael rushes over and kneels, pulling me close to him. "What the fuck have you done?" he spits at the men behind him, then he turns back to me, hugging me tightly as I dissolve into tears. "Are you okay? Are you hurt?" He pulls back and holds me at arm's length as he scans my body, checking for any sort of damage.

I shake my head. And then my gaze slips behind him.

"She's fine," my father says. "Just getting a taste of her own medicine."

He looks nothing like the man I'd grown accustomed to seeing in the cell in the basement. Any of the weakness or the frailty I'd seen before is gone.

"Aren't you going to say hello to your Daddy?" He laughs and another wave of nausea rolls through me. There's a smirk of arrogance covering his face. He's dressed in a white linen suit with a pale pink shirt. Mr Gorman stands beside him.

"Where's Ette?" I want my voice to come out defiant and challenging. It doesn't. It quivers and breaks on her name.

Michael's fingers still dig into my shoulders. He's staring at me intently, shaking his head and mouthing, "I didn't know," as our fathers loom behind.

"You don't need to concern yourself with the girl. She's safe."

My father's words bring me no comfort. How can I believe the words of a monster?

Summoning what courage is left inside me, I remove myself from Michael's grip and get to my feet. Walking over to my father, I glare at him, planting my hands on my hips in an effort to stop myself from shaking.

"I want to see her."

"I'm sure you do." My father's smile is infuriating. "But did you help me when I needed it? Did you have one ounce of pity for your poor father? No. You didn't. Isn't karma a bitch?"

"I haven't broken the law. I haven't held women captive for years. I haven't—"

"Haven't you?" My father lifts his brows. "It seems being an accomplice to murder might, just might, be considered breaking the law. Don't you think, Gorman?"

I step backward, the guilt of the truth in his words hitting me hard. "I don't know what you're talking about," I stutter as he continues to smirk.

"Does the name Keating ring a bell?" Gorman takes the reigns from my father, stepping closer to me with each word he speaks. "It should. It's the name I gave you. The name of the man who was holding—" He turns to my father, "What was it you called her again?"

My father sighs as though remembering something pleasant. "Iris." His tongue runs over his bottom lip. It reminds me of a lizard. "Such a pretty little thing. Pity about the attitude."

I swallow the panic rising at the back of my throat. "What have you done to her?"

"To Iris?"

"To Hope," I spit back.

"Oh, nothing. We left her exactly where she was. We didn't want to be greedy. Taking you and the girl was sufficient retaliation. We don't want to seem like we're being unreasonable, unlike your boyfriend, Priest, wasn't it? We didn't see the need to wipe out an entire family."

My father relishes waving this over me. He starts pacing the cell, hands shoved in his pockets as though he doesn't have a care in the world. His face has already had a fresh layer of spray-tan added, almost giving off an orange tinge.

"You see that's the difference between you and me, daughter. You can't see your own hypocrisy. You see, the man you so quickly spread your legs for, he married this Hope as you insist on calling her. He's her husband. As in, you're the other woman." He waits for my reaction, assuming it to be information I didn't know. I don't give him one. "Under his command, his man slaughtered Keating. There's no other way to put it. He'd already got the girl back.

He could have left without exacting his own punishment, but he chose not to. He also chose to attempt to kill the poor man's wife." He shakes his head and tuts loudly. "The poor woman had been through enough."

"They had Hope locked in a bunker!"

My father whirls around. "They did not! Your little friend did. What was his name?"

My father looks to Gorman. "Dominic," he offers.

"Yes, that was the lad. Strange one, that boy. But he was the one holding her captive, not his father. You see your hero isn't such a good boy, is he?" He chuckles. "You know I never used to take stock in the adage that daughters are attracted to men just like their fathers. Guess I was wrong."

"Jericho is nothing like you! Everything he did was to free Hope, not to imprison her."

"Even if that means killing innocent people?"

"Aaron Keating wasn't innocent."

"Wasn't he? Tell me, what was he guilty of, hmmm?" The way he tacks on the little sound at the end reminds me of his wife. I wonder where she is now. I wonder what she thinks of the man she married. I never liked the woman, but surely she had no knowledge of the crimes he committed.

"Enough!" Michael yells, coming to stand between us.

Mr Gorman leans against the wall, arms and ankles crossed, grinning as though he's enjoying the entertainment.

"It's okay, son. You'll get your turn. I know you've always had a soft spot for the girl."

It feels as though all the blood drains from my body. "His turn? What do you mean, his turn? What are you going to do to me?"

Dread settles in my stomach. The blood pumping through my veins starts to race, echoing a thudding sound in my head.

"Nothing." Michael glares at his father. "They meant nothing by it." Taking my hand in his, he pulls me from the cell. "You're coming with me."

As he drags me down the corridor, I look into the other cells. There are so many of them. Each of them has a woman with sad eyes peering back at me. None of them call out. None of them plead for rescue, they just sit and stare, already knowing their fate. It breaks my heart but it also fills me with fear.

"What's happening, Michael? What are they going to do with me?"

"Nothing if I have anything to do with it."

"Are you going to let me go?"

"You're safer with me."

chapter fifteen

BERKLEY

The doors of the car lock as soon as I'm inside. Michael looks over and shrugs. "You haven't exactly been the most trustworthy person."

I reach for the lock, attempting to pry it open but Michael just chuckles and reaches over to place his hand on my knee. His thumb rubs over my flesh slowly. The feeling of it travels through my bloodstream and twists in my chest, the need to vomit rising. I jerk my leg away and his hand falls. He chuckles again and makes a tutting sound.

"Where are you taking me?" I ask as he starts the car and pulls onto the paved road that's lined with rectangle concrete blocks.

"They were only trying to scare you."

"Well, they succeeded," I reply. "Where are you taking me?"

He just smiles and winks as though this is all a joke. "Don't worry. You'll be safe."

The squat gray buildings line both sides of the road. They're arranged in a grid-like fashion, rows and rows of them. High wire fencing surrounds the compound. I think of all the women I passed along the corridor and wonder if each of the buildings are filled just the same.

"Do all these buildings contain—"

Michael cuts me off. "They're storage units."

"But—"

"They're storage units," he says again more forcibly.

We pass through the gates. "Storage units with armed guards," I mutter.

"Everly," he chides.

It's as though we're living in different worlds. Different realities.

"I don't know how you can just sit by with all this going on." I fold my arms across my chest, sinking deeper into the seat as fields of grass and sheep pass by.

"I don't know how you can sit by knowing that children are basically used as slave-workers to make shoes," Michael mocks.

"That's different."

"Different how?" He shrugs. "It's the way of the world. No point in getting bogged down with feeling guilty about it. Besides, I have very little to do with that side of the business, you know that. It's my job to schmooze potential clients. Sometimes there are pretty women there while I'm doing it." He shrugs as the fields fade away and the houses become more frequent. "Sometimes there's not."

He reaches out to rest his hand on my knee again. He keeps it still this time though, not stroking my flesh with his thumb. The touch burns, but it doesn't bubble up the same revulsion within me as before.

"That's not to say I don't know where our money comes from, or what's involved in obtaining it, but I just choose not to think about it. You should do the same. Just like you do with a million other things in life. Most of which you're probably not even aware of."

I want to fight and argue, but the truth of the matter is I'm too exhausted and I know none of it would matter anyway. It's not as though Michael is suddenly going to be alerted to the evil of his family's ways. But it is something I can work on.

I would have thought the adrenaline rushing through me would have kept me awake, but when Michael's hand joggles my knee, I find we're parked along the circular driveway in front of his house.

My head starts to shake even before I've fully woken. "I don't want to be here."

Michael smiles. It's the same smile that used to make me melt. The same smile I spent hours waiting to receive. Now it just makes me feel sick.

"You haven't really got a choice, I'm afraid." He screws up his face as though he's apologetic. "You'll be safe here. I'll keep an eye on you." The door of the car opens, rising into the air. "Besides, it will give us the chance to hang out again. I think if you get to know me like you used to, you'll find I'm not the bad guy in this, Everly. I'm the one who just wants what's best for you." His smile flashes wider. "You might even grow to like me again. We used to have fun."

I roll my eyes as he comes to my side of the car and offers his hand to help me out. His eyes dart over me as I stretch my legs out of the car and stand.

"Nice outfit." He chuckles.

"Oh, I'm sorry." I stride past him. "I didn't have the time to get dressed as I was violently dragged from my bed, blindfolded and zip-tied as I was being stolen."

"You've always been on the dramatic side, haven't you?"

He runs to catch up with me as I climb the steps that lead to the entrance of the house. I know where I'm going. I've been here before. Just never as a prisoner.

"So where are the cells?" I ask. "Down in the basement? Is that where you're keeping me."

"So theatrical," Michael muses. "Come on, I'll show you the way."

He leads me through the house and up the stairs. There's no one about, no staff, no guards, no family. Just him and me. For a brief second, I toy with the idea of running, but I don't know who I'd run to, or where I'd go. Most of the people I know in the city are friends of the Gormans, dancers who dislike me, or dead.

"Here." Michael opens the door to his room.

"Aren't there enough rooms for me to have one of my own?"

"Yes." He gently guides me inside, his hand resting on the small of my back. "But this way I can keep an eye on you. We don't want you running off back to that Priest. He's not a good man."

"He's not a good man?" I scoff. "That's rich coming from you."

"You've got the entirely wrong picture of me in your mind, Ev."

I walk over to the window which opens onto the roof and try to pry it open. It's locked. As are all the windows. Crossing my arms, I stand and stare, looking out where the pool beckons from below. Michael comes up behind me. He stands close, close enough I can feel the heat of him, but not close enough to touch.

"I'm not the bad guy here." His hand hovers near my shoulder and I take a step away, not wanting him to touch me. "You'll be safe here. I won't let anything bad happen to you."

I turn around, letting the tears well in my eyes. "But I don't want to be here."

Michael tips my chin up. "Give me a chance, yeah? I'm not like them. It's just a business. It's got nothing to do with who I am inside."

He lifts his hands and rests them on my shoulders. Moving his fingers, he scrunches my t-shirt, the material moving up my arms. I jerk away from him again and he sighs loudly.

"Let's find you something else to wear."

Instead of leaving the room like I assumed he would, Michael opens one of the drawers of his dresser and starts tossing through clothing, occasionally pulling something out to examine it before discarding it again. Eventually he decides on something and tosses it my way. It's a summery dress, pale blue with white daisies. It's innocent and sweet. Something I would have worn back during the time he knew me best.

"Seems like a strange thing for you to have in your drawers."

"It always pays to be prepared." Leaning against the dresser, Michael crosses his arms and waits for me to get changed.

"Aren't you going to give me some privacy?"

A smirk of a smile twists his mouth. "I've seen it all before."

"Michael," I warn.

He laughs and turns around. "Happy now?"

Pulling off the t-shirt, I quickly shove on the dress. Michael turns and offers me a smile. "That's better. Now you look more like the Everly I know."

"This is wrong," I say.

"What's wrong?" He looks genuinely confused.

"This." I gesture between us. "Us. Everything that's going on. The fact that you've just taken me out of a cell where there were so many women—"

"I thought we'd talked about this. You need to stop obsessing about things you can't control. It's business. Nothing else. It has nothing to do with my personal tastes. I'm not like that. I like my women keen, eager even." He leans over and grasps the sides of my face in his hand, placing a quick peck of a kiss on the tip of my nose. "I'll win you over. You'll see."

"You really are unbelievable, aren't you?"

He ignores me and flops himself down onto the bed, hands interlocking behind his head.

"Where's Ette?" I ask, cautiously sitting on the edge of the mattress.

"You don't need to worry about her. She's fine. She's with her family now. Don't worry, we won't go to the police."

"The police? Why would you go to the police?"

Michael frowns. "To get Jericho Priest charged with kidnapping." He shakes his head as though he can't quite believe my naivety.

"Jericho didn't kidnap her."

Michael just raises his brows. "I doubt the police would see it that way. But seriously, you don't need to worry about her. She's safe. She's happy. She's with people who care about her and will love and provide for her, rather than lock her away in a castle like some sick freak from a fairy tale."

"That's not—"

Michael holds up his hand. "This is boring me. You've obviously been brainwashed by this Priest fellow. While you're here with me, you won't talk about him, okay?"

"No."

He lifts his brows again and then props himself up on his elbows. "No?"

"No. I'll talk about whoever I want to talk about. I'll say whatever I want to say. I mean, I am a free woman, aren't I?"

Michael twists his face into contemplation. "You're free in a sense, but because of your—shall we say—'innocence,' there are certain restrictions on that freedom. Like you can't leave the house unless I'm with you. Things like that. But don't worry." He scoots along the bed and sits beside me. "I've got your best interests at heart. And it's only for a short period of time, you know, until you gain our trust again." He winks. "That might take a while but I'm willing to give you the benefit of the doubt here."

"So generous."

"Look, Everly, there are two ways of looking at this. One, you fight it. You fight me. You complain and you moan, and you sit here sulking. This will change nothing. Or, you can choose to make the most of this. We were happy together once. We could be again if you'd just give me a chance."

I fold my arms over my chest and look away from him. "Not going to happen."

Michael kisses my cheek. "That's okay. I like a challenge."

He has this swagger when he walks away. It's confidence. It's the knowledge that everything will work out in his favor because it always has.

"He will come for me, you know," I say to his back.

Michael opens the door and turns. "Don't count on it, Ev. He has his wife back now. He has no use for you."

"He will come."

Michael cocks his head to the side. "Maybe. Maybe not. He doesn't actually know where you are, does he? And after that disaster of a rescue where he left two bodies in his wake..." He draws in a whistle of air. "Well, I don't think he'll be rushing in anytime soon, so don't hold your breath."

He flashes me one of his smiles before the door shuts. I hear the slide of a lock moments later.

"Don't worry," he calls through the closed door. "It's just for tonight. You'll be able to earn privileges and gain my trust again. But for the moment, Everly Atterton, you've been a very naughty girl."

His chuckle fades as he walks away.

chapter sixteen

Even though I'm exhausted, I lie awake. Michael sleeps soundly on the other side of the mattress. He sleeps as though he doesn't have a care in the world. He sleeps as though he's innocent.

It's my racing thoughts that keep me awake. Wondering what Jericho is thinking, what he's planning, if he even has any idea who took me. Wondering if Ette is safe, if she's scared, if she's lying awake in bed like me, praying for rescue. Wondering what's going to happen to me.

When Michael left me alone, I searched every inch of his bedroom, searching for some way of escape. But the windows wouldn't open, the door is locked and there is no way of communication with the world other than through a gaming consul.

And even if I did manage to escape, where would I go? How would I get there? I can't call my mother; it would be too dangerous. The Gormans have already let me know they'd be willing to use her. I could land her right back where she started. In the arms of the monster. Just like my father, unspoken threats are their greatest form of control.

I can't call the police because what Michael said is true. Jericho did technically kidnap Ette. He's kept her secret from the world for years, shielding her away at the Sanctuary.

I'd forgotten that Dominic and Michael were related. If I'd remembered that fact earlier, maybe all this could have been avoided. I could have warned Jericho of their family connection.

Michael rolls over. His eyes gleam in the dim light. "What are you thinking about?" he asks sleepily.

"How to get away from you."

He chuckles and moves across the large expanse of the bed to be closer to me. Reaching out, his fingers intertwine with mine and I jerk them away.

"Don't touch me."

All he does is chuckle again. It's infuriating. He makes me feel as though I'm being overly dramatic, that I'm exaggerating the situation, even as I'm literally locked in his room.

"What time is it?" Michael yawns and stretches. He glances at his watch. "It's early, what are you doing awake?"

"I couldn't sleep."

"Do you need something? I've got some sort of pills in the bathroom."

He talks as though there's nothing more than the normal stresses on my mind. As though I wasn't torn from my bed and basically delivered to him. As though it's my choice to be lying in bed next to him.

He scoots closer again and I push myself to the edge of the mattress. "I wish I'd known you were in the city earlier. I feel like we've wasted so much time. It wasn't until Dominic mentioned this girl who'd been outed as the daughter of the monster at his dance company that things clicked into place. He didn't know of our connection. I still don't think he does."

"I heard he's missing. Have you heard from him at all?"

Michael shakes his head and yawns again. "Nothing. And Dad is fucked off about it. But Dominic's always been a strange one. A real mummy's boy. It's not like him to leave her alone for this long."

I swallow the knot of guilt that wants to spill the truth that I know and change the subject. "Why didn't you come find me if you knew I was at the dance company?"

"I wanted to, but you went to work for *him*." He spits out the word as though it's bitter. "It wasn't until Dad told me you were back in the city that I stumbled into you. Stumbled." He chuckles. "Truth was I knew you were going to be there that night. I needed to see you. I thought if I just happened to run into you, you'd remember everything we used to share and—"

"You purposely ran into me that night?"

"It worked, didn't it? You called me the very next day. I can't tell you what that meant to me. I thought you'd forgotten all about me. But it turned out you were just using me, anyway."

"I didn't use—" I cut myself short. That's exactly what I did. I contacted Michael in the hope of using him for information, as a way in. It worked. Rolling over, I turn and face him. "Your Dad knew I was going to be there?"

Michael reaches out to stroke my cheek. I let him.

"Did you think it was just a random encounter? You're so sweet. Nothing is random in the world of our fathers. This was always meant to be, you and me." He tucks my hair behind one ear and trails his finger over my cheek until it catches on my bottom lip. "I wish I'd been able to see you dance."

He's silent for a while, just stroking my face as he stares into my eyes. It takes a lot out of me to lay by his side. To not move. To not shove him away. To not lash out with nails and teeth.

"Did you love him?" he asks quietly.

I know who he's talking about, but I don't answer. Michael just smiles sadly. "It's okay if you did. It doesn't matter. You're with me now."

"I'm not with you."

"Not yet. But you will be."

Sitting up, he tosses the blankets off us. I'm dressed back in my old t-shirt. I like the familiarity of it. I like that it smells faintly of Jericho.

He scans over me with his gaze. Two lines press between his brows. "I'll send Maggie out to do some shopping for you today. We can't have you living in discarded clothing now, can we?"

"How long are you going to keep me here?"

He snorts. "You make it sound as though I'm keeping you captive."

"You are."

"Sure." He grins. "I know a lot of women who would love to be where you are right now."

"Well, maybe you should go find one of them."

Michael clambers off the bed. He's dressed in nothing but briefs and I can't help but notice the way his body has filled out since I last saw him in a similar state of undress.

His chest is bigger, his waist narrower. He must have spent a lot of time at the gym.

"Come on." He pats my leg. "Let's go get some breakfast."

After pulling on the summery dress once again, I follow Michael down the stairs. The Gormans' house reminds me of Dominic's place. Everything is white and sleek, accented with black and gold. It's cold and unwelcoming, but at the same time, fresh and clean and screaming of wealth.

He leads me out to the patio where there's a table laden with every breakfast food imaginable. Mr Gorman sits at the head of the table, my father to one side and Mrs Gorman to the other. A woman sits to my father's left, but I don't recognize her until she glances my way. And then her scars make it obvious.

Her eyes widen when she spots me. "You." She says the word with venom.

"Now, now, Mary. Let's make her feel welcome in our home."

Mary gets to her feet, the legs of her chair scraping across the tiles. She stands, half bent over, clutching at her stomach. "I will not welcome her. Not now. Not ever. This girl did nothing to help me when two men stormed into my home, killed my husband, shot me and left me for dead. She is evil. She is—"

Michael claps his hands slowly. "We seem to be surrounded by hysterical women. Anything you'd like to add, Mother? Maybe some government conspiracy thrown into the mix? Some war on feminist agenda?"

He laughs as Mary lowers herself back to her chair, her eyes hidden behind a veil of hair. I take my seat opposite her, next to Michael. He grabs my hand and places it on his knee, gripping my fingers tightly.

"Everly, my dear," my father croons. "Did you sleep well?"

I feel as though I've stumbled into a sitcom. There's a surreal feeling cast over the atmosphere. It's like no one can see the television cameras apart from me. They act normally. They act as though nothing is strange or unusual.

Mr Gorman sits at the head of the table, stuffing his face with food as he glares at the newspaper folded on the table in front of him. He's distracted from what's going on around him. His entire focus is held by what he's reading.

My father isn't interested in the newspaper. His eyes skip from person to person, a twisted and satisfied smirk on his face.

Mary sits with her head down, her hands in her lap. She's not eating. She's not doing anything. But it's almost as though I can feel the heat of her anger radiating across the table. I don't blame her. She begged me to help her and I merely watched as she was led to what was intended to be her death.

Mrs Gorman is oblivious to it all. She eats absent-mindedly, crumbling a muffin between her fingers and lifting the morsels to her lips every so often. She stares into space, eyes vacant. To look at, she reminds me of my father's wife, Katriane. Severely beautiful but instead of Katrine's sharp tongue and quick wit, there's nothing but emptiness to her personality.

Ignoring my father, I reach for one of the pastries on the table.

My father tuts. "A moment on the lips, a lifetime on the hips."

I shove the entire thing into my mouth, not caring when I have to chew with my mouth open and crumbs fall out. Michael laughs. Apparently, this is funny.

"Do you know where he is?" Mary's voice is quiet when she speaks but it's barely controlled. There's a vibration to it. Almost a quivering.

"I believe she's talking to you," Michael says as he slathers butter onto his fruit toast.

"Where who is?" I ask, lifting my chin and my eyes to look at her.

She stays hidden behind the hair that shields her face. "My Dommie."

A thick wedge of guilt rises in my throat.

"He told me about you." She tosses her head and for a moment, her hair is swayed to the side, her scars on full display. I can't help but stare at them. They are jagged and rough, as though they couldn't afford the plastic surgery to correct them. "He trusted you. He thought you were his friend and now he's out there somewhere, scared and alone, running for his life."

"He's as cowardly as his father," Mr Gorman says, joining in on the conversation for the first time. "I warned you not to marry that man. It's nobody's fault other than your own that he's got his father's spineless blood running through his veins."

Mary lowers her eyes again. The muscles in her arms flex as her hands clench and unclench in her lap. "He's a good boy."

"Is that so?" Gorman taunts. Then he turns his attention to me. "Did you know it was Dominic who alerted me to your presence in the city?"

I reach for another pastry. "So Michael said."

"It was he who informed me that you were leaving to work for the infamous Mr Priest, a name I'd heard of before but had very little interest in until it resurfaced involving you. Really, it was you that brought him to our attention."

"Pleased I could help," I spit sarcastically.

"Dommie would have never held that girl in the bunker if you hadn't told him to." Again, Mary speaks so quietly it's hard to hear her. She darts a glance at the head of the table before lowering her gaze. "He was a good kid. He would have never wanted to hurt anyone."

I stop chewing. It's painful to swallow my mouthful but I need to do it before I choke. "You told him to take Hope?"

Gorman lifts his glass of orange juice and drinks deeply before answering. "I was suspicious of the intentions of your Mr Priest. Turns out I had a right to be. Hope was a safety net in case anything went wrong. Your father went missing days later when we'd worked so hard to set him free. It seemed odd that this would be a coincidence, considering the history of the relationship. Of course, it helped that the boy was so easily swayed. He got his father's genes in both the brains and cowardice department."

"Very forward-thinking of you, Gorman," my father pipes up.

Mary's chair scrapes across the ground again. "I won't sit here and listen to you talk about my son like that, or his father. His dead father. Priest and his side-kick may have been the ones to control the blade that killed him, but you were the one who sent them there. I will never forget that!"

Gorman chuckles. It's the same laugh as his son's. "Oh, calm down Mary, and eat some food. No wonder your husband went elsewhere looking for someone to fuck. With a face and a personality like yours, it makes sense he was hardly ever home."

A giant sob is wrenched from Mary's lip. It's the loudest sound she's made since we walked in. Her chair tips to the ground as she scurries away, her hand hovering protectively at her side.

Mrs Gorman shakes her head sadly. "Do you have to be so cruel to your own sister?" She covers her husband's hand with her own.

"You know the woman just as well as I do. There's not a lot we can do to help her. Besides, I've given her what she wanted ever since she found out Keating was fucking the girl. And now I've given her the kid."

chapter seventeen

BERKLEY

It's late at night when there's a knock at my door. Well, Michael's door. Even though I'm apparently allowed to roam about the house of my free will, I've holed myself away in his room, not wanting to engage with any of the monsters who carry on as though all this is normal.

It's been days since I've seen or heard anything of Ette. Apparently, she's here in the house. Somewhere. I just don't know where.

I keep waiting for Jericho to appear at the door, demanding my release, but he doesn't come. Maybe he doesn't even know I'm here. Maybe he doesn't care. I know better than to think that, but sometimes when I'm laying beside Michael as he sleeps, my mind goes to dark places.

The thing that confuses me the most, though, is my lack of flashes. They've stopped. Completely stopped. I don't get the twists of nausea in my gut. I don't get the panic attacks or the images of depravity. Part of me wonders if it's because I'm at home here amongst the evil. Maybe darkness truly does run in my veins.

It's Mary on the other side of the door when I open it. She stands with her eyes downcast, her hair once again shielding her face. There's a longing to push it behind her ear, make her embrace the scars that grace her and see her stand defiant against the verbal abuse hurled at her by her brother.

"Is it okay if we talk?"

It's the first time she's spoken to me since that breakfast where she ran sobbing from the room. All the other times, she's been like a shadow hidden in the corner, unseen and unnoticed.

She walks in without invitation. Her eyes scan the room until they land on the beanbags in front of the large screens and she sits down delicately, legs crossed at the ankles. She looks out of place. Lost.

"She's okay, you know. Ette," she adds at my confusion.

"You've seen her?"

"She's staying with me. We've got our own wing of the house. Dommie will join us when he's found. He always wanted a little sister. He'll be so happy to meet her."

I don't say anything as I lower myself to sit on the edge of the bed. Something tells me it's better just to let her talk.

"He came back to me that night, did you know that?" She doesn't wait for me to answer. "Your friend had left me for dead. He crept back into the house to make sure I was okay. You have no idea what it was like laying there before he came. I was certain I was going to die. I could feel the blood draining from me. I was so cold." She shivers as though the memory is so strong it's overwhelmed her. "Dommie was the one who made the call to the ambulance. He was the one who saved my life. Then he had to run away to save his own."

She glances up at me then. I recognize the look in her eyes. It's the same look she gave me when she was begging for help. This time, I'm the one who lowers my gaze to the floor.

"He had no idea of the girl's connection to Mr Priest, or to you. As far as he was aware, all he knew was she was the girl his father had an affair with and got pregnant. She was the woman who did this—" she points to her scars, "—to me." She sighs. "He knew that his father thought she was dead and when his uncle came to him and told him she wasn't, he thought he was doing the right thing, he thought he could win his father's favor by keeping her."

I let myself sink to the floor, drawing my knees to my chest and leaning against the side of the bed.

"He was a messed-up child. A messed-up teenager. It makes sense that he is a little messed-up as an adult. But none of it is his fault. All he wanted was for his father to love him."

"I know you love your son, I loved him too, but it doesn't excuse what he did. It doesn't—"

"I was the one who asked my brother to get rid of her."

"Of who?"

Mary swallows. "Of Hope." She pushes her hair back, giving me full view of her scars. "Do you know what it was like for me to discover the man I loved, the man my family hated yet I always stood up for, was fucking a teenager?"

I flinch at her words. For some reason they seem harsher coming from the mouth of someone so quiet and demure.

"I hated her. I truly hated her. It was bad enough coming home one day to find them in my bed, but when I found out he'd gotten her pregnant it all got too much." She lets out a snort of air. "I was going to confront her when it happened. I climbed into the car, drunk and high as a kite on whatever pills the doctor had given me to calm my nerves, but I never made it to her place. This happened first."

Again, she points to her scars. It strikes me strange that after all these years they still appear red and raw, as though they've been freshly opened.

"Once I was out of hospital, I thought that maybe if I had the child to love, the daughter I'd always wanted but never got the chance to have, that I might find some peace with his betrayal. But deep down I knew it would never happen. That's why I went to my brother. He told me he'd had her killed. He told Aaron he'd searched for her and found her dead. The child was supposed to come live with us. She was supposed to heal our family. Instead, all this destroyed it. My brother never liked Aaron and as an extension of that, he never liked Dommie. He lied to me. He lied to us all, and then he used Dommie to exact his revenge. You can't tell me he didn't know what would happen when he sent Mr Priest our way. He knew it would be the end of us."

"But you survived."

"Part of me did, yes. The other part died in that car crash."

"Why are you telling me all this?"

"Because I'm hoping by telling you my truth, you might share your own. You'd tell me if you knew anything, wouldn't you? You'd tell me if that Mr Priest has my son?" She crawls across the ground and kneels in front of me, hands planted on my knees. "I can tell you're a good girl, Everly. You've got a good heart. You're not like your father or my brother or that upstart of a son he has."

It's on the tip of my tongue to tell her. To put her out of the misery of the unknown, but in revealing the truth, it will break her heart.

"Please," she whispers. "The police are desperate for information and so far I've refrained from telling them the truth in the hope—"

Mary's gaze swings to the door as Michael walks in. His arms are laden with various bottles of alcohol. "What are you two talking about, huh?" He places the bottles on the top of his mini-refrigerator.

Mary gets to her feet, running her hands over the wrinkles of her skirt. "She's concerned about the girl. I was attempting to allay her fears."

"Very kind of you, Mary, but you know I can answer any questions she has."

"Sometimes it's nice to talk to someone with a little less testosterone floating through their system." It's the snarkiest comment I've ever heard from Mary and I clap as Michael rolls his eyes.

"You know my mother always enjoys your company."

"She's about as entertaining as a wet rag."

Michael blinks and shakes his head. "What's gotten into you, Mary Gorman? Have you grown a backbone suddenly?"

"It's Mary Keating."

Michael screws up his nose. "But is it still?" He twists the lid off a bottle of whiskey and pours some into a glass. "Your husband is gone, Mary." He takes a sip before pouring another glass. "And as far as we can tell, so is your son." He holds out the glass, offering the drink to Mary. Her eyes blaze as she swipes the glass away and it shatters against the wall.

Michael chuckles and downs the rest of his drink. "If I were you, I'd hold onto the only family I had left."

Mary narrows her eyes before storming out of the room, slamming the door behind her.

"She's always been a little overly emotional." Michael gets out a new glass and starts to pour another drink. "I guess that's where Dominic got it from." He holds out the glass. "Here, I thought we could let off a little steam. It's been a stressful few days."

I'm tempted to copy Mary and whack the glass out of his hand. Instead I turn and walk over to the window. The underwater lights of the pool slowly change color, making it shimmer with deep blue, purple and pink. A lonely inflatable flamingo drifts across the surface, pushed by an invisible breeze.

Michael's footsteps pad across the floor. His arm comes to circle my waist, his chin resting on my shoulder. I tense.

"Don't do that," Michael chides in my ear. "Don't do that around me."

"I can't help it," I say, pulling away from him. "It's a natural response."

Michael groans. "How long are you going to keep this up?"

I whirl around. "What?"

"This." He signals between us before downing the rest of his drink. "This resistance. You know it's futile." He grins lazily. "I know you want me, Everly. You always have." He reaches out to stroke my chin and I jerk away. Annoyance flicks across his expression and he leans close, warm breath washing over my face. "You used to beg me to fuck you. Do you remember that? You'd get drunk. Hell, you'd get shitfaced and then you'd basically grind against me."

"I don't know what I ever saw in you, Michael Gorman."

A smirk twitches at the corners of his lips. "Yes you do." He picks up the drink I denied earlier and holds it out again. "Come on, Everly. Stop this fighting. Stop denying what's right in front of you. I know you've got some sort of fascination with that Priest guy, but I'm your first love. I'm the one you were always supposed to be with. Can't you put everything aside for one night and just have a little fun?"

He shakes the glass in front of me. It's tempting. It's tempting because it would be easy. As much as I despise Michael right now, there's also no denying that he's familiar. That he's—

I shut off my thoughts and reach for the glass, throwing the contents down my throat in one go.

The grin that crosses Michael's face is undeniable. "That's my girl." Grabbing the bottle of whiskey, he turns, pours another and holds it out to me. I snatch it from him, annoyed at my acquiescence.

"To us," he says, lifting his glass into the air.

I simply glare at him and down the drink. He laughs and opens the window that leads onto the roof, beckoning for me to follow him. He drags an over-stuffed cushion out and flops down onto it, not noticing or not caring when his drink sloshes out of the glass.

"Careful," he says when I walk to the edge of the roof. "There'll be no jumping off and attempting escape this time. There are cameras and guards everywhere. Even if you can't see them."

My eyes scan the property. He's right. It looks peaceful and tranquil with no sign of guards or cameras anywhere. Mind you, I thought the same about the Sanctuary, but they were there, just hidden.

"I was gutted you left that night. I was hoping you were going to stay with me, rekindle what we used to have."

I take a quiet sip of my drink as Michael pulls out a cigarette and pats the empty space beside him.

"Come. Relax. Forget the nonsense that's going on for one night and just chill." He struggles with the flame in the breeze but eventually manages to light the cigarette and inhale. He pats the cushion again.

I sigh as I sit down. Michael holds the cigarette out and I take it, inspecting it carefully before inhaling.

"It's not poisonous, if that's what you're worried about." He laughs and places his hands behind his head, stretching his legs out and crossing them at the ankles. "Well, technically it is, I guess. But just the normal sort of poison that comes in a cigarette.

His side of the cushion dips lower than mine and I have to hold myself taut to stop myself from sliding into him. I wrap my lips around the cigarette and inhale. I blink a few times as my head spins, the nicotine flooding my system. I offer it back to Michael, but he waves it away.

"Have another puff." His voice is lazy and low.

I suck on the end once again, closing my eyes as my head spins.

"It's fucking beautiful out here, don't you think?"

He's looking at the stars. Even though we're in the city, the sky is still clear, but nothing like it is at the Sanctuary. But the longer I stare at the inky blackness the more stars appear. It's almost as though some of them are shy and wait for you to pay attention before starting to shine.

"My father wanted him dead." Michael's voice breaks the silence.

"Who?" I ask.

"Aaron Keating. The man was nothing but a waste of space. That's why he gave you the name, why he sent you there. He knew what your Priest would do. He knew he was a killer."

I start to protest but then let my voice fall. There's no point in defending him. Not to someone who has the outlook on life like Michael does. This is a man who willingly looks the other way just so he can maintain the sort of lifestyle he's used to. This is a man who has no problem profiting from other people's suffering.

Michael's arm drifts down from the back of his head and stretches out over my shoulder. I want to move away but my body is too heavy and there's almost a comfort to the warmth of him.

"So you don't need to feel bad."

Tears prick. I try to blink them away, but instead, they come in full force, running down my cheeks as a sob is wrenched from me.

"Oh, shit," Michael curses. "It does that to some people."

"What does?" I hiccup.

He plays with the cigarette between his fingers and wiggles his brows before inhaling deeply. "Do you remember the first time you came here?" He talks with inhaled breath before letting it out slowly. "It was just before you were about to start at school and your father, not that you knew that at the time, brought you over here so you could meet someone before you started."

I nod, my cheek brushing over his arm.

"We lay on the trampoline that used to be in the back yard, you smoked weed for the first time and then we just talked shit and looked at the stars."

I nod again. My body slips across the over-sized cushion, falling close to his side.

"I thought you were fucking gorgeous, even back then. You had these huge fucking eyes, and these plump fucking lips and you were so fucking innocent."

"You swear a lot when you're drunk."

He shakes his head. "More when I'm high."

I twist to look up at him. "Are you high?"

He places a small peck of a kiss on my lips. "Yes, we are high. I was hoping it would relax you." He sits up a little so he's leaning over me. "Are you relaxed, Everly?"

I nod sleepily. I'm so relaxed I feel as though I could fall asleep.

"Good," he murmurs. One finger runs over my shoulder, pushing the strap of my dress aside. The pad of his thumb brushes my collarbone. I shake my head, as he presses his lips to mine softly.

"It's okay, Everly. I'm going to take good care of you." His finger runs down the side of my face. "You're so fucking beautiful, Ev." He presses another kiss to my lips. "So fucking beautiful."

Just as I'm summoning the strength to push him away, he sits up and gets to his feet. "We need another drink."

He's gone only a moment before he's back beside me, helping me sit up a little. He holds the glass and tips it to my lips. "That's my girl," he encourages as the liquid slips into my mouth.

chapter eighteen

He downs his own drink before laying back beside me and wrapping his arm around my shoulder, tugging me close.

"I'm not like my father, or yours," he says while staring up at the stars. "I don't like forcing people to do things they don't want to do. It's a form of power and control I'm simply not interested in. But that doesn't mean I don't get what I want. I always get what I want, Everly." He props himself on his side and looks down at me. "The problem is I don't have much patience. Not with you. Not when I already know what I'm getting."

He reaches down and undoes one of the buttons on my dress. I go to lift my hand and swipe his arm away, but my body won't comply. It's heavy and disobedient, defying instruction from my brain. A spark of panic ignites. I try to get up. I try to twist away but it's like the connection between my brain and my body has been severed and my limbs remain unresponsive.

Michael holds up his glass. "It was in the drink." He smiles slowly. "Yours, not mine, obviously."

I blink away tears. It's as though my body is made of lead. I'm trapped, lying here beside him under the stars.

"Shh, shh." Michael brushes away a tear with the pad of his thumb and lifts it to his mouth, licking it. "You've got nothing to fear. I told you I like my partners keen and eager." He undoes another button. "I'm just reminding you of what could be. Of what you could have. Of who we could be."

Another button pops undone and Michael pushes the material across my body, exposing my breast. He lets out a groan.

Anxiety grips me violently. I want to curl in on myself. I want to escape this place, but I can't. I'm lying here, staring up at the sky and all I can do is squeeze my eyes shut as the flash overwhelms me. But for once the flash is welcomed in comparison to the nightmare of my reality.

Jericho paces in a circle around me as I stand, tied with my arms above my head, the light of the moon pouring in through the stained-glass window and tainting my naked skin. "Tell me to stop," he says.

The tip of Michael's finger caresses my breast. My nipple beads unwantedly and he flicks it, drawing in a sharp breath when the flesh puckers and tightens. His gaze slowly roams up my body until he's looking straight into my eyes. "Your body remembers me," he says.

The sting of Jericho's hand is sharp. Warmth spreads over the cheeks of my ass and tingles between my legs. I squirm, pushing myself toward him. "Tell me to stop," he says again.

His eyes focus in on my scar. He touches it and a wave of nausea washes over me. It still feels numb. It still feels as though there's something wrong with the flesh, like the bullet is still embedded inside.

"I'll never forgive him for marking you like this."

My insides lurch as though trying to toss me up and away from this nightmare, but my body remains frozen. Michael's attention is taken from my scar and drawn back to the exposed strip of flesh between the buttons of my dress. He undoes the final few hurriedly, and pulls the material aside, leaving me exposed to his gaze.

He assaults me with his eyes. They are hungry and filled with lust. The blue that once looked so soft and warm is now hard and cold. My heart pounds but there's little I can do to still it. The only option I have left is to squeeze my eyes shut, letting the flashes overwhelm me.

"I don't want you to stop." My voice is a pant of desperation. My whole body is on fire, waiting for his touch. He slaps me again and the pain sends a delicious spark straight to the coil of lust inside me. Jericho's hand wraps around my throat as he pushes me into the wall.

"Tell me to stop."

"No," I say defiantly. "I want this. I want you. I want the pain and the pleasure of your touch. I want everything."

Michael slips the shoulders of my dress down, full exposing my breasts. The cold breeze tickles my flesh, beading my nipples once again.

"I told myself I wouldn't do this, but just think of all I could do right now but am choosing not to. I'm one of the good guys, Everly." And then his mouth is on my breast. He's grinding against me, his cock thick and hard against my thigh.

I let out a whimper.

He lifts his head, bright eyes darting back and forth between mine. "Shh, shh." He holds his finger against my mouth. "Don't worry your pretty little head. I just want to make you feel good. I just want to feel you and touch you and give you pleasure. I want to remind you of how we used to be."

A wicked grin spreads over Jericho's face. The rope is cut from above and my body slumps into his arms. He scoops me up and carries me across the room, throwing me down on the bed. The black onyx of his eyes gleams dangerously.

"As you wish."

His touch is so gentle it hurts. His fingers feel like needles as he drags them down my skin and hooks them around the lace of my underwear. He tugs softly, drawing them down my thighs.

"Please don't," I manage to whimper although it is mumbled and slurred.

He looks at me then, and I plead with my eyes. My mouth won't work the way I want it to or else I'd scream. My body won't obey my commands. My mind, although filled with fog, is still witness to the plight of my body.

"It's okay," he whispers. "I love you. I've always loved you, right from the moment I first met you. We will be amazing together, Ev."

Jericho clambers over me, knees either side of my body. He doesn't stop until he hovers over my chest, dark eyes staring down at me and utters the command, "Open."

I obey without hesitation. He holds my head with his hands as he eases inside, muttering curses under his breath. I twist my legs together, wetness flooding me as he uses my mouth.

When Michael finds me dry, he spits on his fingers and presses them to me, rubbing in slow circles. He closes his eyes, almost as though he's relishing the sensation. Then he bends down low to whisper in my ear.

"You'd do well to remember this feeling, Ev. It's rather terrifying, is it not? No control over your body. No control over what I could do to you. You can fight this for as long as you want, but remember I have my ways. You are mine, Everly. You belong to me. You always have."

He brushes away another tear before reaching down and using it as moisture to rub over my clit. He rubs, just staring deeply into my eyes before lifting his hand and placing his finger into my mouth forcing me to taste myself.

Every one of his touches has been gentle.

None of them have brought pain.

And yet this has been more terrifying, more aggressive than anything I've known.

He takes his finger out of my mouth and cups my cheek. "I promise never to do this again, okay? Unless you provoke me. Unless you can't see that we belong together, that you are mine. Do we have an understanding?" Michael asks. "Blink if we have an understanding."

I blink. Because I'm scared not to. I'm scared of what he might do.

And then he presses his mouth to mine. My lips are dead under his, but it doesn't seem to worry him. He kisses me gently and softly, sliding his tongue into my mouth. He grinds against me, his body pushing mine into the cushion. He's heavy, crushed against my chest.

"Just remember I love you." Letting out a low whistle, he gets up and lights a cigarette. "That was intense," he says as he leans against the window, smoke billowing into the air. I remain unable to move, unable to speak, unable to fight.

"I'm a patient man." He pulls himself away from the wall, coming to stand over me. "But my patience won't last forever." As he sucks in poisoned air, ash falls from the tip and lands between my breasts. Michael looks at it, head cocked to the side and adjusts himself, the outline of his hardness obvious. He sucks on the cigarette again, flicking it when the ember appears and watches as it falls. It burns when it hits my skin, but I can't brush it away. He watches it until the ember fades.

"I think we'd make the perfect team. I want you on my side. So I'll expect you to be more accommodating in the future." And then he walks back into his room, leaving nothing but a puff of smoke behind him.

My tears fall freely then, unhindered by his touch. They run down my cheeks and soak into my hair. Stars blur above. Music floats through the open window. The cool breeze caresses my flesh and toys with my hair, lifting strands and sweeping them across my face.

I close my eyes to the tranquillity of the world.

Jericho grasps my chin between his fingers. His cock lies hard and heavy between my breasts. His eyes glimmer with darkness as his grip deepens to the point of bruising. His chest heaves with unfulfilled lust. The feathers on his chest dance.

"Tell me to stop," he pleads.

I shake my head, fighting against the grasp of his fingers. His hold falters and slips. Now it's around my throat, cutting off my supply of air.

"Tell me to stop." There's desperation in his eyes.

I push against him, sparks of need firing throughout my body. Black tugs at the edges of my vision, tunneling in on him and blocking everything else out. I struggle to breathe and yet I don't resist him. He gives me everything I crave, everything I need.

"Tell me to stop!" His voice breaks but the grasp of his fingers only gets harder.

The lust coiled so tightly inside me suddenly releases, lashing against my chest and causing a million shards of delirium to shatter throughout my body.

"Stop," I cry out, my body exhausted from the rippling rapture.

And he does.

chapter nineteen

The world is drenched in the gray of pre-dawn before I can finally muster the energy to pull myself up from the cushion. The movement of my body came back gradually. First it was only my fingers, then my arms, my toes and my feet, until finally I was able to pull myself to my feet. My flesh is dotted in goose bumps, cold and numb from the breeze which plummeted with the night. My legs shake. I grip onto the window in order to drag myself inside.

The lights are still on, the music is still playing, and Michael is passed out in the bed. He sleeps contently, as though he doesn't have a care in the world. I scan the room, desperate for some sort of weapon to use against him, but even as I do it, I know it's pointless. I've never felt so weak and so powerless as I do right now. Not even when my body was frozen. Then, I had no choice. He was in control. But now, my body responds to my commands but yet I'm still unable to fight against him.

Michael rolls over, eyes fluttering open. His blond hair is tousled delightfully as though it has no idea of the brute whose head it resides on. His lips are soft and pink. His eyes are brilliant blue, if not a little bleary. He pats the bed absently. "Come to bed."

There's no apology. No acknowledgment of the nightmare he'd just put me through. I turn, dragging my body across the room to the beanbag on the floor but Michael's voice stops me in my tracks.

"I thought we had an understanding?" His voice belies his words. It's soft and gentle. Sweet and affectionate.

He lifts the covers, raising his brows. I almost stumble as I make my way over and slide beneath the blankets. His arm drapes over me and pulls me close. He tucks his chin into the crook of my neck and inhales deeply.

"You're shivering," he says, his voice deep with slumber. His arm tightens even more. "Don't worry," he mumbles. "I'll keep you warm."

My chest pounds, my heart beating rapidly. But all Michael does is fall back to sleep. I want to say I can't sleep in his arms, that the repulsion keeps me awake, but I'm so exhausted, so cold and so tired that I fall to sleep quickly.

I'm shaken awake what feels like only moments later. "Sleep okay?" Michael asks.

For a moment, I think it really was a nightmare, that none of it is true. But then I sit up and my eyes fall to my dress, open and exposed, and the small red welt burned into my skin.

I look up at Michael and blink back tears of anger which he ignores.

"Come on," he says. "You've been cooped up for days. It's time you got out and about. We're going to take the boat out today so get ready. Breakfast is in half an hour and then we leave."

Leaning forward, Michael presses his lips to mine. I don't respond. My lips are limp and cold and motionless but when Michael pulls away there's only concern in his expression. "Didn't sleep too well, huh?" He pats my shoulder before walking over to his dresser and opening a drawer. "Maggie has been shopping. You should find everything you need in here." He sorts through the clothing and pulls out a few pieces of what I assume is white string. "Here, put this on." He tosses it to me.

"What is it?" I try to make sense of the tangled mess.

Michael laughs. "A bikini, silly." He rummages through the drawer some more. "You can wear this over it."

The outfit is loose and flowing and also see-through. It's made out of a finely woven white mesh that almost resembles linen. Michael watches as I drop my clothing to the floor and thread the strings of the bikini over my body. I try to act unaffected by his gaze. The triangles of white barely cover my breasts. I try to hold them in place as I tie the string, but they keep slipping. Michael moves behind me, taking control and tying the knots. His hands are hot when he places them on my shoulders. "There," he whispers in my ear. "All sorted."

I pull on the wide pants and flowing shirt, tying it at the waist, before pulling on the sandals Michael places on the floor.

"Are you coming down for breakfast?"

I shake my head. I have barely uttered one word to him since last night.

"The water always makes me hungry. You should eat something."

I turn and walk toward the bathroom.

Michael sighs. "Suit yourself."

I expected it to be just Michael and me on the boat, maybe a couple of staff, so I'm surprised to find both our fathers already on board.

My father clamps my shoulder and breathes in deeply. "Isn't it great to be out and about? Nothing quite like fresh salt air."

"I hope someone sees you and reports you," I snap.

But my father just laughs. "No one cares out here, my dear." His gaze falls over my outfit. "Pleased to see you making some effort for the boy. He's besotted with you, you know. If it weren't for him, you'd still be trapped in that cell awaiting your training."

"And if it wasn't for you, my life wouldn't be a complete and utter mess," I reply, lifting my chin and pushing past him.

"If it wasn't for me, you wouldn't be alive. Remember it's my blood that flows through those veins, Everly Atterton."

"Don't call me that," I hiss.

He just chuckles. "No matter how hard you try, my dear, you will not be able to wipe the smile from my face today. The only thing that would make this more perfect would be if your mother was here. Do you think she'd come if we invited her?" He laughs loudly. "You should see your face, my girl. It's priceless." He keeps laughing as he strides past and joins Mr Gorman at the helm. "All we need now are some playthings on the boat, my friend."

Mr Gorman shakes his head. "That was always your problem, Sebastian. Too fond of the product. And it was your downfall in the end."

My father laughs as though the last few years he spent in prison were nothing. "What's the point of offering the product if you can't indulge every once and a while?"

"The point is to make money. And to put enough people between you and your business to ensure you are the one never to take the fall. You could learn a thing or two from me, my friend."

"No talk of business on the water," Michael interrupts. "That was always the rule. Don't see why we're changing it now."

"Right you are!" Mr Gorman throws his arm around his son. Twin smiles beam back at me. "Let's get this thing on the water."

I move to the front of the boat as the men pop the champagne. I don't know what they're celebrating, and I don't care. They grow louder and more raucous the further we go out to sea. I concentrate on the scenery, the way the waves roll away as the bow cuts through the water, the small islands dotted in the blue, the flight of the seagulls overhead. Laughter floats on the breeze. The salt air fills my lungs.

I grip onto the railing, head tilted to the wind, and breathe deeply. Michael comes up from behind, offering me a glass, and wrapping his arms around my waist.

"All this could be ours," he says. "This life, this world. Everything is ours for the taking, Everly."

I remain stiff in his arms. I don't want this life. I don't want him.

"Think about it, Ev. It's everything we ever dreamed of. Everything we ever wanted. All you have to do is want it again." He presses his face into the crook of my neck and breathes deeply as though inhaling the scent of me. "You can't resist me forever, you know."

I turn slowly, his arms still looped around my waist and take a sip of the champagne while looking straight at him. "You won't ever have me, Michael," I say with all the sweetness I can muster. "You might think you do. I might pretend you do. But you will never truly have me." I lean forward and talk against his ear, letting my breath flow over his skin. "Your little stunt last night worked. I was scared. I was terrified in fact. You have control over me in ways no one has before, and I will no doubt comply. But know this. Every time I touch you, I will recoil with disgust on the inside. Every time you kiss me, bile will rise at the back of my throat. Every time I feign affection of any sort, it will not be real. It will not be true. And if you ever think, even for a moment that I am falling for you, please know that it is all a lie. I do not love you. I will never love you. I love Jericho."

I press my lips to his, keeping my eyes open, letting him feel the rage that's bubbling just beneath the surface. His mouth is cold and hard.

I pull away, battering my lashes repeatedly. "Blink if we have an understanding."

He moves so quickly, I don't see it coming. A slap sounds and then a stinging pain burns across my cheek. "Don't push me, Everly."

"Or what?" I hiss. "You'll force me? You'll break me? I thought you weren't like your father?"

His chin quivers with barely controlled rage. I cup his cheek and press another kiss to his lips. "He will come for me and he will make you pay. Because I am his."

As quickly as it rose, Michael's anger fades. "I wouldn't be so sure of that." And then he winds his fingers into my hair, pulling my face toward his and smothers me with his mouth. He laughs when I pull away and wipes his lips with the back of his hand. "The reason I'm not like my father is because I choose not to be. Don't be the one who makes me regret that."

chapter twenty

She's been gone for over a week. I keep looking back at footage of her, obsessing over where she might be, what might be happening to her. It's torture, plain and simple. The pain hasn't lessened with the days. I want her back. I'm desperate for her return and each day that passes only increases the rage that's bubbling inside. I learned patience in searching for Hope. But I don't want to do it again. I won't.

Gideon saunters into my office and flops himself down on the chair opposite my desk. "You summoned?"

He blows a stream of air upward, unsettling his mop of curls. And then it's as though he remembers. Remembers that Berkley and Ette have been taken. Remembers that we've gone through this before. Remembers that he shouldn't be acting like the insolent asshole that he is. He sits up a little straighter and leans forward, rearranging his face into something that resembles concern.

"Have you heard anything?"

I shake my head. I don't want to talk about her with him. He made her life here miserable.

"I can't stop thinking about Ette."

There's a tightness in my chest at the mention of her. To be honest, I've tried to block it out of my mind. I purposely don't add her in during the imagined scenarios. It gets me too enraged and that helps no one. I should do the same regarding Berkley, but I can't.

I clear my throat. I called him in here for a reason. There's no point in drawing it out. "I've found Alice."

Gideon blinks. His head tilts to one side as though deciding whether to accept the information or not. "What do you mean, you've found Alice?"

He's wary. I don't blame him. As far as he's concerned our mother has been out of our lives for years. He thinks she may even be dead. He has no idea that I've always known where she was or that I've been in contact with her ever since she left.

"It's exactly what it sounds like, Gideon. I've found our mother."

Gideon gets up from the chair, eyes narrowed in suspicion. Walking over to my desk, he slams his hands down, leaning close. "How long?" he asks.

"There are things you don't know. Things I've kept hidden."

Gideon shakes his head slowly, processing the information. He's handling the news better than I thought. Then again, he doesn't know the truth. Not yet.

"No shit." He walks back to the chair and takes a seat. It's a controlled response from him. Not normal. "So, keep talking." He crosses his arms over his chest, already defensive.

Where to start? I'd gone over this conversation in my head a million times but none of the possible scenarios played out like this. They didn't involve the relative calm on behalf of my younger brother.

I take a deep breath.

"Fucking spit it out!" Gideon splutters, more like the way I thought he'd react. "Is she okay? Does she know about us? Does she care?"

"She's fine." It's best to start with the good news. If you can call it that. "She's a little messed up, got a few substance abuse problems, but nothing unexpected."

Gideon snorts. "So you just fucking lied to me for all these years? Killed our father and then lied about our mother?"

"No." I chew on my bottom lip. "Well, yes, just not in the way you think."

"This better be good," he mutters. Then he looks up, eyes clouded in suspicion. "You made her leave, didn't you? You told her—"

I hold up my hand. "Let me speak."

"Well, fucking speak then."

"I never killed our father. Alice did." I expect there to be some sort of response to this revelation, but Gideon doesn't react. "Did you hear me? I said that—"

"Yeah, I heard you." Gideon rolls his eyes. "I just don't believe you. It's all very well for you to claim this years after when it all happened, but I was there, Jericho. You confessed."

"I confessed in order to prevent our mother from going to jail. She wouldn't have been able to handle it. It would have killed her."

A smirk creeps across Gideon's face. "So you're the hero now instead of the villain? How convenient."

"Gideon," I warn, my voice falling to a low growl.

"Jericho," he mimics. He slaps his hands to his thighs and then stands. "Look, I know you have this need to be adored—"

"That's not what this is."

"But why would you say this now? Why not tell me then? What's changed?"

"I told you. I've found her."

"Once again, how convenient. You want to change history, bathe yourself in some sort of sacrificial light, but regardless of how you look at it, I was the one who got left behind. I was the one who spent those months at that horrible foster home. Mother wasn't there for me, she was in hospital, remember? Another thing that was your fault. She couldn't stand you. She couldn't live with the knowledge of what her son had done."

I get to my feet and slam my hands down on the desk. "Enough!"

Gideon winces at my outburst and for a moment, I see the little boy again. The little boy who cried as I was taken away. The little boy who waited at the window for a glimpse of Hope when she'd visit him in the foster home. The little boy who went from having a family, as fucked up as it was, to having nothing within a matter of days.

"Look, I know you don't want to believe what I'm telling you but it's true."

There's a knock at the door and before I can call out, Hope walks in.

"Did you know?" Gideon snaps at her.

"Know what?" She looks between us questioningly.

"Who killed my father?" he demands.

"I told him the truth," I say, knowing Hope will want to defend me.

Hope's face softens and she turns to Gideon. "Yes. I knew."

"You two are fucking unbelievable. Did you tell her to go along with this story? Was there some sort of agreement between you?"

Hope nods toward the door. "Go ask her."

Gideon's eyes snap to mine.

"I hadn't told him yet."

"She's here? She's fucking here? My mother, who I haven't seen in years, is fucking here?"

"I thought you knew," Hope says apologetically.

"She wasn't in a good place. I thought it would be best to wait for a few days before I told you, give her some time to come to terms with all this. Same for you."

Gideon's chin quivers even as his eyes blaze with anger. "I can't take this all in right now. I need a minute." He strides from the room, slamming the door behind him.

"That went well." I lower myself back to my seat.

"Sorry, I just assumed you'd told him everything."

"I was trying to, but it didn't exactly go as planned." Resting my elbows on my desk, I let my head flop to my hands, dragging my fingers through my hair.

Hope has calmed down somewhat from the first few days after we discovered Ette was gone. I didn't think it would happen. She was hysterical, crying and pacing the sanctuary as though it might somehow hold the answer to who had taken her. Then a calmness descended. One that scares me. There's a deadness to her eyes. Almost as though she's given up.

"How's she doing?" Hope asks.

"Getting stronger with each day. She actually managed to keep down some of the soup Mrs Bellamy gave her yesterday. That in itself is a huge improvement. Doctors say it will be a while before she's back to normal, whatever that is."

"That's good, that's good," she mutters distractedly.

"She admitted that she accepted payment for information on me. Can't believe my own mother would do that. It was a deliberate overdose too. Not sure if the intention was for her to survive."

"She's an addict, Jericho. She would have done anything to get her next hit."

"She's still an addict," I say as the door opens again. This time there's no knock.

"Sorry to barge in, sir." Barrett's gaze flicks between Hope and me hesitantly.

I sigh. "Barrett, I've told you—"

"The Gormans and the Keatings are related."

It takes a while for the information to sink in. "How?" I demand.

"Mary Keating is Michael Gorman Senior's sister."

"And why the fuck did we not know this?"

"It must have just slipped through the cracks. They're not a—"

"That fucking Montgomery. Don't use him again. Ever."

"Yes, sir. I mean, Jericho."

Hope lowers herself to the chair recently vacated by Gideon. The color has faded from her face. "Does that mean…" she doesn't finish the sentence, and instead, lifts tear-filled eyes to mine.

The thin thread of patience I have left snaps. "We should go right now. We should—"

"No!" The vehemence in Hope's voice surprises me. "You don't know them like I do. We can't go rushing in there unprepared."

"I agree with her," Barrett says, coming to stand by her side. There's some sort of strange vibe between them. It's almost as though Barrett's presence brings her comfort.

"I'm not going to just sit here when they could be right under our noses. We've been searching for someone who could've helped Dominic, that might have some stake in this and now we've got confirmation. I knew there was something fucked up about that family."

"I spent years with Sebastian Atterton. If this Gorman is anything like him, I'm not risking him doing anything to Ette. We need more information."

"More?" I roar. "What more do you want?"

"They're siblings, Jericho. It's not a fucking crime!"

"It's obviously retaliation. We killed her husband. We tried to kill her too." I can't believe they're fighting me on this.

"I've got an idea, but you're not going to like it," Barrett says, breaking my eye-line with Hope.

My heart is pounding. It's taking all my strength to merely stand here when I want to knock the fucking doors off the Gorman's house and hunt for Berkley. The image of Michael's gaze on her, the way he looked at her so possessively, echoes through my mind.

"Spit it out," I bark.

"Invite them to the next game."

"Invite them here?" I almost choke.

"Why not? He fits in with the clientele perfectly. It would give us a chance to suss them out. It would also ensure they weren't at home for the evening, an ideal chance for me to scope the place, see what sort of security they have."

I hold my hands out in front of me. They're shaking. They want blood. They want to feel the crush of flesh beneath my knuckles.

They want vengeance.

Hope gets up and comes across to hold my hands in hers. "Don't put my daughter at risk, Jericho. We've got to come up with a plan. We can't just barge in there all guns blazing and risk their lives."

I know they're talking sense. But I don't want to listen. I want to listen to the primal scream for blood that's pulsing through my veins.

"The last time we rushed something without checking it out first ended badly."

"Thanks to you," I snap at Barrett and then instantly regret my words when I see the pain flash across his eyes.

"Yes, it was my fault. I didn't do the job properly. I will take the blame for that. But if you recall, sir, I advised you to wait."

Hope squeezes my hands again, looking at me pleadingly.

"We have nothing to go on other than the familial connection," Barrett continues. "There's been no talk, no suspicious behavior, no motive—"

"We haven't exactly been watching them day and night though, have we?" I need them to be the ones. I need to have someone to blame, someone to exact my revenge on.

"No, we haven't. So we need to do that. We need time to ensure that we're making the right move here. The last thing we want to do is add to the danger Berkley or Odette may be in." Barrett and Hope exchange a look. It's one of relief. "So, we're in agreement then? We proceed with caution?"

I nod, and it takes all my strength.

Hope looks at me, eyes narrowed. "We need to make sure there are enough people there to dissuade anyone from creating a spectacle."

I know the 'anyone' she's talking about is me.

"Rather than the more intimate affair you usually host, we could consider a casino themed occasion. Bring in some of the staff from the club. Set up different gaming tables. Get in some live music."

"Yeah," I wave, dismissing him. "Whatever you want."

I don't care what sort of theme it is. Standard practice is we cater the night to appeal to whatever client I've got the most interest in obtaining information from. I don't see why this should be any different.

chapter twenty-one

BERKLEY

I'm sitting in a chair in front of the mirror staring at my reflection. It's one of those mirrors that has lightbulbs dotted along its edges. They make my skin appear paler than usual, but there's also a dullness to it, almost an insipidness. I don't recognize myself. My shoulders are weighted with defeat. There are dark marks beneath my eyes. I'm dressed only in lace underwear.

Reflected in the mirror, through the crack in the door is Michael. He's sifting through the shopping bags his assistant Maggie just dropped off.

"I think you should wear this to dinner tonight, what do you think?" He holds up a dress. It's pale pink with a key-hole neckline. He mentions the name of the designer, a label I've never heard of.

I give him a weak smile. "Sure. Whatever you want." It looks too elegant for a family dinner, but what does it matter? If he wants me to wear it, I'll wear it. He could ask for worse.

"Come," Michael calls out. "Try it on."

I stare at myself one last time before walking out of the bathroom. Michael holds out the dress, a smile covering his face. Whether he knows the torment within me, or whether he's oblivious, it doesn't matter. He's made one thing clear. He doesn't care. As long as I behave, he's happy. Whether I am or not is of little consequence.

I step through the dress and Michael pulls it up my body. He turns me so I'm facing the full-length mirror on his bedroom wall and smiles over my shoulder. "Beautiful," he whispers reverently and pecks a kiss to my cheek.

Michael hasn't touched me since that night. Not sexually anyway. He's affectionate, but not like I feared he would be. He lies with his arms wrapped around me each night but never takes it any further. He sits with his arm draped over my shoulder. He comes up behind me and pulls me close, hands possessively clinging to my waist. He walks holding my hand. He presses kisses to the top of my head.

"What do you think?" he asks, stepping away to face me.

"It's nice," I reply.

"Nice? It cost a fucking fortune."

"I never asked for it."

"No, you didn't. And you'll never have to ask for anything again, Everly. I'm going to give you the world."

It's as though he truly believes his words. He truly believes that one day I will love him. One day I will choose him. He's unconcerned about the deadness in my eyes, or the way I drag myself through the day. He chooses to ignore my hesitation, my repulsion, and lives in a world unconnected to reality. A world where we are a couple. A happy couple. Where I am on his side.

"Keep your hair down like that for dinner. I love the way your hair looks when it's out, but you so often tie it back. It's a shame." He runs his fingers through the dark strands. They get caught on a knot and my hair snaps when he tugs them out.

Walking over to the bed, he pats the space beside him. "Sit."

I do.

"You can smile, you know. I'm not asking you to do anything you don't want to."

I want to tell him I don't want to be here. I don't want to be with him. And I don't want to smile. I want Jericho. But I don't say any of those things, because the memory of lying frozen, vulnerable and unable to move, is too present in my mind. I may have shown strength on the boat, telling him I would never be his, but that strength has faded. The defiant girl is gone.

"I want to tell you my plans," he starts. "Well, our plans. My father wants me to step up, take a more active role within the business. He's been wanting it for months now, but it wasn't something I was interested in. I was too busy partying. I liked my life. But now…" He takes my hands in his. "Now, I've got you and I want it all. I want to give you everything, Everly. The life you've always wanted. Can't you just picture it? Us dripping in money, traveling the world. You always wanted to travel, didn't you?"

I merely nod.

"Name a place. Any place and I'll take you there. It will be my gift to you. You know," he adds, "once everything has died down a little." When I don't say anything, he pats my hand softly. "I'm getting ahead of myself. I was thinking of bringing a few suggestions to my father, you know, to prove to him that I'm serious, I'm ready, but I wanted to run them by you first." He clears his throat. "I was thinking about the idea you brought to me, the business you pretended you and Mr Priest were interested in running. The more boutique shopping experience. One where people put in the orders of what they want, and we provide them with the closest match we could. It would be different from how things are run now. Of course, we'd still run the auctions, still offer the 'off the rack' options, so to speak, but this merchandise would attract a more specific clientele. One that would be willing to part with a premium rate in order to have their requests fulfilled. What do you think?"

"It's wonderful," I lie. "It's almost as though I thought of it myself."

Michael sighs with relief. It's as though he believes the words coming from my mouth. Surely, he can detect the sarcasm in my tone. Surely, he must feel the waves of hatred pulsating from me.

"Okay." He shuffles closer to me excitedly, as though he's fuelled by my lack of enthusiasm. "Here's my other idea. I'm not sure how my father will react to this one, but in this day and age we need to move with the times." He takes a deep breath and says, "Males."

I wait for more, but he just sits there, looking at me expectedly.

"Males, what?" I ask.

"Males in the auctions. We've always concentrated on females as they've always been in the highest demand. But the world is changing, and we've got to change along with it. It's a good idea, don't you think? Obviously, it's been done before, for many, many years, but there's limited competition. I've done my research and I believe the demand is there if we just offered the supply."

"What sort of research did you use to come to that conclusion?"

He laughs. "You don't want to know. But it's a good idea, isn't it? Modern. Equality and all that."

I can barely believe the words coming from his mouth. It is like he lives in some alternate reality. One where he cannot fathom that what he's proposing is wrong and evil. To him it is merely a business proposal. He doesn't consider it toying with people's lives.

He's still looking at me, waiting for my answer.

"No," I say finally. "I think it's a terrible idea."

"You don't think there would be much of a demand?"

"I don't think you should sell people."

Michael rolls his eyes. The action reminds me so much of Dominic it hurts. It's the only time I've ever seen a similarity. "And we're back here again." He flops himself onto the bean bag. "You've got to stop thinking like that, Everly. You've got to stop thinking of them as the same as us, as though you could be one of them."

"But I could be."

"Your father wasn't serious when he said he would have left you in that cell, you know that right?" He places his hands behind his head, looking up at me without a care in the world. As though we are discussing something as simple as ice cream flavors. There's no point in arguing with him. He believes he's right, no matter how twisted his logic.

I smile weakly. "I know."

"Good." He slaps his hands onto his thighs. "You are a part of this family, now. The Gormans and the Attertons are on the same team."

Only I don't want to be an Atterton or a Gorman. I want to be just Berkley.

"Let's go down for dinner. I've got a surprise for you."

The last time he said that my mother was at dinner. But there's no way they'd invite her now. Not with my father, the man who kept her captive for years sitting at the same table.

Michael walks out the door, expecting me to follow, but before I do, I dash into the bathroom and twist my hair back into a ponytail as a silent protest. It's all I can do.

I'm filled with apprehension as I approach the dinner table. I look up, bracing myself for the worst, but instead I find bright blue eyes sparkling with excitement.

"Berkley!" Ette shouts.

She launches herself from the table, tipping her chair over in the process, and races toward me. I fall to my knees, wrapping my arms around her as she catapults into my embrace.

I start to cry, unable to say anything and just hold her tightly. She's crying too, her sobs loud in my ear.

"I thought I'd never see you again!" Ette cries.

"Sit back up at the table, dear. There's no need to make a spectacle at dinner." Mary pats the seat beside her.

Ette pulls herself out of my arms, wiping her tears away and does what Mary asks. But she drags me with her, our joined hands hanging in the space between our chairs. And that's the way she stays. She does not let go of my hand when the food is served. She does not let go even as she tries to slice her meat. She clutches on tightly, her eyes darting to mine every so often.

I want to ask her if she's okay, if they're treating her well, but with everyone's eyes on us it would bring too much attention. So instead, we just cling to each other, fingers threaded through each other's to the point of pain.

"We've received an invitation," Mr Gorman says once he's finished eating and pushed his plate to the side. "Michael and I have been personally invited to one of Mr Priest's famed poker games."

Michael's eyes snap to mine at the mention of Jericho. I look down, toying with the food left on my plate. I may look calm on the outside, but my heart is beating wildly. He knows something. Or at least he suspects something. There is no way he'd invite them otherwise.

"I hope you're not consid—"

"I think we should go," Mr Gorman says, talking over his son.

Michael's knife clatters onto his plate. "You can't be serious," he splutters.

"Why wouldn't I be?" Mr Gorman lifts a glass of wine to his lips and takes a sip.

"It's got to be a trap of some sort. He wouldn't just invite us for no reason."

Mr Gorman just raises his brows. "I've accepted his invitation."

Michael gets to his feet. "But why?" He sounds so much like a whiny child I have to hold back my laughter. Ette squeezes my hand tightly.

I take the opportunity of the table's distraction to lean close and whisper, "Are you okay?"

Mary clears her throat. "Dominque, please inform Everly that it is rude to whisper in front of other people."

"Dominque?" I echo. "Her name is Odette."

Ette's brows bunch together. "But why would anyone need to whisper if no one was around?"

"Don't talk back!" Mary snaps. Then she attempts to recover herself, smoothing her hair and schooling the expression on her face back to one of passivity. "It's rude," she adds, her voice now calmer.

Tears spring to Ette's eyes but she doesn't say any more. I'm dying to reach out and embrace her, tell her everything will be okay. If Jericho searched for Hope for years, there was no way he was going to give up on us. He will find us.

Michael is still standing, glaring at his father.

"We're going," Mr Gorman says with finality, daring his son to defy him further by meeting his glare. Tension floats around the room, infecting us all until, after a few breath-holding moments, Michael sits back down.

"It's time for you to leave the table, Dominque. The adults are talking," Mary instructs.

"But I haven't finished eating."

"You would have had the time to finish if you didn't insist on holding Everly's hand the whole time."

"Her name is Berkley, not Everly," Ette mutters under her breath.

"And her name is Odette, not Dominque," I don't mutter.

Mary bends low and whispers in Ette's ear. She lets go of my hand, her eyes sliding to mine and her chin trembling. "Yes, Mary," she says.

"I've told you to call me Mother."

"She has a mother," I say, lifting my chin.

Mary ignores me and gestures to Ette to leave. She slides off the seat and walks with her head down. Before slipping through the door, she stops and looks back at me.

"When will I see you again?"

My heart breaks at the tears in her eyes.

"Now!" Mary screeches.

Her voice startles me. My heart breaks and tears spring to Ette's eyes and she scurries through the door. Anger simmers. I place my knife and fork down on my plate and push it away, most of the food left uneaten. I can't look at anyone. I can't look at them because if I do, I will explode.

There are noises, a chair scraping across the floor and then I feel Michael's hands on my shoulders. Hot and heavy. He tugs at my ponytail, freeing my hair and presses a kiss to the top of my head.

"It's Everly's birthday in a few days. I was thinking it was about time we had a party, introduced her back into the world. Again."

"Great idea, son." Any of the tension between father and son vanishes, or at least gets pushed under the surface.

Michael pulls out Ette's chair and sits down. "You could even invite some of your friends from the dance company."

"I don't want a party."

"Don't be so ungrateful," my father says.

"You could dance!" Michael says, ignoring my insistence of not wanting a party.

Mrs Gorman looks up, the first time she's shown any interest in the conversation. "What a wonderful idea! We could theme the entire décor around Swan Lake. I can picture it. Oh, it will be so beautiful. And we could make it a masquerade party, that way your father could be there too and no one would even know."

"Brilliant!" My father can't contain his grin. He's been complaining that he's stuck here, unable to participate in any of the social engagements that the Gormans attend. "And Everly could do that scene where the swan dies." My father winks.

"That's not even from Swan Lake," I mutter.

"Yes, it is," he insists. "The Dying Swan I believe it's called. Rather apt, don't you think?"

Michael's hand comes to rest on my shoulder again. He's rubbing back and forth, back and forth. I want to shake him off. I want to jerk out of his reach. But I don't.

"It's not. It's a dance performed to Le Cygne from Le Carnaval des Animaux, and there is simply no way I can perform it. I'm not good enough. The pointe work alone is an impossibility. I don't have the skill. I'm out of practice."

"I'm sure you'll be able to get some training in before the party," my father says.

"And from what I've witnessed," Michael's face twists into a mocking smirk, "your ability to move your body is exceptionally good."

I glare back at him. "Strange, as I don't seem to recall you giving me the chance to move at all."

chapter twenty-two

BERKLEY

The final notes of Camille Saint-Saëns's Le Cygne fade as I sink to the floor, chest heaving, muscles aching. Over the last couple of days, I've pushed myself into a grueling routine in the hope of being somewhat able to perform. My feet are bruised and bleeding, my toenails black. And even then, I've only been able to manage to perform a stilted version of the dance at half pointe.

But at least Michael isn't here watching me this time. He and his father left to attend Jericho's famed monthly gathering. He's been moody since his father insisted on them attending. He snaps at me and insults Jericho, attempting to elicit a response. But I don't bite. I don't give him the pleasure.

I'm trying not to imagine them shaking hands, acting civil, pretending I don't exist. I don't know what Jericho's plan is, but I trust he has one.

Each day I spend here I miss him more. There are times when I wake in the morning, trapped in Michael's arms and for a split second, I think it's Jericho. In my half-dream state, I'm happy. A warm glow radiates from my chest, but then I open my eyes and realize where I am.

I haven't had any flashes over the last few days. I'm beginning to miss them. Not the twisting in my stomach. Not the shortness of breath or the pounding of my heart. But because I don't see him. As confusing and vivid as they were, they allowed me to be close to him even when I wasn't.

My only joy is seeing Ette at dinner each night. Not that we're given any time to talk. But at least I get to see her. I get to check that she's okay. Physically at least. It's given me some peace.

Pulling myself to my feet, I walk over to the stereo to start the song again. Michael cleared out his gym for me, pushing all the weight machines, treadmills and rowers to the side. It doesn't allow me a huge space to practice in, but it's better than the cramped space of my apartment where I used to train.

It's the first time he's truly left me alone since I came here. He made sure to show me the feeds of the cameras and introduced me to some of the hidden guards before he left. But knowing I'm not being watched by him, even if I am by others is a weight lifted from me. I feel lighter than I have in days, even if my body is exhausted.

My feet are too sore to even attempt full pointe, so I concentrate on the movements of my arms. They are still too stiff, still too human-like to replicate the movement of wings.

I take my position as the rolling notes of the piano start. My arches and toes protest when I lift to the balls of my feet and hover my way across the room as the cello joins. I wish there was a mirror so I could see my progress. I wish I had something to record myself so I could watch it back. Even though I don't want to perform, I know I have to, so I want to do it well.

I close my eyes, allowing myself to get lost in the beauty of the music, the sadness of the dance. It tells the story of a swan who has been wounded. She's fighting against it, fighting against death, but she loses her battle. The melancholy strains of the cello are haunting but it's the final note which brings my tears. It quivers almost as though the cello itself can feel the pain.

When I'm collapsed on the floor again, a slow clap echoes about the room. I lift my head to find my father, the monster, leaning against the doorway, watching me.

"I told you all you needed was a little practice."

After taking off the slippers Michael arranged for me to use, I get up and turn off the stereo. "I'm not even close."

"It looked beautiful to me."

I turn, waiting for the next comment, the barbed remark but it doesn't come. He pulls himself away from the doorway and steps into the centre of the room.

"You have it good here, daughter. You must have something rather appealing between those legs considering you've now managed to trap two men between them. I guess you're more like your mother than I thought."

He chuckles and the sound runs through me as chills. I grit my teeth, determined not to give him the satisfaction of seeing me upset. It doesn't work.

"Oh, come on now. You know how enamored Michael is with you. You should be grateful."

"Grateful?" I splutter before I can stop myself.

"Yes, grateful." He narrows his eyes. "Fucking grateful in fact. He's offering you a life you don't deserve. If it were up to me, I would have left you in that cell, given you a taste of what your life could be. But Michael wouldn't hear of it. He insisted on bringing you back here. Insisted you were part of the family even though I'd told him you'd already spread your legs for that excuse of a man, Jericho Priest."

He's purposely trying to provoke me.

"You know." He slowly stalks around the room, running his fingers over the gym equipment and rubbing them together when he finds a speck of dust. "Everything good in your life is because of me. I was the one who raised you. I was the one who paid for your life." He glances up, no doubt hoping to see the anger in my expression, but I push it deep down and hope I'm showing nothing but nonchalance. "I'm still paying for your life," he adds, pushing the barb in harder. "And yet you've done nothing but disappoint me. You owe me everything, daughter, and you've done nothing but turn your back on me."

"Enjoy this while you can, Father." I spit out the word as an insult. "I won't be here for long."

"Still praying for your Priest to arrive? I hate to break it to you, my dear, but priests don't ride white horses."

"He got Hope back, didn't he?"

My father snorts. "You think he did that? He did nothing but follow the line of crumbs Gorman lay for him. Of course, we only had to do that because of you. We had everything planned but then you got in the fucking way. Do you think your Priest would have even looked at you if you weren't my daughter? You are nothing without me. It's about time you realized that and showed some fucking gratitude."

He reaches for me, but I jerk out of the way. "Don't touch me!" I hiss.

"I'll fucking touch you if I want to fucking touch you." He lunges toward me, grabbing my arm and digging his fingers in painfully. "I'm going to teach you a lesson, show you what your life would look like if Michael hadn't pleaded on your behalf. Maybe then you'll realize how fucking grateful you should be."

He starts to drag me from the room. I fight against him, trying to rip myself out of his grasp but he's stronger than I thought.

"Don't make me call the guards," he growls when I flail against him. I ignore him and level a kick at his shin. He winces and bends over but doesn't let go. Without warning, his elbow cracks against the side of my head. I see stars for a few moments, the world swaying before coming back into focus. I'd be on the ground if it weren't for his grip on my arm.

"Don't test me," he warns. "I'm not Michael. I'm not swayed by tears in your fucking eyes. I'm your father. I'm not tempted by what's between your legs." He spits as he speaks, little globules of saliva hitting my face.

I start yelling as he grabs a fistful of my hair and yanks hard, demanding my obedience. I try fighting him. I try resisting as he pulls me outside. My bare feet scramble against the gravel, trying to find purchase. The bruises are soon joined by cuts and scrapes. My hands are held over my father's, trying to relieve some of the pressure on my scalp.

Opening the car door, he tosses me inside. "Fucking stay!"

He slams the door shut before I can bar it. I fumble with the lock, trying to release it, but it won't open. Clambering over to the other side, I try once again but it too won't open. My father gets in the driver's seat as I'm banging on the glass, desperate for someone to hear me.

Out of the corner of my eye, I see Mary wandering through the garden. She lifts her eyes, peering through the darkness only to smile faintly and wave when she sees my fear.

I guess I deserve it.

As the car starts to pull away, I feel the familiar tug of anxiety.

"No, no, no," I chant. "Not now, not now."

I brace myself for a flash, but it never comes. But the nausea in my gut does, the rapid beating of my heart does, and so does the panicked breathing.

"What's wrong with you?" He glances at me, lying on the back seat, the palms of my hands pressed to my eyes.

"First, second, third, fourth, fifth. First, second, third, fourth, fifth." I open my eyes.

"What's fucking wrong with you?" The monster yells, spittle spraying the windscreen.

Even though my breath is still ragged and my heart is beating wildly, I heave myself forward, lunging at my father and wrapping my hands around his neck.

"You fucking little whore!" he splutters.

His elbow rams me in the face again. The force of it whips my head back but I keep my grip on his neck. I squeeze with all I'm worth as the car swerves over the road, controlled only by one hand of the monster. The other is tearing at my fingers, attempting to pry them from his neck. Then his elbow comes back again. I see it, but in order to avoid it, I'd have to let go.

He hits me in the jaw this time and the taste of blood fills my mouth. The pain is too much, and I'm forced to let go, falling back onto the seat.

"Stay there." The monster curses as he rubs his neck.

Tears tighten the back of my throat, but I refuse to let them push to the surface. I close my eyes again, counting internally, attempting to calm myself. I stay like that as the car slows and I hear him talking to the guards. I stay like that until we pull to a stop. The door opens and the monster grabs a fistful of my hair again, dragging me out and onto the ground. He allows me enough time to get to my feet before pulling me inside.

He seems to know the guards. They greet him by name, some of them giving him a high-five as he passes, dragging me along behind. Some of them glance at me with an amused look in their eyes. Others ignore me. None of them care.

Metal clangs against metal as a guard opens one of the doors to a cell. I expect to be thrown inside, the door locked, and the key thrown away, but it's my father who enters, yanking me behind him.

"That will be all." He nods to the guard as he releases his grip on my hair. I fall to the ground and shuffle myself into the corner, as though somehow the concrete walls will protect me.

"We're not supposed—"

"That will be all!" My father screams.

My body starts to tremble. I can't help it. I wish I was stronger. I wish I could get to my feet and face him, but I stay huddled, my knees pressed to my chest.

This cell is different from the one I was in. It has a window. There's a patch of moonlight on the ground, a perfect rectangular shape, mimicking the window. I hazard a look around, and that's when I see her. Blonde hair highlighted by the moon, making it look like a halo on her head. Naked body, skinny and bruised. Hands bound by rope.

"No," I whisper.

The girl looks up as my father advances. She tries to push herself into the wall, make herself disappear, but she knows there's no escape. She shakes her head as he approaches and whispers the same word I am.

"No."

Tears fall as my father strokes her hair. And then she lifts her eyes, meeting mine across the room. I see myself reflected in her gaze. We're mirror images of each other, both pressed to the wall in fear, both with scrapes and bruises and cuts. I lift my hand, reaching toward her and she shakes her head, eyes locking with mine.

"This, dear daughter, could be your life."

The girl whimpers as he runs a finger down her cheek before cupping her chin and tipping it up to face him. There's something almost gentle in the way he's touching her. But I know it's a lie. I know it's the calm before the storm.

"She hasn't been here more than a few days, have you, sweetheart? Only just started her training. And judging from the state of her, I'm guessing obedience doesn't come naturally for this one." He chuckles and tightens his grip on her chin.

She tries to jerk out of his grasp, but he grabs a fistful of her hair, forcing her head back sharply and bends low to hiss in her ear. "You will do as I fucking say." As he lets her go, he pushes her down and spits. She starts to sob. "Get on your knees."

The girl faces away, burying her head against the concrete wall as though she can hide from him.

"Get on your fucking knees!" the monster roars. When she doesn't comply, he starts to undo the buckle of his belt, tugging the leather through the loops of his pants.

I've seen this part before.

I've dreamed this part before.

I know what's coming.

"No!" I pull myself to my feet. "Don't you fucking touch her!"

The monster turns his gaze to me, lifting his brows. "Watch, my daughter. Watch and be fucking grateful it isn't you."

I scream as I race toward him, shoving him to the ground and clambering on top of him, fists, knees, and feet thrashing, attempting to hurt him. My screams are primal as I lose control, lashing out in any way I can. The girl stares wide-eyed as I scratch my nails down his cheek, blood pooling in their wake.

"Help me!" I beg her.

She shakes her head as the echo of the guards' footsteps sound down the corridor. Metal clangs against metal but I don't stop. I barely register what I'm doing as I thrash and flail, beating my fists against any part of him I can. He cowers beneath me, attempting to save his face from my disjointed attack. My throat tears as sounds I didn't know I could make are ripped from my mouth.

And then hands are on me, dragging me back. I twist and turn, attempting to escape their vice-like grip, but I can't. I'm held in place as my father lifts himself from the ground, wiping his mouth with the back of his hand. He stares at the smear of blood and then back at me.

A shudder runs through me at the coldness behind his eyes. The devil is reflected in them. He walks forward, breath labored, and stands in front of me. I struggle against the guards but there is no hope of escape. My father punches me in the gut and pain radiates through my side. The breath leaves my lungs and I fold over on myself, the only thing stopping me from collapsing is the grip of the guards.

When I lift my eyes again, the monster smirks. "Now, my daughter, you will watch, and you will be fucking grateful it isn't you." He wraps the end of his belt around his wrist.

I've had nightmares about the cruelty my father inflicts on others, but I've never been witness to it. But now, I'm trapped, forced to watch as the monster is unleashed.

chapter twenty-three

"You're afraid of getting hurt."

Barrett is staring at me as I lay where he deposited me on the mat on the gym floor. A fine layer of sweat covers my body. My muscles ache. My breathing is labored with exertion. He's been training me in self-defense techniques, something he insisted on before teaching me how to handle a knife.

"Of course I'm afraid of getting hurt." I sit up and cross my legs, using my hands to prop myself from behind. "Who actually wants to get hurt?"

Barrett grins lopsidedly and lowers himself to the ground. There isn't a lick of sweat on him. Not even a flush. "You'd be surprised." He chuckles. "I guess it's not a matter of being unafraid, it's more about teaching you what to do when you are afraid and using it to your advantage. Right now, you've got no fear of losing. I'm not a threat to you. If you don't fight me, all that happens is you end up on the ground. But if you do, you have a chance of hurting both yourself and me."

"I have no problem with hurting you."

"Good to know." He laughs. "You've got to decide which you fear the most, the possibility of getting hurt by me, or the possibility of being controlled by someone."

"Control. It's definitely control." I shudder. Even though I force back specific memories, that feeling of being used, of being unable to stop it, unable to fight back, still lingers in my bloodstream.

"Well, you need to use that. You need to muster it right here, right now and fight back when I attack, okay?"

I let my hands slide over the mat, lowering myself back to the ground. "I'm not sure I can. Can you just teach me to slit his throat?"

"You plan on always carrying a knife, do you?"

"Why not?"

"Because it can be used against you."

"They'd have to pry it from my cold dead fingers first." I stare at the rafters of the ceiling as Barrett jumps back to his feet.

There's something appealing about the thought of using a knife. I keep imagining myself running across the throat of those who have hurt me. I keep imagining the way their blood would gush out and flow down their chest. The way their clothing would turn dark with the stain of it.

Barrett is waiting for me expectantly. He's got way too much energy. "Come on." His face appears in my vision. "Let's go again. You ready?"

I shake my head and moan. "Nope."

"Oh." Barrett blinks in mock concern. "Well, I'll just sit here and wait until you catch your breath. Bad guys are usually pretty accommodating like that."

Before I can even blink, Barrett throws himself on top of me, crushing his body against mine. My reaction is instant. The panic. The vice-like tightness in my chest. I push against his chest feebly, forgetting everything he's spent hours trying to teach me.

Barrett laughs menacingly in my ear. "Is that all you've got?"

I twist and turn, struggling to get out from under him. He grabs my wrists, pinning them above my head. I fight against the panic, determined to use it rather than let it use me.

"Stop trying to push me away," he says. "Pull me closer. Stop me from being able to get to you."

I thrust with my hips, causing the smallest amount of leeway against his grip around my wrists. And then I heave myself up, hugging his torso, removing any of the distance between us.

"Good, good," Barrett huffs. "Now the leg. Trap my leg."

He's helping me. He's not using his full strength or ability but I'm assuming I wouldn't stand a chance if he did. Not yet. I wrestle my arm up and over his shoulder and plant my free leg down heavily, using the leverage to drive up with my hips and roll him off me. But the way we're entangled means I end up on top of him, my knees resting either side of his hips.

He grins. "And now this is where you decide to run or fight. You've got the advantage, you're now on top. But you've got to weigh up whether you think you can keep that advantage. Personally, my recommendation is, whenever possible, run."

I nod, my words not coming due to my heavy breathing. Even though he was helping me, he didn't exactly make it easy. It's not a simple thing for a person of my size to toss a person of Barrett's size off.

"You okay?" he asks when I'm still struggling for breath.

I nod again, bringing my hand up to press against my rapidly beating heart. "Just need a minute," I manage to say.

"I did what I could while I was," I pause for a moment, "while I was away, but there wasn't exactly gym equipment on hand."

Barrett cocks his head. "Take all the time you need."

He looks at me then. And for the first time in years, a warmness creeps up my neck and flushes my cheeks. Barrett isn't handsome in the same way Jericho is handsome. He doesn't cause women to turn and stare as he passes. He doesn't have a killer smile or a wicked grin. But there's something about him that makes me feel safe. And that's more important than anything else.

I grin sheepishly and slide off him, flopping onto the floor. "Are we done for the day?"

Barrett jumps to his feet. And when I say jump, I mean jump. His energy is boundless. "If you want to be done, then we're done."

"I don't think I have any strength left."

Barrett snorts. "Of course you do." He holds out his hand, tugging me to my feet. "You are one of the strongest people I've ever met, Hope. What you've been through requires more strength than most people ever have to demonstrate in their lives. Don't ever doubt how strong you are."

My hand is still encased in his. He holds it close to his chest, his eyes boring into mine as though pleading for me to believe him.

I smile and nod, tucking a loose strand of hair behind my hair because I'm not sure what else to do.

"I mean it, Hope."

"Mean what?" Jericho strides into the room.

"Nothing." Barrett drops my hand and grabs a towel, looping it around his shoulders. His eyes flick back to mine before facing Jericho.

"Good," Jericho says. "Because you're supposed to be getting ready for tonight." Jericho's tone is snappish, like he's searching for someone to argue with.

"I'm all sorted," Barrett informs him.

"Shouldn't you be on your way, then?"

"Just leaving now, sir." Barrett spits out the word 'sir' purposely and Jericho's frown deepens.

He narrows his eyes. "If you don't think you're up to this…" Jericho leaves the rest unspoken.

"I'm not the one I'm worried about."

"Have you got something you want to say?" Jericho puffs his chest out, as though challenging him to a fight. Barrett is discreet when he looks at me, rolling his eyes a little. I stifle a laugh.

Barrett clamps Jericho on the shoulder. "Not at all. Hope everything goes well tonight."

Jericho lets out a noise that resembles a growl as Barrett leaves the room.

"He's got a lot on his plate today. He doesn't need to be distracted by you wanting him to—"

"I think Barrett can decide what he does and doesn't want to be distracted by. You, on the other hand, look as though you could use a distraction."

Jericho sighs and runs his hands through his hair. "I don't know if I can just sit there and watch them without wanting to put my hands around their fucking throats." He mimes the actions as though the Gormans are right there in front of him. "Fuck!" he curses. "What if they have her? What if Berkley and Ette are right there while they're sitting in my fucking house!"

Walking over to the punching bag, he lets loose, his blows swinging the bag wildly. He keeps punching and swinging until his face is red and his hair is damp with sweat.

"And what if they're not?" I raise my voice to be heard over the sound of the punching. "We can't risk—"

He stops, narrowing his eyes and speaks between gritted teeth. "I know, okay? I know. I'm not going to do anything to put Ette at risk. You should fucking know that by now."

He turns back to the boxing bag, hugging it with one arm while punching it with the other.

"Wow. Calm down, psycho," I mutter.

Jericho whirls around at the sound of my voice. "Calm down?" He steps toward me. "Fucking calm down? I was calm. I stayed calm for years. I stayed calm when you went missing. Calm when the police said they had no fucking clue what had happened to you. Calm when I started searching on my own. Calm when I hit dead end after dead end, and calm when I had to sit there and watch the news knowing that that fucking monster had his hands on you. I'm done being calm." He throws a few more punches at the bag, grunts littering the air with each blow.

I place my hand on his shoulder. He stops, but he doesn't turn to face me.

"She really means something to you, doesn't she?"

"She means everything."

"We will get her back. She and Ette will come home and they will be safe."

He looks at me with eyes filled with desperation. "How do you know that?"

"I don't. But I have to believe it. If I don't, there's nothing left for me."

Jericho covers his face with his hands and rubs vigorously. "I'm a selfish fucking bastard. I'm so sorry, Hope."

"You don't have to hide your anguish around me. You can be yourself. You can let it all out. Just rein it in tonight, okay? If they are the ones who have taken them, we'll make them pay, okay?"

Jericho nods and pulls me to him quickly, squeezing me tightly.

We have been bouncing between each other. At times he's the one comforting me, talking me off the precipice of insanity. Other times, like now, I'm the one trying to placate him.

His jaw is locked tight when he releases me. He turns to walk out of the gym but I stop him.

"How's Gideon?"

Jericho lets out a snort of air. I'm not sure if it's one of annoyance or resignation. "I don't know. He won't talk to me."

I lay my hand on his arm. He stares at it as though it's a foreign object he hasn't seen before. "He'll come around."

The look Jericho gives me is cold. I know I haven't seen him in years. I know we're both different from the naïve kids who got married all that time ago, but the look in his eyes right now is like nothing I've seen before. There's a darkness there which makes me shudder. It's as though he's given up. It's as though his need for revenge has consumed him.

"Jericho?" I say his name because I don't know what else to say. It's like there is a dark cloud slowly overtaking him, threatening to devour him. "You will get her back."

For a moment, I imagine I see a tear in his eye, but then he shakes, ridding himself of my hand on his arm and the wall of darkness comes crashing down.

"I've got to get ready," he says. Then he stalks from the room, his shoulders weighted, his steps heavy.

I spend the rest of the evening aimlessly wandering until the sun sets and the shadows of the house push me back to my room. There is a ledge below my window. If I climb outside and hold tight as I walk down the slope of the roof, I can sit there and look out over the world. It's my favorite place at the Sanctuary. There's something both peaceful and depressing about it. So that's where I go.

I've never considered giving up before. Not when faced with the cruelty of men. Not when faced with the ever-dwindling hope of freedom. Not when pain and suffering afflicted me. But now, facing the loss of her, of my daughter, well, I've never known a feeling like this.

Even though it is my name, Odette has always been my hope. In my darkest hours, I'd allow myself to think of her.

To hold onto the fact that she was okay, that she was living a life I couldn't. It made it bearable.

And now she's gone.

The graveled driveway lies below. It's as though I can picture myself lying there, legs broken, blood pooling from my head. There is something almost poetic about it. As though it's a memory rather than a premonition. Of course, I will not do it. I will keep fighting because that's what I've always done.

I think back over the first few weeks of my freedom and curse myself for allowing the anger I felt to taint the time I had with her. I'd foolishly assumed we'd have a lifetime together, that my life of captivity was over. But even though my monster no longer cages me, he's still found a way to hold my chains.

I try to keep my despair hidden from the others. Especially Jericho. In front of him, I act calm and collected. Because I have to. If she has been taken by the Gormans like he suspects, they also have Atterton. And I know him. I know his level of cruelty. I will not provoke him unnecessarily. I know how to bite back the urge for revenge. I know how to bide my time.

I only wish they'd taken me instead of Ette. Maybe then I'd have peace. Maybe this electrified tension inside me would be quelled. She is the only innocent left in all this. She is the only one worth protecting. And I failed her.

At nights, I imagine kneeling before him and looking deep into his eyes as the life drains from his body. And with God as my witness, if he's placed a hand on my daughter, he will face death.

The night has already bloomed. The moon is just a sliver in the sky. Dark clouds huddle around it as though searching for warmth. A breeze sends ripples across the water of the pond and the swans are hiding under the branches of the weeping willows, forewarning of the storm to come. Rain looms, held back by an invisible force, waiting for release.

The party, or whatever they call these gatherings of Jericho's, has already begun. Car upon car is parked in the circular driveway below. Men were shown inside, through the entrance to the ballroom, by pretty girls with fake smiles.

As the first drop of rain falls, I reluctantly give up my perch on the ledge and climb back up and inside my window. Both Jericho and Barrett warned me to stay out of sight tonight, but I am sick of men telling me what to do.

My footsteps echo through the empty passages of the Sanctuary. I pass through the dining room, through the kitchen and outside. If I wander around the side of the building, I'll be able to peer in the windows, the darkness of the night keeping me hidden from prying eyes.

The glowing windows shine with secrets. Inside, the ballroom is abuzz with commotion. There's a roulette table with men in tuxedos crowded around it, watching the colors spin. Men are seated at blackjack and baccarat tables, their eyes eager and hopeful. At the back of the hall, a woman is leaning into a microphone, the soulful vibrations of her voice seeping through the glass. Smoke swirls, rising to the ceiling. The chandelier shimmers and flickers as though lit by candles.

And in the centre of the room is the poker table. The eyes of the men seated around it are distrusting and suspicious. It is there that Jericho, Michael and Mr Gorman have chosen to take their stance.

Michael and Jericho sit opposite each other, their eyes locked in silent battle. Michael looks a lot like his father, although it's only his father's mouth that's curved with mirth. He's loud, bellowing for drinks and throwing Black Swan poker chips into the centre of the table with wild abandon. He laughs at one stage, tossing back his head in glee and the sound causes me to freeze. I know that voice. I've heard it before.

Keep fighting. It makes me hard.

I swallow back the panic.

He was there. He was there with Dominic.

Darkness toys with the edges of my vision, just like it did then. I want to bang on the glass and alert Jericho. I want to scream. I want to run inside and hold a knife to his throat and watch his blood spurt over the table. Instead, I take a step back, and then another and another until the damp grass is under my feet and drops of rain are falling on my face. Lifting my hands, I watch them tremble. It's strange that I can't feel them, that their quivering went unnoticed. Bunching my fingers together in a fist, I crush them tightly until I know I've left marks.

chapter twenty-four

I stare at my trembling hands as I sit in the car, waiting for the monster to return. When he appears, he doesn't look like a monster. He doesn't walk like one. Doesn't sound like one. Doesn't smile like one.

Swinging open the car door, he gets behind the wheel as though nothing has happened. Glancing over at me, he makes this tutting sound, as though he's disappointed.

"It's over now, daughter. Wipe away those tears."

When I don't move, he leans over, attempting to swipe his thumb across my cheek, but I press myself against the door, placing as much distance between us as possible.

He shakes his head as he starts the engine. "It's over now." The tires crunch over the gravel as he pulls away. "I only did what I did to show you your place. Which is here, in this world. By Michael's side. You'll thank me for it one day. You'll realize I did it out of love. We'll move past it now."

I keep my eyes fixed on my hands, trying to stop them from trembling.

"You remind me of Katriane." It's the first time I've heard him speak of his wife. I've thought of her often over the years, wondering if she knew. If she tried to stop any of it. "She wasn't always the strong woman that you knew her to be. She had to adjust. She knew her place and learned how to use it to her advantage." There's silence for a few moments and then he says angrily, "You won't even look at me."

I hold my hands together tightly.

"Look at me, goddammit!"

I turn my head, lifting my eyes to meet his. He glares at me before returning his attention to the road.

"This life offers you privilege in the world, Everly. You'd be a fool to waste it. From now on, you'll be grateful. You'll know your place. You'll accept it and you'll help Michael. It's not too late for us to be a family, Everly. I'm planning on going into business with the Gormans. A nice little stud farm on the outskirts of the city." He winks." Play your cards right and you could help run it. You always loved being around the horses when you were little."

"I know nothing about horses."

"You'll learn."

He prattles on like this for the rest of the car trip. It's as though his mind has been wiped of what he just did. As though he doesn't give it a thought at all.

It's different for me. Once back at the house, I walk up to Michael's room almost in a trance.

I long for a flash or even the familiarity of twisting nausea in my gut, but all that races through my head are memories. It's like my mind is stuck, forced to replay the vision of what my father did to that girl over and over like a broken record. I lie under the blanket of Michael's bed as though it can block out the memories, but it doesn't.

I feel each of the tears she shed. I feel every lash of the leather as it bit her skin. I taste the sobs as they were wrenched from her mouth. I wish I could have taken her place, maybe then the heaviness of guilt wouldn't sit like a weight inside me.

My father is a monster. And I am his daughter. Cowering in fright, hiding under the covers.

Unable to take anymore, I toss the blankets aside, ignoring the pain as I run to the door and yank it open. I start to run, racing blindly through the house, searching for a way to escape. I run out onto the patio, around the pool and start sprinting through the garden. Desperation guides my steps. I run until I come across the winding driveway and push myself to the gates. My hands grapple with the bars, slippery in the rain as I try to climb.

Floodlights blind me. I hear the footsteps of the guards. I scramble, trying to climb as they push nearer and nearer. But then I remember her. I remember Ette. And I know I can't leave.

I let myself fall, not caring when I collapse on the hard ground.

There's the static buzz of a radio and someone says, "I've got her." Someone else nudges me with their boot. "On your feet."

I don't move.

I can't move.

I'm lifted, someone cradling me against them. If I close my eyes, I can imagine it's Jericho. It takes me back to when I thought I had to escape him. If only I'd known.

"What happened?" It's Michael's voice now. He must be back from the Sanctuary.

"She tried to escape," the guard explains as he lowers me.

I don't know how I manage to stand but I do.

Michael grabs my chin, turning my face to his. I leave my gaze unfocused, staring through him

"What the fuck did you do to her!" he roars.

The guard is quiet, no doubt contemplating what to say. "It wasn't me."

"Well, who was it then!"

"Her father," the guard replies. At least he's honest.

Michael bends and scoops me into his arms. He strides past the guards, past his father, past his mother and Mary, who have come down to see what all the commotion is, and carries me up the stairs and back into his room. The place I started. He lowers me to the bed.

"What happened?" There's concern in his tone, but I don't care. I lie down and roll over, placing my back to him.

"Tell me what happened," he demands.

"The monster came," is all I manage to say. But it doesn't sound like me. It's the voice of someone broken. Someone defeated.

Michael flicks the light on, and I bury myself under the covers, unable to stand the brightness. There's movement as he undresses then he climbs in behind me and cradles me close. I gasp when he presses against my side, the pain of the punch my father inflicted sharp and intense.

He jerks away as though I burned him and pulls back the covers. Peeling up my shirt, he gingerly runs his finger over the red welt which is growing darker by the second. Then he cups my face, turning it toward him, a frown pressing between his brows as he examines my wounds.

"He did this?" he whispers.

I nod, not caring when the tears fall.

"I'm going to fucking kill him." He moves to lift off the bed but a sudden need to not be alone overwhelms me.

"Please stay," I beg, my fingers digging into his arm.

His eyes travel slowly from my face to where I'm gripping onto him in desperation and then he sighs, crawls back into bed, and pulls the covers back over us. Even though I hate him, I don't want to be alone.

"What did you do?"

Of course he assumes I deserved it, that I did something to earn the wrath of my father.

I let out a cold laugh, even though it hurts. "I was born."

His body feels warm next to mine. I huddle closer. I don't care if he is the enemy. Right now, he's all I've got.

We lay in silence.

Visions of my life to come stretch out through my mind. Me by Michael's side, a fake smile on my face, my body stooped with sadness. A life of wealth and riches. A life built on the misery of others.

"I don't want to do this, Michael. I don't want to be here."

"Shh," he says, tightening his grip and ignoring the way I wince in pain. "You're in shock. You're hurt. You don't mean what you say."

I roll over to face him. "Yes, I do. I don't love you. I never will." I don't care what reaction my words could bring.

"You've got no choice," he whispers in my ear. "You're mine."

You're mine.

Formed by the lips of someone I love those words brought me joy. Spat from the mouth of someone I loathe they bring nothing but fear.

"One day you will love me, Everly. And even if you don't, you will still worship me. You will learn to fall at my feet. You will learn to beg me for affection. The alternative is only pain."

Reaching out, I cup Michael's cheek and look deep into his eyes. "I will only worship at the feet of my Priest."

I expect him to respond with rage but all he does is stare, his gaze cutting through me. A cold smile stretches over his face and then he rolls over, turning his back to me.

I don't sleep. I'm too plagued by the tears of the girl in the cell. Michael sends a nurse to treat me the next day. She sponges away the blood. She cleans my wounds and wipes away my tears.

I stay secluded in the room, not wanting to face anyone, but when dinner time rolls around, Michael demands that I accompany him. It is my birthday after all. He says I need to get in the mood for tonight's party. He helps me dress. He brushes my hair. He bends down and slips my shoes on my feet.

Everyone is already seated at the table by the time we walk in. They all murmur 'Happy Birthday' but Ette gasps when she sees me.

"What happened to your face?" she cries, escaping the dart of Mary's hand and running over to me. There are tears when she looks up and I smile, hoping to shed some of her fear.

Michael bristles when he sees my father. "You fucking coward," he spits. "Look what you've done to her."

My father glances up as though noticing me for the first time and shrugs. "It's nothing a little makeup won't fix."

"I think we'll eat in our room tonight," Mary says, getting to her feet.

"But it's Berkley's birthday!" Ette cries.

Mary snaps her fingers and holds her hand out. "Come, Dominque."

I don't bother to correct her. Maybe this is our life now. Maybe she is Dominque. Maybe I will never escape being Everly.

Ette looks to me as Mary drags her from the room and I force a smile and a small wave.

"The fucking party is tonight," Michael hisses.

"You should be thanking me," my father says. "She needed a lesson in gratefulness."

The room falls into an uncomfortable silence, everyone picking at their food hesitantly and avoiding each other's eyes. My father doesn't seem to notice though, or if he does, he doesn't care.

"I heard from Katriane the other day," he says.

Mrs Gorman looks up, relieved the conversation is headed in a more civilized direction. "And how is your dear wife?"

"Ex-wife," my father corrects. He directs his gaze toward me, ignoring Mrs Gorman's question. "Apparently your brother has absconded from the facility where they were holding him."

"He's not my brother," I say through gritted teeth.

My father rolls his eyes. "Your half-brother then. You didn't have anything to do with it, did you, Gorman?"

Mr Gorman looks startled at his question. An amused look passes over his face. "Of this sin, I am innocent."

"Good," my father says, shoveling food into his mouth. "It's the best place for him. God knows I tried to help that boy, but there's more than one screw loose in that kid's head."

"I wonder why?" Michael mutters under this breath.

Mrs Gorman looks over at me, blinking as though it will wipe away the tension. "How is the practice going, dear?"

"Good, from what I saw," my father answers. "I'm sure she'll give a splendid performance, won't you, Everly?"

I toy with my food, moving it around the plate rather than eating it.

My father slaps the table. "Won't you, Everly?"

I jump, startled by the sound and slowly lift my gaze to the monster. "I'm sure you'll be very proud, Father." I push my chair back from the table. "I should probably go practice now, just to make sure."

Michael reaches out as I pass him, his fingers tugging on mine. "I'll come with you. I've got a surprise for you."

I turn, not registering any emotion on my face. "Wonderful. I can't wait."

He smiles as though he's made me happy. Maybe he thinks he has. Maybe he has no concept of the emotions of others. Maybe he doesn't care.

chapter twenty-five

Michael holds up the costume and honestly, it's beautiful. At any other time, at any other place, gifted by any other person, I'd be in awe. The outfit looks as though it's been made of feathers. They curl up the bodice and cup over the breasts, made to look like wings. The skirt is a classic bell tutu, the white feathers realistic and drooping with a hint of melancholy. Wilted roses have been stitched into the lower hanging layers of the tulle.

"What do you think?" He's waiting expectantly, a look of anticipation hovering across his expression.

I know how he wants me to respond. With gratitude. With amazement. So I say the right words, even if there's no emotion behind them.

"It's truly beautiful. Thank you."

"But that's not all." He opens the door to his bedroom. "Come in, come in," he waves in the woman waiting in the doorway. She smiles brightly, a large toolbox grasped tightly in her hand. Her gaze immediately moves to the swan costume and her eyes widen.

"It's amazing! Oh, Michael, it turned out so wonderful. Are you happy?" She walks straight past me and into the bathroom, placing her toolbox on the vanity.

"Come, come, hun. Take a seat."

Michael nods, waving his hand as though to shoo me away. I sit down.

"You must be Everly. I'm Natasha. Michael thought that since this is a special occasion, he would hire me to do your hair and makeup." She starts rifling through her toolbox. "Do you have any particular look in mind?"

She looks at me then. Actually, looks at me. Her eyes pop open a little in surprise. "Oh, hun." Her expression softens to kindness. "What happened to you?"

She strokes the side of my face. Tears well uncontrollably at her gentle touch. Her eyes meet mine in the mirror and then dart to Michael. He steps forward, hands resting heavily on my shoulders.

"It wasn't him," is all I say at the same time as Michael makes a throwaway comment about how clumsy I am and laughs.

"Don't worry, it's nothing a little makeup can't fix," she echoes the words of my father. I can tell the woman isn't fooled, but she merely smiles tightly and gets to work. "So, Michael tells me it's your birthday." I nod and close my eyes as she starts to lather some sort of cream over my face. "You are very lucky. I've heard he's got quite the party planned."

She's pulling my hair back tightly, getting it off my face when I look at her next. I don't say a word. But she knows. She knows I'm unhappy. That this isn't my choice. That something not right is going on. But she chooses to ignore it and instead starts prattling on about the looks she has in mind for me.

Simple, elegant, but dramatic, is how she explains it. Michael leans against the vanity, watching the whole time. He and the woman talk easily, as though they've known each other for years. I don't care how or why. All I want is for this night to be over.

I keep my eyes closed until the woman pushes a band into my hair and announces she's finished. Michael lets out a low whistle of appreciation as I blink, my eyes adjusting to the brightness of the lights around the mirror.

My skin is flawless. My lips are a pale shade of pink. The only thing dramatic about the makeup is my eyes. Thick lines of black curve above and below, accented by white. My cheeks are sprinkled in silver glitter. They look like tears. The headpiece sparkles like a crown dusted in diamonds, some of which hang in a triangular point over my forehead. The sides of the headpiece are covered in the same feathers as the dress.

"So beautiful," Michael says reverently. He reaches out, a finger tilting my chin up to look at him. "Do you like it?"

He's so eager for me to say yes. It's as though he truly wants to please me. How he can be so blind is beyond me.

"It's perfect," I say, because there's nothing else to say.

The woman starts collecting her things and placing them back inside her toolbox. She hovers for a while, as though hoping she might get to speak to me alone, but Michael ushers her out the door, promising to reward her well for her efforts.

As soon as the door shuts, Michael instructs me to get into the costume. He walks behind me as I stand in front of the mirror. I don't even look at the costume because my hatred for him dominates the reflection. I keep my expression schooled to indifference as he paces behind me, hands clasped under his chin as though deep in thought.

"It's perfect, is it not?" I nod and he rolls his eyes. "You could at least say something."

"It's perfect," I mimic.

Michael frowns. He turns and collects a jacket from one of the shopping bags on his bed, rips the tag off and holds it out for me. "You're going to be late for your own party."

The jacket has been made to cover the costume. It's black and ruffled. Michael does the buttons up, claiming he doesn't want anyone to glimpse the final product until I'm on stage. He pulls a mask out of the shopping bag and I have to do up the tie at the back of his head. It's a plain black mask. Nothing special. But it makes his blue eyes appear even more brilliant. And cold. Then I follow him out of the room.

I am used to anxiety. Used to the nervous twisting of my gut and the rapid beating of my heart. But I'm not used to this.

Nothing.

It's as though I'm floating, ungrounded and out of place. I glide through the room, ever so slightly in Michael's wake. There are people I know and others I don't. Everyone is dressed glamorously, some wearing masks which cover their entire face, others wearing more the suggestion of a mask. I am the only one free of one at all.

I pass through the crowd in a haze. I smile when I think I'm supposed to. I answer the questions I'm asked. Michael has his arm draped over my shoulders, tugging me from person to person protectively, as though I'm nothing more than a possession to show off.

We pass by my father, the monster. He wears the mask of a wolf. It's gold, and the shape of it is menacing. It has his smile. He grips my arms as we pass, fingers digging into my skin.

"Don't forget our little talk, my daughter."

I simply stare at him until Michael jerks me forward, pulling me toward another group of strangers. It isn't until Miss Marchand opens her mouth that I realize they're not strangers at all. I'm standing in front of the members of my old dance company.

"So pleased you could make it." Michael kisses her cheek. "I thought it would be a lovely surprise for Everly. She had no idea you were coming."

Miss Marchand's hair is down and hanging loosely around her shoulders. I've never seen her wear it like that before. She looks a lot younger. Monique is there as well. And the girl with the name starting with J. They all hold champagne flutes in their hands but none of them are drinking.

"Lovely to see you again, Everly." It's as though Miss Marchand takes pleasure in calling me by that name. "And happy birthday."

I nod and smile demurely, as though I imagine Michael would want me to. He wraps his arm around my shoulder and tugs me close.

"I thought you were still working for the Priest?" Monique flicks her hair over her shoulder.

Michael winks and answers for me. "She got a better offer." His hand slips from my shoulder and he winds his fingers through mine instead. "But I guess we better get the birthday girl backstage. You'll be amazed at her performance."

Previously, I would have felt sick at his praise and the expectation put upon me. Now I don't care. I will dance, but I will dance for me alone.

The room I am to perform in has temporarily constructed stage. Bunched and draped tulle covers the walls and branches and feathers dotted with fairy lights hang from the ceiling. It gives off a fairy tale type feel. Whimsical and ethereal, as though we've stepped into an enchanted forest.

"You ready?" Michael asks as he peels the jacket from my shoulders.

I nod. Because there's nothing else I can do.

"We'll call everyone in and then we'll start the music. You know your cue."

The few minutes I spend alone, I merely stand still, waiting for the time to pass. I hear the flurry of the audience as they fill the room. I hear their murmured voices and their exclamations of adoration at the decorations.

Michael's voice rings out, announcing the special event.

The crowd hushes.

The stage is shrouded in darkness.

The rolling notes of the piano begin.

The strains of the cello join.

I lift to pointe and step out onto the stage.

The spotlight turns on, both illuminating and blinding me.

There's nothing but me and the music.

So I dance.

chapter twenty-six

JERICHO

My hands grip the wheel tightly. I'm driving idiotically fast. My eyes keep flicking to the rear vision mirror, but I don't know what I'm looking for. All I can think about is Berkley, and the moments that have ticked by since Barrett confirmed she was at the Gormans' house.

Hope sits beside me. She's quiet, and has barely said a word since we got into the car. I tried to stop her. I told her it would be better if she stayed behind but she wouldn't listen. No doubt her mind is obsessed with finding Ette, just as mine is obsessed with Berkley.

The tale Barrett told when he returned from scoping out the Gorman home wasn't easy to listen to. He was there only to find out the number of guards stationed around the place, hidden and otherwise. Maybe he'd get a glimpse of the cameras. But the information he came back with chilled me to the bone. I wanted to leave there and then. I wanted to storm inside, kill everyone in sight and run away with Berkley in my arms. Because while Michael and his father were outfitted in their finery, sitting at the table of my poker game, the monster dragged Berkley to a car and drove her away.

But Hope and Barrett had convinced me otherwise. They said we needed to assemble a team. They said we needed to be prepared so we didn't put either Berkley or Ette in any further danger. I knew they were right. But that still didn't mean I liked it.

I spent the entire night pacing the floor of my bedroom, an ever-dwindling bottle of whiskey in my hand. Everything reminded me of her. The stained-glass window that was supposed to be in honor of Hope, now only made me think of Berkley. It was as though I could see her there, her skin tinted by the colors of the glass, her finger tracing the etching of the swans. My bed smelled of her. My sofa reminds me of the time she climbed on top of me, forgiving my confession. Even the shirt slung over my clothing rack reminds me of her. She's everywhere. She's permeated every aspect of my life.

And I will kill anyone who keeps her from me.

The screen on the dash lights with Barrett's name. Hope's eyes flick to mine and then she presses accept, knowing my fingers are too tightly wrapped around the wheel to let go.

"Did you manage to find everyone?" I say without preamble. Barrett's used to my direct manner but even for me, it comes out snappish and stern.

"They're all here. Ready to go."

"Good," I bark. "We'll be there soon."

Barrett clears his throat. "We have come across a bit of a problem though."

"Spit it out, Barrett."

"They're having a party."

"A party?" Hope speaks for the first time since she got in the car.

"It appears it's Berkley's birthday. The party is in her honor. It's masquerade, judging from the people going inside."

Hope looks at me. I know what she's thinking. What if Berkley was in on this the whole time? What if she's happy there? What if I'm a fool?

"Don't," I growl.

She turns over a hand, palm up. "What? I didn't say anything."

"Sir?" Barrett says.

"I heard you. I'm still coming."

"But there's no way we should consider—"

Hope presses the end button. "We're still doing it, aren't we?" There's both anticipation and resignation in her tone.

I nod and push the accelerator down further.

We make a short detour before meeting Barrett at a hidden spot near the Gorman's house. I've changed and am now dressed in a tuxedo; a mask, reminiscent of one worn by the Phantom of the Opera, is clasped in my right hand. It was all they had.

Barrett starts shaking his head before I've even fully got out of the car. "They've got guards all over the place, dressed as guests. The cameras are operating. There are people everywhere. You can't go in there."

"I can and I will."

Barrett grabs my arm. I freeze, staring at his fingers until he lets go. "There are other ways to do this."

"I'm not going in there to make a scene, but I am going in there."

"What if it puts them in even more danger?" Hope says.

I run my hand through my hair, frustration and hesitation controlling my actions. I'm torn.

"They're not going to do anything while all these people are here."

This time it's Hope that grips my arm. I glare at her fingers but she doesn't remove them like Barrett did. "You don't know these people like I do, Jericho. You don't know what they're capable of."

I lift her hand, peeling it from my arm. "And you don't know what I'm capable of. If they're as bad as you say, we shouldn't wait another minute. They won't stop me and I won't do anything. Not now. Not yet. But I can't just wait around any longer."

And then I stride away, shoving my mask on and ignoring their pleas as I head toward the house.

The men at the door are guards. They're dressed like butlers, but you can tell from their stances and stiff manners they've never greeted guests before in their lives. They look me over suspiciously but don't say anything as I enter. There's a maid who shows me down the hall and into the room with the other guests. I'm late. Everyone else is already here. I arrive just in time to see Michael step to the front and announce a special event in the other room. I follow as the guests file their way through the door.

"I didn't expect to see you here," Mr Gorman's voice sounds behind me. "I don't believe you were invited."

I turn, plastering a grin on my face and hold out my hand. "I figured I'd give you a chance to return the hospitality I showed to you last night. Michael was kind enough to mention it."

"He was?"

I nod and clamp my hand on his shoulder. "He was."

A man is standing beside him, wearing the mask of a wolf. It takes a few moments for me to realize who he is. The monster. He's smirking beneath the mask, twisting the expression of the wolf into something even more sinister.

"I don't believe we've met." He extends his hand.

There are a few tense moments as I stand there, refusing to accept his offer. As I glance around the gathering crowd, I can't help but feel the heavy gaze of eyes on me. There are at least six guards in the room, maybe more.

The wolf-like monster waits, hand extended. I take a step toward him, closing the gap between us and he startles, moving backward, his eyes scanning the crowd for protection.

"That's what I thought," I hiss in his ear. "You will pay for your sins."

He laughs but there's fear in it. Part of me wishes I could rip the mask from his face and expose him then and there. But sending him back to prison isn't in my plan.

Michael gets on the stage, calling for the attention of the room. Everyone quiets as the lights dim to darkness and then music starts. At first, the stage remains shrouded in the shadows and then the spotlight appears, shining on white feathers.

It's Berkley.

She dances on pointe, her movements graceful and elegant and melancholy. Her arms flutter like wings. Transfixed, I take a step toward the stage. A guard moves toward me.

A hushed reverence falls over the crowd. Even the monster watches. I keep my eyes fixed on her as she twists and shapes herself into the embodiment of the swan. I watch as she struggles, fighting the death that threatens to overtake her. She commands the stage, every eye focussed on her. And then, as the music slows, she succumbs, wilting to the ground as silence swallows the stage and it falls into darkness.

The room is left spellbound by her performance until the lights flick back on again and then it erupts in thunderous applause.

Berkley is back on her feet. She smiles sadly, gives a small wave and as her gaze sweeps the crowd, her eyes lock on mine. They widen, filling with tears. She takes a step forward, but Michael comes up behind her and grabs her arm, thanking the crowd and pulling her off the stage. He's whispering something in her ear as she looks back at me desperately. When he thinks they're out of sight, he digs his fingers into her arm, jerking her viciously and spitting words in her face. She lifts her chin, eyes blazing and slaps him.

I move toward the stage, ready to rip her from Michael's grasp, but the guards stalk toward me, stand either side, and wordlessly guide me from the room. I'm almost trembling with the need to fight my way back to her, but now is not the time. Not yet.

Is everything okay?" Someone says, threading their way through the crowd toward us.

"Everything is fine," is the clipped response from one of the guards.

The man removes his mask. It's Officer Conway, the little upstart who came to the Sanctuary to interview me and then later appeared at one of my games.

"Mr Priest, isn't it?" He narrows his eyes as though trying to peer behind my mask. "You aren't causing any problems now, are you?"

I don't get a chance to respond before the guards push me past him, ignoring the surprised look on the faces of some of the guests as I'm unceremoniously shown the door.

chapter twenty-seven

BERKLEY

Michael drags me through the house, his fingers savagely digging into my arm, swiping a bottle of vodka on the way. He doesn't care that people look on with alarm, that they mutter under their breath and shake their heads.

A man approaches, extending his hand to Michael and grinning at me beneath his mask. "Truly splendid performance, my dear," he says.

"Judge Ross." Michael nods and shakes his hand but keeps walking, tugging me behind him. The man frowns, then shrugs and takes another sip of his drink.

Once we're at his room, he shoves me inside and slams the door behind us.

"What the fuck was he doing here?" Michael says, twisting the lid off the bottle of vodka and bringing it to his lips. "Want some?" he offers. I shake my head and he laughs. "Don't worry, it hasn't got anything in it." He paces the floor, lifting the bottle time and time again. "Did you know he was coming? Have you been in contact with him?"

I lower myself to the edge of the bed, fluffing the tutu of my costume over the mattress. "And how would I have done that?"

Michael scowls. "Just answer the damn question."

"No," I reply. "I did not contact him. I did not know he would be here."

There was a pull in my chest the moment I laid eyes on Jericho. It was like he had reached inside, wrapped his hand around my heart and physically tugged me toward him. It was only Michael's grasp on my arm that had stopped me. Otherwise, I would have leapt from the stage and ran to him. Even then, I wanted to fight Michael. I wanted to rip myself away and run to him. But Michael's heated words whispered in my ear had stopped me in my tracks.

"I wonder how Ette will fare without you here."

That was all it took for me to obey. The reminder that it was more than just my life at stake.

"Well, how the fuck did he know!" Michael bellows.

"You hosted a birthday party in my honor. You hardly kept it secret. He will have been searching for me." Michael's eyes flick to mine as I speak, but he keeps pacing, keeps drinking. "He won't give up until he gets me back."

"Well, he has some nerve walking in here. There's no way I'll…" He stops talking and blows out a long stream of air. "I need something stronger."

He starts to rifle through his drawers, through the cabinets in the bathroom until he finds what he's looking for. Tapping the white powder onto the coffee table, he lines it up then inhales it, pinching his nose and shaking his head before his eyes spring open and focus on me again. "That's better," he announces. He holds out his hand, his eyes glazed and wide. "Dance with me."

"Michael, I'm—"

"Dance with me!" he roars.

I take his hand and he tugs me to him, plastering my chest against his. His hand grips my back possessively. My costume is crushed between us. His grin is maniacal.

"All I wanted was to make this night perfect for you, Ev. I wanted to show you how much I love you. How perfect we are together."

I don't say a word as he jerks me around the room. His movements are frenetic. His eyes skip from object to object as though expecting someone to jump out and surprise us. Then he suddenly shoves me away, pushing me to the floor.

"Your father was right. You are an ungrateful bitch. I'm offering you the world, Everly. I'm offering you everything you could ever want and you're throwing it back in my face as though I'm nothing to you."

"You are nothing to me," I say, gingerly getting up from the floor. "And the only thing I want is him."

Having searched the room and found his vodka bottle again, Michael chugs on the liquid as though it is nothing more than water. "Him," he snorts. "Jericho fucking Priest." He guzzles some more. "What can he offer you that I can't?"

I rearrange myself on the bed, attempting to look as though his ranting doesn't affect me. But it does. There's something unhinged in his eyes. Something crazed and deranged.

"Answer me!" he demands, lifting his voice to yell again. He stalks toward me, and I tell myself not to flinch when he grips my chin between his fingers and jerks my head upward. "I should have left you in that fucking cell. That's what your father wanted. Did you know that?" He lets go of my chin and shoves a finger into his chest. "I'm the one who rescued you. I'm the one who loves you, who wants you. Why can't you see that, Ev? Why won't you love me?"

I lower my gaze as he stares at me, pleading through blood-shot eyes. I can't help it when my lips start to tremble, signaling the arrival of tears.

Michael sighs. "I'm sorry." He sits beside me, leaning against me heavily. "All I want is for you to love me. That isn't too much to ask, is it? You loved me once. Can't you love me again?"

His blue eyes implore me, begging me to consider loving him. As if it is an option. For a moment, I'm taken back to a time when I would have given anything for him to look at me like this. But now I know who he truly is. Now I know him by his actions and not just by the prettiness of his face. Now my heart belongs to another.

He cuts his gaze away from mine, not finding what he was searching for. "Let's go out onto the roof," he says, grabbing my hand and tugging me to my feet.

"I don't think you're in any state—"

He whips around suddenly, holding a finger to my lips. "Shhh," he hisses. "No one is asking you."

He struggles to open the window to the outside while still holding my hand and the bottle of vodka, but he manages somehow. Music pulses from below. There are glasses and bottles scattered around the pool. The lights are all on, as though the party is still in full swing, but the place is deserted.

"Where did everyone go?" I ask as he pulls me tight to his chest and starts swaying, the hard glass of the vodka bottle digging into my back.

"Dad sent them home. I think your Priest's little stunt pissed him off."

Michael's swaying movements pull us closer to the edge of the roof. I try to guide his steps away, but he's stubborn and strong. My heart beats wildly as his feet hover dangerously close to the edge. A wicked thought of pushing him off streaks across my mind, but I know he'd take me with him.

I don't know whether it's the drink or the drugs or merely the excitement of the night, but his body is sweaty and hot. The warmth of it soaks into my skin. His hair is damp, sticking up in odd directions from the swipes of his hand. He keeps running his tongue over his teeth and swallowing heavily as though his mouth is dry.

"We should jump," he says, dropping his grip on me and looking over the edge at the pool below.

"Don't be silly." I take his hand and tug him back.

He doesn't move, merely stares at our joined hands. His gaze lingers on them, almost sadly, and then moves up my body, eyes skipping over the details of my costume.

"I only wanted to make you happy. That's what all this was for." He waves his hand still holding the bottle of vodka out over the scenery as though it's still littered with people from the party. Lifting the bottle, he downs the remains then throws it over the edge, the glass shattering below. "Why won't you do the same for me, Ev? Why won't you try to make me happy?"

He tugs on my hand. "Come on, where's that carefree, bold girl I used to know? Let's jump."

"Michael, no." I push against him as he pulls me toward the edge.

"Come on, it will be fun."

"Michael, you're drunk." A wave of panic washes over me as he keeps tugging, keeps pulling. "Oh, come on, Ev. You've done it before. Why not do it again."

I fight against his grasp, knowing how dangerous it would be for him to drag us both over. He's in no state to coordinate his movements.

"Michael, please," I beg. "You're scaring me."

"You? Scared? Everly fucking Atterton scared?" He laughs and then looks at his free hand as though surprised to find it empty. "Where did the vodka go?"

"You drank it all." His nails are digging into the skin of my hand. "Michael, you'll ruin my dress if you pull us over."

He rolls his eyes. "What do you care? You didn't pay for it. You don't care about any of this. About us. About anything."

"Michael, please!" I plead again.

He laughs, a cold smirk covering his face. "I kind of like it when you beg. Maybe eager is overrated."

After wrestling a little more, I'm able to rip my hand from his grasp. But Michael comes after me, lunging toward me and not caring when he slips and has to grab onto the roof for support. He laughs again. I run toward the open window, but despite his drunkenness, Michael is still quick enough to grab my ankle, and my feet slide out from under me.

"Okay, okay," I say, holding up my hands in surrender. "We'll jump, okay? I'll jump with you."

Michael grins as though he's won the lottery and holds his hand out. But instead of taking it, I get to my feet, dash past him and leap, arms and legs flailing as I fly.

The water is colder than I expected, and I rise to the surface, gasping for air. Michael is laughing above, still trapped on the roof.

"There's my girl!" he yells into the night. "There's the girl who's spontaneous and reckless."

I power through the water, fighting the awkwardness of the tutu wrapping itself around my legs, and pull myself out. Some of the glass from the shattered vodka bottle rests on the edge of the pool and I cut my hand, leaving behind a smeared splatter of blood.

Michael is still laughing and hollering as I start to run.

"Hey!" he calls out. "Where the fuck do you think you're going? You know there's no point in running! You're mine, Everly Atterton. You're fucking mine!"

There's a splash of water behind me as I keep racing. I ignore the pounding of my heart, and the sharpness of the stones beneath my ballet slippers as I sprint as fast as I can. I reach a patch of grass. I can hear Michael behind me. He calls out, excited by the chase.

"I've always been faster than you, Everly. You won't be able to escape me!"

I only make it a few more meters before an arm snags around my waist and I tumble to the ground. Michael falls on top of me, wrestling as I attempt to fight him off. He sits over my hips and I try to pound my knees against his back, but he doesn't budge. He manages to grab both my wrists, pinning them to the ground above my head.

Michael's face twists into a cruel smirk as he glares down at me. "This is fun," he slurs. "I think I like it."

I keep fighting, keep writhing and twisting beneath him, but he's too strong and has the advantage of being on top. Leaning down, he plants his mouth on mine, laughing once again as I try to twist away from him.

"Stay still!" he orders.

I don't. I keep struggling. Yanking my hands down to my sides, he traps them with his knees, before reaching behind, and yanking at my tights.

"Michael, no. Michael, please stop. Think about what you're doing. Who you're doing it to."

But he's deaf to my words, tearing holes in my tights as he rips them down.

"Michael, please," I beg as the tears begin to fall. "This isn't who you are."

"It's who you think I am!" he roars. "Maybe it's in your blood to like it this way. Maybe that's what your father passed onto you. A love of depravity."

"Stop!" I scream. "I don't want this! I don't want you!"

He's managed to rip away my tights enough for me to be exposed beneath the skirts of my tutu.

"Stop fighting!" He lifts a hand and slaps it across my face. I barely feel the sting.

"We're friends, Michael! I'm not some nameless plaything for you to do whatever you want with. It's me, Michael. It's Everly. We've been friends for years. You were my first love."

"I know who the fuck you are! And I've given you every opportunity to come to me willingly, but you keep fighting me." He leans down low to hiss in my ear. "So now I'll give it to you the way you've been asking for it all along. The way I know that deep down you want it."

Coldness washes over me. He isn't fooling around. He isn't doing this to scare me, or teach me a lesson. This time he means it.

"Is this how your fucking Priest did it? Is that why you fell for him? Because he didn't ask? Because he fought you for it?" His laughter fills the air as I buck and wrestle beneath him. He fumbles with the buttons of his pants, freeing his cock. "Look at me, Ev. I'm so fucking hard."

Involuntarily, my eyes fall to where his cock pulses, red and angry just like the monster who owns it.

"It's all for you, baby." He grunts as he pushes himself against me, grappling with the layers of tulle.

Tears fall down my cheeks freely. I stop wrestling. I stop fighting. I look up at the sky, tracing the patterns of the stars as he fumbles, plunging his fingers against me.

"That's my girl," he says in a hushed whisper. "You know this has to happen. You know you're mine. There's no point in fighting."

My body is numb. I no longer feel his hands on my flesh. His cock feels like nothing as it pushes against the side of my thigh.

Directing my gaze back downward, I look into his eyes. Those brilliant blue eyes. So cold. So cruel. He sneers, as he prepares himself to push inside.

Then his head jerks backward by fingers fisted in his hair. Something gleams, capturing the light of the moon and then a warm spray covers my face, neck and chest.

Blood gushes.

It gets in my hair, my eyes, my mouth.

His body is tossed aside, the weight of it gone as I scramble across the grass, gasps of shock falling from my mouth.

I taste his blood.

I gag.

Wiping my face, I desperately try to rid myself of his blood.

"Berkley."

Someone kneels before me. The world is tinted in red. I can't make out their face, but I know the voice.

"Jericho!" I lift my arms and he scoops me up, holding me tightly against his chest.

I laugh. I cry. I collapse against him.

He holds me so tightly it hurts. "Are you okay? Are you hurt? Did he hurt you?"

I don't answer and instead, search for his lips. The metallic taste of blood coats our lips but I don't care. I'm still laughing, still crying as our lips crash against each other. My hands cup his face.

"You're here," I say, attempting to look at him through the splatters of blood that still stain my eyes.

He wipes his thumb across my cheekbone. "I'm here," he says. "You're safe."

I let out a sob, barely believing it to be true. Part of me thinks Michael has drugged me again and this is all some narcotized dream.

But then Jericho pulls away from me, holding me at arm's length and my eyes fall to the body slumped on the ground behind him.

"Michael?" I utter his name.

Jericho grips my face, directing my gaze back to him. "He's gone. Don't think about him. I need you to get Ette. Hope is waiting in the car and I need you to take Ette to her and then stay there until I return. Can you do that?"

"What about the guards? What about the—"

Jericho presses his lips to mine again, silencing my words. "They'll be taken care of. All you need to do is get Ette and get out of here. Can you do that? Do you know where she is?"

I nod, my vision starting to return as Jericho's face comes into focus. Splatters of Michael's blood are across his skin. His brow is bunched with worry.

"I've got to go, okay? Can you do what I asked?"

I nod, swallowing the fear at the back of my throat.

"Good," he says. "Good." He lets go of me. "I'm not finished." And then he stalks into the night, toward the house.

chapter twenty-eight

HOPE

We'd stayed hidden as the guests drifted from the party and into the waiting cars. Jericho had prowled like a caged animal, anger visibly rippling through his body.

They'd thrown him out of the party, just as he knew they would.

Then he'd waited for his revenge.

"Stay in the car," he ordered as he, Barrett, and the team they'd assembled slipped into the night.

I did. But not for long.

The house is fully lit as I creep toward the main entrance. Music seeps from indoors but there are no accompanying voices. No sound of life at all. It's as though everyone has disappeared, hiding from the failure of the party.

The door creaks as I push it open. I'm greeted by an eerily empty entranceway. My footsteps are clipped against the tiled flooring. The music floating through the house is familiar, but I don't know why.

It's classical. Theatrical. Haunting.

I move into a room scattered with memories of the party. There's food on the tables. Discarded glasses, still half full on the mantle. Lights still glow amongst tulle draped down walls and twisted around chandeliers. The music is louder in here. It encourages the heavy beating of my heart, urging my blood to flow faster.

I find the stairs and creep up them, eyes continuously scanning for signs of life. Unlike the first level of the house, this one is dark. In the dim light, I pass by closed doors, wondering if Ette is behind any of them. But for now, she is not my focus. She is not who I seek.

There's an open door at the end of the hallway. Blue light flickers from its opening. My fingers close around the knife in my hand. In my other hand, my fingers are gripped around the cold metal of a gun. Barrett gave it to me before he left. He told me it was for protection. But I think he knew what I was planning. He knows what I have to do to find peace.

He's sitting alone at a desk in the room. He's wearing an open bathrobe, eyes fixed on the porn flashing across the screen in front of him, one hand gripped around his flaccid cock, the other gripped around a glass of whiskey.

He's trying to stroke himself, trying to pump some life into his limp cock, but it's not working. He growls in frustration. But he doesn't see me as I step into the room. He doesn't notice as I lift the knife gripped tightly between my fingers.

"Hello, Master."

His bloodshot eyes, glowing in the reflection of the screen, shoot toward me in shock. "How the fuck—"

"Shh," I warn him, waving the knife a little to remind him that it's there.

He looks toward the door.

"The guards are gone," I say. He gets to his feet, attempting to step toward me but I shake my head slowly. "No one is coming to save you."

He attempts to arrange his face into a smile. "Iris," he coos.

"My name is Hope."

He holds up his hands. "Hope, yes I know, but I always rather liked Iris. It suited you, did it not? My beautiful flower."

"Stop talking." I come closer, pressing the tip of the knife under his chin.

He lifts his hands higher. "Now, now—"

"Stop talking," I repeat. I expected to have adrenaline pulsing through my veins, but I feel nothing of the sort. There's a silence within me. Calm. This is what I came to do. There is no regret, no hesitation.

His Adam's apple bob up and down as he swallows. "I loved you," he says, ignoring my order. "You always meant so much to me. I regretted the day I sold you."

I move to step behind him, keeping the blade press to the skin of his throat the entire time.

"What do you want?" he asks. There's a hint of fear in his voice now. He knows I'm serious. "I'm sure we could work something out. I've got money. I could get you out of the country. You and your daughter."

I push the knife a little harder against his skin, causing a trickle of blood to flow.

He laughs but it's tight and uncertain. "Are you into even sicker games than you used to be, Iris my dear?"

He lifts his hand, wrapping his fingers around my wrist. The images on the screen keep flashing. He's watching a scene where a woman is struggling, her arms bound, her mouth gagged. During the parts when the screen darkens, I can see our reflection imposed over the images. There's a gleam of triumph in my eyes and a glimmer of despair in his.

"Let go of my hand," I warn.

He tries to jerk my wrist down and away from his neck, but I just press the blade harder against him, and shake my head, reminding him of who has the power.

"You won't do it," he hisses. "You can't. You haven't got it in you. Despite your resistance and your rebellion, you loved what I did to you. You always will. You're nothing but a worthless whore."

Still standing behind him, I bend low and whisper in his ear. "Those are some strong words from someone with a blade pressed to his throat." I press a little harder, creating a fresh dribble of blood to run down his neck and pool in the dip of his collarbone. He hisses, this time feeling some pain. "Tell me, Master," I say, my lips moving over the tip of his ear. "Have you said your confession?"

And then, before he has the chance to struggle or fight back, I run the blade across his throat and watch as a spray of blood arcs through the air and splatters across the floor.

His arrogance allowed me to do it. He didn't think I would and therefore he never even considered putting up a fight. I didn't need the training provided by Barrett. Left alone without control, he was nothing more than a weak old man.

Moving away, I watch unaffected as his body slumps to the ground. I step over him, as he gurgles and splutters, gasping for air. There's shock in his gaze. He didn't think I would do it. He thought he still had some domination over me. Or maybe he thought there was a part of me that loved him. There isn't.

He tries to say something, his mouth open and shutting, flapping futilely, but I don't even turn as I walk out the door, leaving him to die in a pool of his own blood.

It's what he deserves.

chapter twenty-nine

BERKLEY

The music of Swan Lake plays on repeat, mocking me as I slip back into the house via the pool entrance. There are no staff cleaning the mess of the party. None of the family lingering in the aftermath. It's as though everyone decided to go at the same time, leaving the house in a state of abandonment.

Mary's room is at the opposite end of the house than Michael's and the music fades the further I walk. Her door is unlocked, so I creep inside and over to the bed where Ette sleeps soundly.

"Ette?" I shake her gently.

She wakes with a frown of confusion that melts into a smile when she sees me. She extends her arms, wrapping them around my neck.

"What are you doing here?" She whispers and her eyes dart over to where Mary's asleep on the opposite side of the room.

"We're leaving," I tell her, pulling the covers back.

"Are we going home?"

I nod and hold my fingers up to my lips, reminding her that we don't want to wake Mary. I grab a cardigan next to her bed and wrap it around her shoulders. Taking her hand, I pause as we pass Mary. She looks peaceful in her sleep. Even the scars look less harsh. For once, her hair is pushed away from her face, fanned out over the pillow. A wave of sympathy washes over me. I imagine her as a young woman, fresh-faced and eager for what the world would bring. I imagine her as a bride, walking down the aisle to the man who would break her heart. I try to imagine the thoughts that would have been racing through her mind when she got behind the wheel, alcohol-fueled, emotionally wrecked and desperate for revenge. She watched her husband die. She lay and waited for her own death, while saying goodbye to a son she would never see again.

"Wait for me in the hall, okay?" I whisper to Ette. "If you see anyone come back to me. I won't be long."

Ette looks confused but does as I ask. I'm gentle when I wake Mary, not wanting to startle her, but she sits up abruptly anyway, her eyes scanning the room for signs of danger.

"What's going on? Why are you out?"

"I just want to tell you something before I leave," I say.

"You're leaving? Michael's letting you leave?"

A vision of Michael's slain body left bleeding on the grass comes unbidden. I'm surprised at the sadness I feel. I thought maybe I might find some relief in his departure, but there's only sorrow, despite everything he put me through.

"They found Dominic," I say.

"Where?" she leaps out of bed as though ready to leave here and now.

"It doesn't matter where. He's gone."

Her eyes narrow. "What do you mean, gone?"

I struggle with the words, still not knowing the truth of what truly happened. "He's dead," I say bluntly, choosing not to shelter her from the one aspect of what I know to be true.

She sinks back to the mattress, sitting on the edge and shake her head. "How?" is all she says.

"He took his own life." Tears well in her eyes, but she doesn't question it. It's as though she knew it was an option.

"Thank you for telling me." Gathering the covers, she lies down and pulls them over her head, turning away from me.

"Mary?" There's no answer from the mound under the blankets. "Leave. Start a new life away from all of this."

Still no answer. I shake the mound. She pushes back the covers, her eyes lifeless and blank, and merely blinks in my direction.

"Go now. Find Mrs Gorman and leave, okay?"

"Sure," she says, pulling the covers back over her head.

Ette appears in the doorway. "I hear footsteps."

Peering down the hallway, I take her hand in mine, and then we run. Our footsteps echo loudly. I keep checking behind us, certain we're going to get caught. The house seems larger, now that we're trying to escape. There are more doors, more rooms than I remember. I pause, looking down one hallway, wondering if it leads to an exit.

There's a scuffle in one of the rooms next to us. Grunts and moans. The sound of a body getting slammed against a wall.

Ette looks at me wide-eyed. I hold my finger to my mouth once again and shake my head, not wanting to alert anyone to our presence. We share a look before I tighten my fingers around her hand and we step out, choosing our path.

The sound of a gunshot echoes through the house. There's a cry of pain and a door flings open. Jericho stumbles out of the room. He's covered in blood. His face is swollen and darkening in patches. There's a gash above one eye. Another over the bridge of his nose.

"Berkley," he says my name quietly as he clutches the wall for support.

"Jericho!" I run to him and with his free arm, he crushes me to his chest, burying his nose into my hair. He breathes in deeply and then coughs a little, his entire body flinching in pain. I feel the rapid beating of his heart. I cling to him desperately, as though afraid he's going to disappear.

"Did you miss me?" he says. He coughs. And then he groans in pain. My only answer is to squeeze him tighter. "Careful," he warns. He attempts a chuckle and a bubble of blood forms at the corner of his mouth. "I think I might be hurt." He presses another kiss to my head. "We need to go." His words are stilted, his breath held tight.

"Here," I wrap my arm around his back, trying to support him.

He takes one step, then his body falls heavily against mine. He's too heavy. I can't hold him up. I scramble, trying to find purchase but he slumps to the ground.

"Jericho!" I screech, falling to my knees beside him.

Ette screams. But she's not looking at Jericho. She's looking at me. The white feathers of my costume are stained red. Blood red. It blooms like a crimson petal across my chest.

For a moment, I think it's my blood. My hands fly to my stomach, checking for wounds, but then the truth hits. The blood didn't come from me. It came from Jericho. I tear at his clothing, shoving his top up and exposing his stomach. And that's when I see it. The nasty gash on his side, weeping blood.

"Jericho." I shake his shoulder, but he's out cold. "Jericho, please wake up." I hold my hands to the wounds, but the blood keeps coming, seeping out between my fingers.

"Is he dead?" Ette's pressed against the wall, face ashen.

"Give me your cardigan." I reach toward her as she pushes it off her shoulders and hands it to me. I press it to the wound and tell Ette to come and kneel beside me. "Press hard, okay?" I say, placing her hands under mine, and pushing down hard so she understands.

She swallows and nods. But as I get up, she looks up in fear. "Where are you going?"

"We need help, Ette. I can't carry him and we need to get him out of here before the police arrive." I look around the still deserted house, the finals strains of Swan Lake floating down the hall. "If the police arrive." It's too quiet. There are no running steps of the guards. No wailing sirens. "You need to wait here, okay? Keep pressure on his wound and I'll be back with help as soon as I can."

Her chin trembles, tears well in her eyes but she nods.

"You've got this, okay, Ette? You can do this."

And then I turn and run, desperately hoping to find Barrett. I go into the room Jericho came from first. There's been no noise, no sound since the gunshot, and as soon as I open the door, I know why.

Two guards are lying on the ground. Both of them dead. Their bodies don't shock me like others have before. I've already seen too many. Aaron Keating. Michael. I was looking into their eyes the moment they died. But these men mean nothing to me. I barely give them a glance as I run through the next door.

This room is empty, but there are traces of a fight. Turned over chairs, the top of a desk shattered and broken. I find the bodies of three more guards. All of them still and lifeless. All of them dead.

Did Jericho do this?

Is he responsible for all this death, because of me?

But I don't have time to consider the state of my monster. His life is in danger. He's bleeding out on the floor.

Giving up on an effort to remain quiet, I start to yell. "Barrett!" I round another corner. The stairs beckon me. "Barrett!" I scream as I race up the steps. "Barrett!"

Mr and Mrs Gormans' room is at the end of the hall. I push the door open hesitantly, scared of what I'm going to find on the other side. The room is dark apart from a slice of moonlight falling across the bed from an open split in the curtain. Even though I know Barrett is not here, something pulls me in. I creep across the floor and study the lone figure lying on top of the covers. It's Mr Gorman. I step even closer, needing a better look, and feel something damp beneath my feet. A glass has tipped over on his bedside table, the contents having spilled on the floor.

Looking back up at Mr Gorman, I see his eyes are open. But they don't move. They don't blink or come to rest on me. His body is still, but there's no sight of a wound, no blood. Cautiously, I touch his shoulder.

"Mr Gorman?" He doesn't reply so I shake him gently. His arm flops off the bed, and I jump, startled by the movement, a gasp escaping me.

He's dead.

Another body to add to the tally.

Running out of the room, I resume my desperate search for help, aware that every second that passes puts Jericho more and more at risk.

I start yelling for Barrett again and barge straight into him as he races up the stairs.

"Are you hurt?" he asks, his eyes locking in on the blood over my dress and scanning me for any sign of damage. "Did you find Ette?"

"It's Jericho," I say breathlessly, then keep running down the stairs, expecting Barrett to follow.

When we reach Jericho and Ette, Hope is there, pressing against his wound and begging him to stay alive. Ette is at her side, hands covered in blood, eyes wide and somber.

"He wouldn't stop bleeding," Ette whimpers.

"What the fuck did you think you were doing leaving her all alone like that?" Hope yells at me.

I ignore her outburst, falling to the ground and cradling Jericho's head in my lap as Barrett rips off his shirt and ties it around Jericho's waist. Jericho moans as Barrett twists the knot tightly.

"It's okay," I croon, cradling his cheek in my palm. "We're going to get you out of here. We're going to get you help."

"No hospital," he grunts, his eyes flickering open and closed.

"I'm going to need both of you to help," Barrett instructs, pushing me away and moving in place to loop his arms under Jericho's. "Take a leg each. Ready?"

Hope and I both nod, bracing ourselves as we hoist Jericho between the three of us. Somehow, we manage to stumble through the house. Somehow, we manage to get him to the car. Somehow, we manage to heave him into the backseat.

I climb in after him, once again cradling his head in my lap. There's a handprint in blood from the last time I did it and I try to wipe it away, letting the tears fall as I do so. Hope and Barrett are talking of security cameras and destroying footage and a missing guard. But I don't care about any of that.

"Please don't die," I beg Jericho.

He doesn't reply. At some stage of us moving him, he slipped into unconsciousness again. I lean down and press my lips to his forehead. His skin is hot. I push back the hair stuck to his skin.

"Please don't die," I whisper again.

Hope turns around in the front seat, Ette on her lap. It strikes me how not all that long ago the roles were so different. She was in the backseat with Jericho as we sped away and I was in the front, looking on with envy, even as my mind struggled against the horror I'd just witnessed.

It's different this time. There's no anxiety twisting in my gut. My mind isn't filled with images of depravity. It isn't focused on the dead bodies we've left in our wake. I'm not thinking about Mr Gorman, or Michael or any of the guards. All that consumes me is Jericho. And the desperation, the agony that's rippling through me only confirms one thing.

I love him.

My tears fall to his cheek as his body is jostled and tossed by the movement of the car. Someone's hand rests on my knee and I look up and into Hope's eyes.

"Berkley?" she says quietly.

I blink back tears, trying to focus on her through the blurriness.

"I killed your father."

chapter thirty

BERKLEY

The monster is dead. I wanted him dead. So why is there this heaviness inside me?

I'm leaning against the stained-glass window in Jericho's room, watching the drops of rain slide down the glass. Even though I'm looking at the landscape, the darkening clouds of the sky, the gentle ripples on the water created by the rain, the slight sway of the trees, I don't really see any of it.

Because my mind is stuck on him.

My father. The monster.

The moment the words had come from Hope's mouth, something had overtaken me. Not joy or peace, like I thought. But an unbearable weight. A feeling of guilt, of responsibility.

We'd taken Jericho straight to the doctor's house. He stitched up his wounds, placed his arm in a sling, given him medication, and then sent us on our way. He's visited a few times since, checking in on his patient, but Jericho seems to be recovering well.

The only issue we're having is keeping him in bed to aid his recovery. He's a terrible patient. Grumpy and sullen. Snappish and demanding. But I wouldn't have it any other way.

He's here.

And my father is not.

But it's hard not to look at him, look at Jericho, and not see glimpses of a monster. Knowing what he did to rescue me fills me with both gratitude and dread. When I lie in bed beside him, images of the bodies of the guards, of Michael, of Mr Gorman, and of Aaron Keating loop on repeat through my mind. I'm not sure if he was the one to kill them all. I haven't asked. But I know it was by his command.

I've been waiting for the crunch of gravel beneath the tires of police cars. But they haven't come. I've been waiting for wailing sirens and flashing lights, but the Sanctuary is as tranquil and isolated as it has always been.

"Hey," Jericho's voice is rough and worn.

I turn my back on the window as he clears his throat. "You're awake."

Jericho holds his hand out, beckoning me to him. "You look sad," he says as I lower myself to the bed, taking comfort in the feel of his fingers wrapping around mine.

"Just thinking," is all I say.

"Are your flashes worse?"

I shake my head. I haven't had any since the night Michael drugged me, but I haven't told Jericho about that. I'm not sure if I will. He's already asked me what they did. But it's too hard to tell him the truth. Too painful to relive the memories, even though they haunt me.

I feel guilt for the sadness I'm experiencing over my father, but it's uncontrollable. As though my blood knows it's missing a strain of its existence.

"You've barely spoken to me since it all happened." Jericho's eyes travel over my face. I know he's taking in the bruising left by my father. "Come here." He tugs me toward him and lifts up his arm, the one not bound in a sling.

"I don't want to hurt you," I say.

"You won't."

Jericho's chest blooms with patches of blue and purple, some of them completely blocking out the feathers that usually float there. His side has been wrapped tightly in a bandage. There are stitches in the gash over his eye and the one that trails over his nose. Some of the swelling has gone, but his face is still a patchwork of pain.

I snuggle into his side and he holds me tightly to his chest. His heart beats steadily, comforting me with its rhythmic counting.

One, two, three, four, five.

First, second, third, fourth, fifth.

"I was so scared I was going to lose you," he says, his lips moving against my hair. "Please don't tell me I have."

I sit up, my gaze honing in on his. His eyes are so murky there's no blue to be found. Not even a glimmer in the darkness.

"Never," I reassure him. "I just can't help but think that some of this is my fault. That if I wasn't here, none of this would have happened."

"None of it is your fault, Miss Berkley." He smiles faintly and reaches to tuck a strand of my hair behind my ear. "It's okay to move on from this. It's okay to be okay. None of it can be undone and it is me who must bear the burden of their deaths, not you. I will carry that weight. You don't deserve any of it."

I sigh deeply. I wish it were as easy as taking him at his word. Simply believing him. But I know it won't be. I know I'll be haunted.

Pulling myself away, I get up from the bed, knowing I should go check on the rest of the household.

"Where are you going?" Jericho asks.

"I've just got to go check on a few things."

"I'll come with you." He starts to lift himself off the bed, his face twisting in discomfort, but I push him back down. "You've got to stay in bed. Doctor's orders."

He lifts a brow as he relaxes back against the pillows. "Can't you stay with me?"

I laugh when his eyes darken even more as they fall to scan my body. "You're injured."

"You could be gentle."

I laugh again, moving to walk past him but he reaches out and catches my wrist. He looks at me with a need so dark, I have to swallow the small knot of nervousness that has lumped in my throat.

"Please," he says. Only it doesn't sound like a question. It sounds like a command.

A small coil of lust unwinds inside. I want nothing more than to climb on top of him, but I'm scared of making his injuries worse.

"Jericho, you're—"

He tugs, pulling me across the bed. He winces as he leans over and drags me on top of him. "Please," he commands again. "I need you, Berkley. I need to know I've still got you. That you're mine. There's this feeling inside me, this fear that I've lost you that just won't leave. It hurts more than any of my physical injuries and you're the only one who can make it go away."

"But what if—"

"Kiss me," he growls. "Fucking kiss me."

Leaning down, I gently press my lips to his, careful not to lean too hard against him, careful not to cause him any pain. But he winds his fingers into the back of my hair, and jerks me toward him, crushing our lips together. My chest falls to his and he lets out a low whistle of air as I squash his arm.

"See!" I peel myself from him. "I'm hurting you."

"I don't care. I need you more than I care about the pain. I would go through a million times worse just to see your smile. Now shut up and kiss me, Miss Berkley."

Once I surrender, the lust swirls through my body uncontrollably. Our mouths battle. His hand fists my hair again, yanking back my head, his mouth continuing its assault down the pillar of my throat. He makes these growling noises, these noises of need and desperation and dominance.

"Take off your top," he orders.

I don't hesitate to obey. I surrender quickly and easily, my need as strong as his. Holding my breath, I anticipate his touch. But it doesn't come.

He's staring at me, his eyes drinking in the sight of my nakedness as though he's starved. My nipples beads under his gaze and he takes a breath in, his bottom lip drawn in between his teeth.

When he does reach out to touch me, it's to trace the pattern of the freckles flecked across my skin. My breasts seem heavier with the anticipation, begging for the stroke of his finger. Moisture pools between my legs and I wonder if he feels the heat of me spread across his waist. My ass is pressed to his groin and his cock pulses as though begging to be inside me.

"Touch yourself," he orders.

"Jericho." I burn with embarrassment.

"Cup your breasts. Play with your nipples. I want to watch."

I ignore the blush creeping up my cheeks as I lift my hands, running them over my breasts, down my stomach and then back up to pinch my nipples.

Jericho moans. His cock pushes even harder against my ass. "Oh, the things I'm going to do to you when I'm healed."

His eyes remain fixed on my hands, following their every move as I skim them over my body, toying and teasing, taking delight in the way his breath hitches when they touch my flesh in ways I know he wishes he could.

He lifts his knees, pressing them to my back and tipping me closer to him. His head lifts and his lips descend on my breast, drawing it into his mouth and sucking deeply.

"I cannot wait to teach you things, Miss Berkley. You will be my student and I will show you ways of wickedness even that dark mind of yours can't imagine."

I push against him, winding my fingers into his hair, encouraging him to take more of me into his mouth. His tongue twists around my nipple and my hands fall to his shoulders, digging my nails into his flesh, moans of ecstasy tumbling from me.

Then his tongue travels back up the column of my throat and our mouths collide again. His hand skims down my back and under the cheeks of my ass, encouraging me to lift. And then he guides me, adjusting himself so I sink onto his hard cock.

We stop kissing, our foreheads pressed together as I breathe in the feel of him inside me. He's hard and smooth. He feels perfect.

My hands drop to his chest as I lift myself, rising up his length before sinking down onto him again.

"Good girl," he growls and a flood of pleasure washes over me at his praise.

His legs fall back to the mattress, and I arch back, gripping his thighs and grinding myself onto him. His fingers brush over my knees, drawing small circles in time to the rotation of my hips.

The rolling of thunder rumbles outside.

A crack of lightning whips across the sky.

I lose myself in him. I lose myself in the sensations rippling through me. My body trembles in unison to the thunder. Jericho jerks his hips when the lighting crashes and the force of it, the way he feels inside unleashes a blaze of desire so strong, I cry out, falling forward onto his chest as he pulses and shudders.

And then I lay, panting and clutching onto him as I ride the waves of rapture. Jericho cradles me, his fingers running through the strands of my hair flowing down my back.

I feel safe in his arms.

I feel secure and happy.

Content and, for once, unafraid of what my future might bring.

I am free of my father. Free from being the daughter of a monster.

Now I am slave to one.

I'm not sure how long we lie like that. I'm not sure if we sleep, or if we just drift in and out of consciousness, content in our bliss. Rain splatters heavily against the glass, the soundtrack to our place in paradise.

It's only when there's a faint knock on the door that we move. Jericho slides himself out of me, and I slump to the side of his body.

"What?" Jericho snaps, calling out to the visitor behind the door.

It almost makes me laugh. The sternness of him. The surliness that appears mainly when others do.

The door creaks open as Jericho pulls the covers around my shoulders, but no one enters. "Mr Priest," Mrs Bellamy's voice calls through the crack.

"What?" he snaps again.

"The police are here."

chapter thirty-one

BERKLEY

They separate us almost immediately. First, they stay with Jericho, while I wait anxiously downstairs, scared they are going to lead him down in handcuffs. But when the door opens and footsteps descend, it's only Officer Conway who greets me.

"Is there somewhere we can talk privately?"

I'm not sure anywhere in this house is truly private, but I don't tell him that. Instead, I lead him to the library, sitting myself down on one of the overstuffed armchairs and tucking my feet in beside me. I'm trying to look casual, as though the reason for this interview isn't eating inside me.

"I suppose you know why we're here?"

I nod. "I saw it in the newspaper."

The headlines had been sensational. 'Entire Household Slaughtered.' 'The Monster's Revenge?' 'City Shocked by Mass Killing.'

They were hard to read. Truth always is.

The officer pulls out a small notepad and a pen. He clicks the cap repeatedly before asking any more questions.

"And you were there that night?"

I nod. "I was."

The policeman arches a brow. I'm so scared of giving away something I shouldn't, I've made him suspicious already.

"It was my birthday," I add. "A surprise party."

"A surprise party that you danced, in costume, fully prepared for?"

"The surprise was that I was having a party at all. I'm not a huge socializer. But Michael insisted."

"Michael Gorman?"

I nod again.

"The deceased Michael Gorman?"

"Sadly, yes."

"You danced very well, I must say."

"You were there?"

"Michael and I were friends."

"That's right. I remember seeing you at his pool party."

The young officer locks eyes with me. He knows there's more to the story, he knows I know more than I'm letting on, but he doesn't voice it.

I smile tightly. "I left later that night. After the dance. Before…" I look down at the floor, studying the patterns of the carpet. "Before everything happened."

"Did you know your father was there that night?"

"Yes, I've found out since. It was a masquerade party. Everyone was wearing a mask."

"And you didn't recognize any of the guests as your father?"

"I wasn't expecting to see him, so no."

"And you left without seeing anything suspicious?"

"Last I saw of the party, everyone was having a marvelous time."

"Were you there when Mr Priest was asked to leave?"

I shake my head. "I was getting changed. I left afterward." The lies flow easily. I don't even need to school my face. It remains impassive. Innocent.

"And where did you go?"

"After the party?"

"Yes, after the party."

"Here."

"With Mr Priest?"

"Yes. I had a job to return to."

"I see." Officer Conway clicks two more times on the cap of the pen and then sets it and the notepad down, balancing them on the arm of the chair. So far, he hasn't recorded any notes.

"Can I be honest with you, Miss Atterton?"

"I go by the name Berkley." I smile demurely. "Go ahead."

"None of this adds up. You're a little too involved not to be considered suspicious."

"I can see how you could think that, but I assure you, I did not kill my father, or indeed any of the men that died that night."

"No one said you did."

"You implied it."

"I implied you're not telling me everything you know."

I shrug. "Maybe you're not asking the right questions."

So far he's been leaning forward, elbows rested on his knees. Now, he sits back, hooking the ankle of one foot over the other knee.

"Here's the thing. I've been working undercover with these guys for months. And the things I've seen, the things I've witnessed, have made me very eager to see those men in jail. Now that it won't happen, I'm hoping the wrong people don't end up punished for their sins. I would like to see them held responsible alone. My friendship with Michael Gorman allowed me access into their circle, and their willingness to take advantage of my position blinded them to the fact that I may have been using them, rather than the other way around."

"Congratulations."

He narrows his eyes. "Ever since the bust with your father, we've had the Gormans under surveillance."

"I'm surprised the police allowed this to happen under their watch then."

"Allow me to offer my perspective on the situation. Correct me if I'm wrong at any stage." He clears his throat. "The Gormans were working with their lawyers, the same lawyers your father has, to get him released. We know this for a fact. They were successful in their plans. Your father was released on bail. Then they allowed the world to think he'd gone missing, but in reality, your father was tucked away safely in their house this whole time."

Officer Conway pauses, waiting for me to respond to the information he'd shared so far.

"I can see how they'd be capable of that."

"We don't have any witnesses to that fact, but I'm sure with the right persuasion, someone who had been at the house, perhaps someone at the party, would be able to bear witness to seeing him there. Do you understand?"

I tilt my head, his meaning dawning on me. "I'm following so far."

"Perhaps your father got jealous of their freedom when he was stuck inside. Perhaps he wanted to claim their kingdom for his own. It's happened before. Wealthy men, once friends, jealous of each other's successes. A clash resulting in the death of both sides, no one rising as the victor."

"It would be a little strange for my father to be able to kill all those men on his own though, would it not?"

"Unusual, yes. Impossible no. I had heard rumors floating about. Some of the men who worked for the Gormans did not believe Michael Junior would head the company in the right direction. Their loyalties may have lain elsewhere. Mr Gorman was poisoned, that would not have been difficult to do. And as for the guards, other men were working for the Gormans that night who could have made a surprise visit under the instruction of your father."

"And then killed him as well, accomplishing what, exactly?"

"That's where my version of the story falls apart. I was hoping you might be able to shed some light on the situation."

"What about the women?"

"What women?"

337

"The women in the house. Mrs Gorman? Mary Keating?"

"You knew Mary was there?"

I shrug. "I'm assuming. She was Mr Gorman's sister, wasn't she?"

"Both women claim to have slept through the entire thing. We found traces of a sedative in their blood."

"They didn't see anything?"

"Not that they're telling the police, anyway. All Mary Keating wanted to talk about was her missing son. She insisted he was dead somewhere and wanted us to find his body, though she wouldn't reveal what made her think that."

"And did you?

"Did I what?"

"Did you look for him?"

"There are more pressing matters at the moment."

Part of me deflates. I would have liked them to have found him, at least so he could have a proper burial and Mary could get some closure.

"Can I ask you a question? Off the record."

Officer Conway sits up a little. "This whole thing has been off the record so far, Miss Atter—Miss Berkley."

"What would happen to a woman held captive who say, killed her captor in order to escape?"

"It would depend on the circumstances, but I wouldn't hesitate to say it would be hard for anyone to charge her in that situation, especially if her life was at risk."

"So, say there was someone who had been held captive in the bunker of someone's house. And then someone who wanted that woman, broke in, stole her, and killed, or at least attempted to kill the occupants, and took her back with him to be held captive again. Say this woman then witnessed this man killing other people and she had the chance to kill him and escape, she wouldn't be charged with anything?"

He chuckles. "That's a little hard to follow, but I'd imagine that woman would be offered immunity in exchange for her testimony against the men who held her captive and any further information she might have."

"I feel as though we're talking in riddles."

He nods. "We are. But I feel you understand where I'm coming from."

I nod and unwrap my feet from where they are tucked in beside me. "I do. Might I suggest you request Hope to join us later? She may have some information of interest to you."

"Who is Hope?"

"Jericho's wife. She went missing years ago and has only just returned. My father held her captive."

Officer Conway blinks, but that's the only sign of his surprise. He picks up his pad and paper, scribbles something down and then flicks on a recording device.

"Shall we start then? Please state your full name for the record."

"The name I go by is Everly Jane Berkley, but please just call me Berkley."

"Right, Miss Berkley. Were you there on the night in question?"

"Yes."

"And did you witness your father, Sebastian Atterton as present at that party?"

"Yes, I did."

epilogue

HOPE

My dreams are the only place monsters still haunt me. I don't have nightmares often, maybe every few weeks, but each time I wake and find myself safe with my daughter sleeping soundly in the room next to mine, the relief is so acute it almost makes the nightmare worth it.

This morning's nightmare melded all my monsters into one. It's the way they appear now. Nothing specific. No particular memory is burned into my mind. It's always an obscured face and an unidentifiable body, but the thing that stays with me is the sensation.

The sensation of being alone. Trapped. Helpless and at the mercy of another. That feeling may never leave me. Or the brief moment of panic that follows it. And I'm not sure I want it to. Because when I open my eyes, even while my heart still races and my skin is prickled with a cold sweat, I know it is nothing more than a dream.

That part of my life is over.

The police never charged me over his death. I guess they figured I'd been through enough. It may have also had something to do with Berkley organizing a deal for my immunity if I told them what I saw. It may not have happened in the order I presented to the police, but it was all truth in some form or another. Besides, the police were too caught up in all the drama that followed to be worried about what happened to me. They found the storage facility. They became heroes because of all the women they rescued. They prosecuted a crime syndicate, and they didn't even have to get their hands dirty by bringing down the kingpins. According to what the world knew, the infighting and conflict meant they had destroyed themselves from the inside out.

And because of that, Ette and I are free.

We are free to live our lives.

Free to exist in the world.

Free of monsters.

Free.

In the months that followed, builders constructed a cottage in a clearing on the hill behind the Sanctuary. The bitterness I felt after I was first rescued faded away. I slayed my beast. Now I get to live my life in peace.

Apart from the constant noise coming from the renovations happening at the Sanctuary. Berkley put all the money she received from her father's will into the restoration. It's just about complete. In a few days, there will be a grand opening. It's to be a Sanctuary for women in need, funded by the money from the monster. Jericho's mother, Alice, and I will run it. She's doing better now. She's clean. We'll offer classes in order for them to gain employment. We'll offer protection for them from those they fear. We'll provide them with a home, a family, a life. Control over their destiny.

And it's as though the building has come to life, flourishing under the purpose of what it's always been meant for. The ghosts of the past no longer haunt it. It has a new purpose. A new life. Just like me.

When I wake early, like I did this morning, I don't try to go back to sleep. I get up, creeping across the floorboards so as not to wake Ette, make a cup of tea and take it out onto the deck.

And then I watch the world begin to wake. I watch as the mist that hangs around the crumbling walls of the Sanctuary garden lifts and fades as fingers of the sun stretch between the trees. I listen to the birds sing. I touch the scattered leaves that have fallen to the deck, crumpling them between my fingers. And then, closing my eyes, I take a deep breath and then open them slowly, knowing I will smile when everything is as it was before. Perfect.

Nothing changes.

This is not a dream.

This is my life.

Ette is not an early riser. She sleeps until I wake her and then she runs about the cottage in a fluster, complaining about not having enough time to get dressed properly. She takes great pride in her uniform.

"Mum!" Ette calls when I'm back inside and preparing breakfast. "Mum! I can't find my socks!"

I take a sip of my third cup of tea before calling back. "They're in your drawers like always."

"I can't find them! I'm going to be late for school!"

I smile as I pour the pancake batter into the pan. Of course, she can't find them. She never can. Moving the pan off the heat, I walk into her room, open her drawer and pull out a pair of socks.

"Here." I force a small frown when I hand them to her.

She ignores it. "Where did you find them? I've been looking for ages."

"In the same drawer as they always are."

Ette dumps herself on the edge of the bed and proceeds to pull on her socks. She's dressed in a navy kilt, white shirt and red jersey. Her socks go up to her knees and the leather of her shoes is red. She fell in love with school on the very first day, although I had a little more difficulty.

It was hard saying goodbye, even though I knew it was only for a few hours. As soon as she disappeared behind the school gate, a wave of panic washed over me.

What if something happened to her?

What if something happened to me?

What if I never saw her again?

Even though I hadn't said a word of how I was feeling, Berkley turned up on my doorstep only minutes after I arrived back home, and dragged me over to the Sanctuary to make renovation decisions despite the fact they'd already been made. She never mentioned Ette. But she kept me busy and distracted until it was time for Ette to come home again. It was an act of kindness neither of us ever acknowledged.

"There," Ette says, getting to her feet, shoes on and laces tied. "I'm ready for breakfast now."

Having forgotten about the pancakes, I rush into the kitchen and put the pan back on the heat. Ette pulls out a chair and sits at the table expectantly.

After years of not being able to choose what I ate, when I ate it, or even how much I had, cooking for my daughter and myself has brought tremendous joy. It's the little things that matter.

Brushing Ette's hair and twisting it into the plaits she likes to wear to school. Making myself as many cups of tea as I choose. Leaving the house. Driving the car. Going for a walk. Cooking. Choosing what to wear. Even washing my own clothes.

We are both seated at the table, tucking into our pancakes, when a car appears along the driveway and pulls to a stop. Barrett opens the door, gets out, and leans against the bonnet. He doesn't say anything. Doesn't call out to announce his arrival. Just waits.

After quickly collecting Ette's bag, I follow her outside.

"Morning, Barrett!" she greets cheerfully.

Barrett nods. "Morning, Miss Odette."

Ette laughs as she skips down the steps. "I told you that makes me feel like I'm about to be told off."

Barrett walks to the side of the car and opens the door. "Which is precisely why I do it."

Ette climbs inside and slides the seatbelt over her chest as Barrett shuts the door.

"You know, you don't need to drive her to school each morning," I say. "I'm quite capable of doing it."

"I know." He winks. "But I like it. Gives me a chance to catch up with her each day." He tilts his head, peering over at me. "And you."

He's standing with his hand on the handle, but he doesn't open the door. It's like he's waiting for something. Or maybe he wants to say something.

"Did you get everything settled in the city the other day?" A faint blush of color creeps over his cheeks.

I bite back my smile. "Yes. Jericho and I have officially filed for divorce. It might not even take two years, you know, due to the circumstances." I shrug. I don't like to talk about it. I prefer to look forward, not back.

"Suppose it makes sense." He looks at the ground as he speaks. "Give both of you the chance to move on with your lives now that things are more settled." Barrett peers up, squinting into the sun.

"What about you? Have you decided what you're going to do?" I ask after a few seconds of awkward silence.

"I heard they were looking for security here at the Sanctuary, so I thought I might just stay here. What do you think?"

The car window rolls down. "Come on, Barrett! I'm going to be late for school," Ette whines.

I reach out and rest my hand on his shoulder. Apart from my self-defense lessons, it's the closest contact I've shown any man. "I think that would be nice. You know, if it's something you want to do. I'd imagine it will be a little different than your security role with Jericho."

He chuckles. "That's what I'm hoping."

I let my hand drop. "Will you come get me before you collect Ette from school? I'd like to come for the ride if it's not too much hassle."

"You're never a hassle."

"Barrett!" Ette moans.

"I'm coming. I'm coming." He opens the door. "I'll see you later." It's said as more of a question than a statement. I nod, letting the slightest smile cross my lips.

"Bye Mum!" Ette shouts as they reverse down the driveway. "I'll see you later!"

And I wave back, safe in the knowledge that she will.

Berkley lies beside me, one hand flung over her head, the other resting on her chest as though she'd somehow swooned when she got into bed. Her hair is spread over the pillow. There's a faint smile on her lips. She's wearing the same threadbare t-shirt she's always worn and it's twisted about her body, exposing the lines of her collarbones. She lies still, the gentle rise and fall of her chest the only motion to her body.

I always wake before her. Even during the months my body was healing, I'd wake early just to watch her sleep. It's the only time I get to see her motionless. Unless, of course, there are other restraints that ensure her stillness.

We moved into my apartment in the city not long after her return. I told her it was to avoid the hassle of the renovations, but that was a lie. Here, I have her all to myself. Here, I can ensure her safety. Here, there is no ex-wife, no mother, no Ette, no Gideon, no Barrett, no Mrs Bellamy, no Alma.

It's just us.

After waiting what seems like an entirely for her to wake, I reach out and trail my finger along her collarbones. Her movements lazy with slumber, her body searches for mine, shuffling across the mattress, and curling into me. Her head comes to rest on my chest and she lets out a contented sigh. Her leg hooks over my thigh and her hand drapes over my waist. My body responds instantly to the feel of her flesh pressed against mine.

My desire for her is insatiable. It's as though my body craves her. I feel restless unless I'm around her. Unsettled unless I can feel her close. I wake in the middle of the night and pull her to me. I reach for her during the day, needing the feel of her skin under mine. My mind gets caught on all the things I want to teach her. All the sensations she's yet to experience. Despite all we've been through, I buzz with the excitement that this is only the beginning of us.

Placing my hand on her hip, I bunch the material of her t-shirt between my fingers, pulling it up her thigh until bare skin is beneath my touch.

She smiles, nuzzling into my chest and her eyes flutter open. My stupid heart swells. There's nothing better than seeing her smile and knowing it's because of me.

"Morning," I say, pressing kisses to her hair.

My body is taut and tight, eager in its need for her . I want to drag her over, slide her onto me and entangle our bodies until she cries out my name.

"Morning," she replies lazily.

She stretches, twisting onto her back and lifting one arm into the air. I take the opportunity to slide my hand up her body, a moan escaping me as my hand cups the soft flesh of her breast.

"I've been waiting for you to wake," I murmur in her ear while rolling to clamber over her.

Tugging her t-shirt up, I lower my mouth to her breast, swirling my tongue over her nipple. She sighs again and relaxes under me, submitting her body to my control. I kiss her stomach, the dip of the belly button, each of the freckles that dot her skin, the slope of her hips, the groove of her thighs. She twists and turns, writhing beneath me until I grip her hips possessively, holding her in place.

My cock swells to the point of pain. I need to be inside her, to feel the sensation of her wrapped around my hardness. Last night I had been rough and commanding. I'd tortured her with my touch. Tormented her, held her in that exquisite place between pleasure and pain until she begged me for release. But this morning I'm gentle. I want to hear her sigh rather than her scream. I want to listen to her moan my name.

I drag my lips down her left thigh and then lift her leg to kiss the soft spot on the back of her knee. I playfully sink my teeth into the muscle of her calf and she gasps, her leg jerking under my touch, so I hold her firmly and scold her to stay still.

There's this sound she makes. It's in between a laugh, a sigh, a gasp and a groan. It's a sound I try to elicit from her each and every time I'm inside her as it's a sound of perfection.

But she doesn't make that sound. She gasps, but it's a gasp of shock, not of overwhelming lust.

Berkley sits up. "What's the time?" Her eyes dart about the room as though in search of a clock.

"It's early," I growl. "Lie back down and stay still."

She slips her legs out from beneath me and swings them over the side of the bed. "I'm going to be late."

"Late for what?" I force myself not to reach for her. Not to grab her and toss her back onto the bed.

"Dance class."

"Don't go." I can't help the commanding tone of my voice.

But Berkley ignores me, darting across the room while pulling off her t-shirt and tossing it to the ground. The sight of her completely naked just about undoes me. It always does. She has no idea how much control she would have over me if she ever chose to use it.

I flop back onto the bed but keep my eyes trained on her every move. "Since when do you have class in the morning?"

"Extra training," she calls from the bathroom. She turns on the shower and lifts her voice to be heard over the spray. "Miss Marchand has made it well known that I need to earn my place back in the company. She would not be impressed if I didn't turn up."

She's left the door open and the steam of the shower begins to seep into the room. In the reflection of the mirror, I watch as she lathers her body in soap and then lets the water wash the suds away. I lose sight of her when she steps out of the shower.

"How long are you going to be?" My voice almost breaks, my need for her deepening it to the point of fracture.

Gripping the doorframe, she swings her head around the side, holding her body behind the wall. "Why? Are you going to miss me?" She winks and disappears again.

Tossing off the blankets, I rise and stride over to the bathroom, catching her as she's drying herself. I rip the towel away, grabbing her and pressing her against the wall to assault her lips.

She's breathless when I finally let her go and stares up at me with eyes flamed with passion and her hair in disarray.

"I'll take that as a yes," she says with a small smirk.

I'm still pressed against her even though our lips are no longer entwined. My cock presses into the softness of her belly. I slide my hand up her throat, hooking my fingers under her jawbone and tilting her face up to mine.

"Don't go," I say, my voice a low rumble.

She makes that sound. That sound that sends my lust-filled body into overdrive. It's enough to make me want to toss her over my shoulder and throw her onto the bed. But she smiles teasingly and lifts her hand to mine and peels away my grip.

"Keep that thought for when I get back." She slinks out from under me and I let my fist fall against the wall in frustration. "You know," she says as she pulls on her tights and a leotard, covering that tantalizing body of hers. "Maybe you should pop into the club today. See how things are going?"

"Are you trying to get rid of me, Miss Berkley?"

I follow her out of the bathroom and lean against the wall as she collects her things. She tries to act as though I'm not a distraction, but her eyes keep sliding to my body which I'm unashamedly displaying. And this small shudder runs over her when I say Miss Berkley. I know what it does to her. And it's a level I'm willing to lower myself to.

She licks her lips before speaking. "It just seems like you've been a little bored lately." She tries unsuccessfully to pull her gaze up to my face.

"I can assure you I've been far from bored." There's no misunderstanding in what I'm saying. Even my cock stands taller at my words. I let my eyes scan over her brazenly. I know she won't succumb. I know she needs to attend this class, but it's still fun to try.

"My therapist thinks you're just putting everything on hold simply to make sure I'm safe."

There is some truth to her words. I barely want to let her out of my sight. I never want to be without her again. I never want to run the risk of someone taking her from me.

"Your therapist is a wise woman." Pulling myself from my position against the wall, I walk over to where she's stuffing extra tights into her bag. "Do you still have the flashes? Do I still do terrible things to you in your mind?"

She swallows and her gaze scans me slowly. "Jericho," she says in a lower warning voice as she gets to her feet, her body dangerously close to mine

"What?" I tease.

She rises to her tiptoes, pressing her lips to my ear as she speaks. "The terrible things you do to me are no longer in

355

my head. And now, thanks to you, all the time I'm going to be in class, I'm going to wonder which version of you I will come home to. Whether it will be the one who will bind me and torture me in the most delicious of ways, the one who will slap me, command me, consume me. Or the one who will hold me tenderly as he fucks me."

Closing my eyes, I groan at her words, all the different scenarios of her suggestions running through my head. And when I open them again, she's got this grin on her face, knowing how quickly she reversed the roles of our temptation.

Hoisting her bag over her shoulder, she walks toward the door. "You realize you pretty much killed everyone who wanted to hurt me? There's no need to worry about me."

"Didn't you say your brother went missing from his hospital?"

She shrugs. "I haven't heard anything more so they must have found him." She waits in the doorway. "Speaking of brothers, did you see the email from Gideon?"

I glance toward my laptop sitting on the table. "Did you read it?"

"Only a quick scan. He seems happy. I think it was a good thing you did, setting him up as the manager of one of your clubs. It will give him a chance to grow up. A chance to make his own way. Sort of."

"I'm nothing if not generous."

She just lifts her brows in amusement.

"At least let me give you a ride."

"It's not far. I'll be fine walking." Her eyes dart up and down my body one last time before she shuts the door and leaves.

I wander over to the laptop and open the email from Gideon. Berkley is right. He seems happy. The last few months have been a big change for him. He discovered the truth about his father, his mother and his brother. And in doing so, he found out I'd been lying to him for years. He was angry at the start. Angry with me. Angry with Alice. It was Hope who helped him in the end. She was the only one who was able to get through to him and convince him to move forward, rather than look backward.

The amount of emails waiting to be read has greatly diminished ever since Berkley gained access to her father's trust fund upon his death. She purchased the Sanctuary from me, allowing me to pay off all my debts. And now she's established a trust, assigning my mother and Hope in charge of running it.

It gives us the freedom to pursue our dreams. Whatever they may be. For we have all the time in the world now. We could travel around the world, visiting each of my clubs. Or we could sell the whole lot and spend our lives living on a secluded beach. But whatever we choose, for now, I'm content to be where I am. With Berkley. Just soaking in the luxury of being together.

There's a noise as a key slides into the lock. The door is pushed open and Berkley's smiling face appears. "I forgot to say I love you," she says, blowing me a kiss. She's gone again before I can reply.

So much has changed since I first locked eyes with her at the dance studio. Back then, I saw her as a damaged doll, tattered and torn from life itself. I knew then and there that her broken parts would be a match for mine. But I didn't know her strength. I didn't realize her beauty. And I didn't know just how much she would come to mean to me. There's still a part of me that feels she'd be better off without me. I am nothing more than a monster and she deserves better. But I know I'd never have the strength to leave her. And she seems to want to stay.

In the beginning I wanted Berkley so I could exact revenge.

Now there is only one reason I want her.

Because I love her.

BERKLEY

The wrought-iron gates no longer groan when they open. I press my head to the window, peering up at the concrete pillars and twisted iron. The lanterns perched on top almost give off a cheery glow, as though welcoming us back to the estate we used to call home.

Reaching over, I entwine my fingers through Jericho's as he drives us down the tree-framed winding road. He lifts my hand and brushes a kiss across my knuckles as the Sanctuary looms above us.

There's something different about it now. It doesn't seem so imposing. It's as though its ghosts have vanished and it's finally able to stand in all its glory rather than stoop under the weight of its past. The crumbling ruins of the gardens have been given a new lease on life, fresh flowers and shrubbery perfectly placed around the property. The walls of the Sanctuary, which had cracked and tumbled, now stand strong and tall. And above the arch of the entrance the words 'Swan Sanctuary' have been set in the stone. Even the pond somehow seems to have been renovated. The water is clearer, the pads of the lilies are brighter and there's even more elegance to the way the swans glide across the surface. The gazebo has even been given a fresh layer of paint.

Mrs Bellamy waits on the steps just as she did the very first time I arrived. She's dressed in her usual black and white ensemble, but instead of standing solemnly with hands clasped in front of her, she's waving enthusiastically. As soon as the car rolls to a stop, I open the door, rush over to her and wrap her in an embrace. She's been on a well-deserved holiday over the past few weeks. And she's returned to find all the renovation of the Sanctuary completed and in time for its grand opening tomorrow.

"Welcome back to the Sanctuary, Miss Berkley," she says, pushing back from me and holding me at arm's length, as though her time away requires her to inspect me for differences.

"Just Berkley, Mrs Bellamy."

"Nonsense," she says. "You will always be Miss Berkley to me. Now let me get a good look at you. You look as though you've lost a little weight. Have you been eating okay?"

Jericho is now out of the car and standing beside me. Mrs Bellamy lets go of my shoulders and Jericho moves closer, his hand coming to rest on my waist.

She looks between us. "I do worry about you two alone in that tiny apartment. You are both eating okay, aren't you?"

Jericho laughs and leans forward to place a kiss on her cheek. "How was your holiday?"

"Entirely too long. After the first week, I was itching to get back here and help prepare everything for tomorrow. But it seems as though Hope, Alice and Alma have done a wonderful job. There's barely anything left for me to do."

"Well, that's good. You deserved a break. We're just back for one final stroll around the place before everyone arrives tomorrow. A final goodbye I guess you could say."

"Oh, don't say that. That makes me sad. You better come back lots of times to say hello. And no doubt Miss Berkley will need to come back to keep an eye on her investment."

I look upwards, staring at the stone arch and the words above. "I do get some satisfaction that this is how his money is being spent. I hope that he knows it somehow."

"Berkley!" A high-pitched voice sounds behind me and I turn around to see Ette break away from her mother and skip up the steps. I lower myself and open my arms as she runs into them. "Mum said you weren't coming until tomorrow."

I squeeze her tightly. "We thought we'd come a little early and spend one last night here before it's officially open."

Ette's eyes grow wide and she turns to Hope. "Can we stay here too? Just for tonight? I can stay in my old room." She turns back to me without waiting for an answer from her mother. "It looks so different now. They changed almost everything. But they still have beds so we should be fine." Ette takes my hand, pulling me inside the large doors. "Come on, I'll show you."

Jericho waves me on as Ette tugs me to the stairs. The lighting of the Sanctuary has changed. It's brighter, happier, with fewer shadows and less mystery. But I miss the creaks of the stairs as we climb. I miss the way the banister felt under my hand, worn and smooth. Now it's shiny and glossy with a fresh layer of varnish.

"How did the audition go?" I ask Ette when we reach the top of the stairs. I'd helped her with a dance routine to audition for the school talent show. Although it's a little harder to find the time, I continue with Ette's dance lessons when I get the chance.

She beams a smile back at me. "It was so good. I'm going to be so much better than anyone else there. Well, anyone else who chooses to dance anyway."

"Pleased to see you're not lacking in confidence." I chuckle.

Ette drags me to the kitchen next, wanting to show me the recent changes. It's been extended somewhat, allowing a lot more room for Alma to cook. All the staff have chosen to stay on and new staff have been hired. Instead of the hollow and empty hallways, soon the place will be buzzing with activity.

It's dark by the time Hope comes to take Ette back to their cottage on the hill. Ette protests, wanting to stay one last night, but Hope finds comfort in her own house in a way she never did at the Sanctuary.

I keep wandering alone, submersing myself in the feel of the place. The eeriness and melancholy of the building is gone. It's as though it knows what awaits it. It's as though it's eager to feel the hustle and bustle of life within its walls again.

I run my fingers over the books in the library. I take off my shoes and dip my toes into the water of the pool. I lift my eyes to the chandeliers of the ballroom, and walk from window to window, watching the moonlit landscape unfold from frame to frame.

It's not until I open the doors of the dance studio that I find some tears gathering in my eyes. Nothing has changed. The baby grand piano still sits in the corner, the glossy blackness of it gleaming in the light. The walls are still the same color. Although the wooden floor appears to have been polished within an inch of its life.

I stare at my reflection in the mirrors that flank the wall. I see none of the girl I used to be staring back at me. I'm no longer Everly, no longer just Berkley. I'm a combination of them both. The broken pieces of me, the strong pieces of me, the darkness and the light, it all remains within me, making me the person I am now. I'm no longer just known as the daughter of a monster. I'm also known as the person who helped bring him down.

Lifting my fingers, I touch the skin of my face as though searching to find some of him within my features. But he's not there.

He's gone.

Just like Michael is gone.

Mr Gorman is gone.

Even Dominic is gone.

I'm startled when Jericho appears in the reflection behind me. I didn't hear him enter. I didn't hear his steps as he crossed the wooden floor. He doesn't say a word as he comes to stand behind me, running his hands down my arms and then pushing them inwards. My feet automatically form the familiar position, heels together, toes turned outward.

"First." His voice is low and guttural, his breath hot against my ear.

"Second," I say as we change.

His eyes lock on mine in the reflection of the mirror as he curls one of my arms inward. "Third."

We slide into fourth and finally fifth and then he spins me, turning me so I face him. I bring down my arms looping them around his neck. His eyes are dark like the night sky. His hands grip around my waist possessively.

He cocks a brow. "I want you, Miss Berkley. Right now."

The low gravel to his voice works the same magic as it always does and a tremor of anticipation ripples through me. He dips his head, lowering his lips to mine and kisses me gently before dragging my bottom lip between his teeth and biting.

Moving away, he stalks toward the door, only turning to hold his hand out when he realizes I'm not following. My heart skips a little. A warm flush of arousal washes over me when I think of the dark and dangerous things he could do.

Because there are two types of monsters in this world. There is the kind who revel in their cruelty, not caring about the pain they inflict on the world. They are like my father. And then there are the ones who only rise in defense of others, using their darkness to exact revenge for those who need it.

And Jericho Priest is my monster.

About the Author

Sabre Rose is the author of contemporary and dark romance. She writes about love and lust. Flawed people in messy relationships. Happiness and heartbreak. Loyalty and betrayal.

She lives at the bottom of the South Island of New Zealand with her husband and two children..

Email Newsletter:

www.subscribepage.com/sabreroseauthor

Social Media:

www.facebook.com/sabreroseauthor
www.twitter.com/sabreroseauthor

Website:

www.sabreroseauthor.com

Email:

sabreroseauthor@gmail.com

Black Swan Trilogy Reading Order

Daughter of a Monster

Searching for Hope

Among the Sins of my Father

Other Books by Sabre Rose

Thornton Brothers

(Contemporary Romance Series)

Touched

Tempted

Taken

Torn

Tears

Torment

Turmoil

You Ruined Me

(A Tragic Dark Romance Novella)

Say You Love Me

(Psychological romantic suspense)

Requested Trilogy

(Dark Romance Series)

Don't Say A Word

Until You're Mine

My Sweet Songbird

Printed in Great Britain
by Amazon